GHOSTS OF IWO JIMA

A Story About Battles, Ghosts, and Two Very Special Dogs

JOE JENNINGS

DEDICATION

This book is dedicated to the seventy thousand U.S. Marines and U.S. Navy Corpsmen who, on the morning of February 19th, 1945, assaulted one of the most heavily fortified objectives in military history, and whose bravery and dedication brought them to victory thirty-six days later.

Semper Fi

And To

Betsy, Mac, and Katie

Cover designed by Worlwind Creative, Park City, Utah

This book is a work of fiction. Names, characters, places, and incidents either are products of the author's imagination or are used fictitiously. Any resemblance to actual persons, living or dead, events, or locales is entirely coincidental.

Chapter Five contains excerpts from two articles originally published in the *Marine Corps Gazette*: "CAP November 3; A Pretty Good Little Ambush" (November 1986), and "The Long Night" (November 1996). The *Marine Corps Gazette* has graciously granted permission to use these excerpts.

Printed in the United States of America

First Printing: Aug 2017
Amazon

ISBN-9781522042914

CONTENTS

ACKNOWLEDGMENTS

Since this is my first book, I've been surprised by the amount of effort and expertise required to get from concept to publication. Without the help of some wonderful people, *Ghosts of Iwo Jima* would still be a nice idea floating around in my head. I'd like to acknowledge them here without embarrassing them too much so I'll just use first names.

Nan, for all the work on editing; Annette, for the great cover; David for the expert advice on plot and character; Betsy, for the critiques and feedback; Bonnie and George for reading and supporting; and, of course, Betsy (again), Mac and Katie for being who you are and meaning so much to me.

Sue Bulanda is a professional writer, so I'll use her full name. Sue was very generous in sharing her time, experience, and knowledge, and she helped make *Ghosts* better than it was when she first saw it.

AUTHOR'S NOTES

I once heard Craig Johnson, the author of the *Longmire* novels, say in a dinner speech that the greatest lie that an author can tell is that his characters are solely the product of the imagination and that any relation to actual persons, living or dead, is entirely coincidental.

That statement may satisfy the concerns of the lawyers, but I agree with Mr. Johnson that it is definitely not true. We write what we know, or think we know. I believe that every character in every novel ever written is some composite of all the people the author has known, read about, or observed throughout his or her life.

I know that is the case with the novel you are, I hope, about to read. This is a work of realistic fiction; a story set in a realistic context about things that could have happened to the characters, and in which the characters react in realistic ways. Well, except, perhaps, for the parts about the ghosts.

Some people who know me may believe that parts of this book are autobiographical; they may be partly right. Others will almost certainly think that they know the identity of the four-legged hero of the story; they will almost certainly be correct.

Based on experience, I can vouch for the realism of at least two elements of my story, the combat scenes and the capabilities of military working dogs and search and rescue dogs. If the combat scenes seem fancifully gruesome, I can assure you that my writing skills are insufficient to over-dramatize the horror of infantry warfare. If you are skeptical that dogs can do some of the things I have them do, I would suggest that you find the nearest volunteer K9 search and rescue team and arrange to observe one of their training sessions. I think you will find that, if anything, I have understated what these remarkable animals can do.

I hope that you enjoy reading this as much as I enjoyed writing it.

Semper Fi,
Joe Jennings
Eden, Utah

By their victory, the 3rd, 4th, and 5th Marine Divisions and other units of the Fifth Amphibious Corps have made an accounting to their country which only history will be able to value fully. Among the Americans who served on Iwo Island, uncommon valor was a common virtue.
Admiral Chester W. Nimitz, U.S. Navy

TURQUOISE BOY

Heaven goes by favor. If it went by merit, you
would stay out, and your dog would go in.
--Mark Twain

Snow Peak Ski Resort, Utah
Lightning Ridge near Cache Bowl
Wednesday, 15 January
1030 Hours

THE TEST ARTICLES WERE THREE WOOLEN SWEATERS, each worn for several days by a different person to infuse them with human scent. The scent itself was composed of many millions of skin rafts, microscopic particles of dead skin that people tend to slough off at a rate of about forty thousand per minute.

The sweaters, buried under about two feet of loosely packed snow in the test area, were only about two or three degrees warmer than the snow above them, but that was enough for heat to be transferred and to rise toward the surface. As the warm air rose, it brought with it water vapor and on that vapor rode the skin rafts.

Some of the rafts stayed on or near the snow surface, and others floated into the air to be carried wherever the wind was blowing.

The test area was one hundred yards across and one hundred yards long on a snow slope that was tilted downward at about thirty-five degrees. Thirty-five degrees is the beginning of the sweet-spot for avalanches, the angle at which poorly bonded slabs of snow can fracture under the weight of a skier and send hundreds of tons of snow and the hapless skier hurtling downhill at speeds up to eighty miles an hour. The snow had been chopped up by ski patrollers working back and forth on their skis until it resembled the debris at the bottom of an avalanche slide.

As the skin rafts slowly diffused across the area, their density was just a few parts per billion.

To pass their re-certification test, the team would have to search the ten thousand square yard test area and find all three of the hidden sweaters in less than twenty minutes.

For an experienced avalanche search dog like Gunny, a nine-year-old Golden Retriever, this should be a piece of cake.

Gunny and his handler, Sam Webber, stood at the top of the ridge and waited for the evaluator to signal them to begin. Behind them was a ski patroller with his avalanche probe ready. He would ski down when Gunny alerted on a scent article and verify the find. That way, Sam could stay up high where he could better direct his dog.

The evaluator looked at the team and then at her watch, "Sam, are you and Gunny ready?"

"Sure. Anytime."

"OK, time starts.....Now!"

Holding tight to Gunny's harness, Sam yelled down the hill, "This is Snow Peak Ski Patrol. I have a search dog. Shout out if you can hear me!"

After a brief pause, "Dog on the hill!"

Releasing the harness, he commanded, "Gunny! Go Find!"

Gunny started running across the top of the ridge. Gunny had been fooled once when an evaluator had buried a scent article near the top of the test area, and Sam was happy to see that Gunny wasn't going to let that happen again.

He's not as fast as he used to be, Sam thought, *but he's a whole lot smarter.*

When Gunny got to the side of the test area, Sam called, "This way," and started skiing his grid pattern down the slope closely watching his dog for any change in behavior.

They made two passes across the area with Gunny working about ten yards below Sam. As they started their third pass, Gunny's head suddenly turned downhill—a "head snap." A second later Gunny himself turned downhill and began crisscrossing from side to side as though he was moving inside an ever-narrowing funnel.

"What's your dog doing?" the evaluator asked.

"He's in scent," Sam replied, "He's in the scent cone."

A moment later, Gunny suddenly stopped and turned uphill. Now his nose was very close to the surface and sniffing as fast as it could. He pawed in a couple of places and then thrust his nose into the snow, stood back, and started digging furiously.

"Prober, we've got a dog alert here!" Sam yelled.

The ski patroller skied quickly down and confirmed that Gunny had found the first sweater.

Gunny looked back up at Sam.

"Gunny! There's more! Go Find!"

Gunny and Sam started off on their grid search again.

A few minutes later, the process was repeated when Gunny found the second sweater. Two down, one to go.

About halfway across the slope on their next pass Gunny made another head-snap, but this time instead of working a scent cone he immediately put his nose to the snow and started following a straight track down the hill.

"Your dog is following my scent trail!" the evaluator said.

"Yep," Sam said.

"That's cheating!"

Sam grinned, "If he ain't cheatin', he ain't tryin' hard enough."

The evaluator swore to herself, *Dammit, I should have been more careful with an experienced dog like Gunny. He knows my scent, and somehow, he knows I put in the scent articles.*

But Sam's right. You gotta love a dog who does whatever it takes to find his target, and there's nothing in the test standards that says he can't do this.

Gunny followed the scent trail until he was a few yards away from the last article, and then he caught its scent and went right to it. A few seconds later, he was digging in the snow and, when the prober confirmed the find, the test was over.

Total elapsed time—nine minutes.

Sam skied quickly down and dug a ratty old piece of rope he'd had since Gunny was a puppy out of his pocket. As he held the toy out, Gunny leaped up joyously and grabbed one end starting a game of tug that went on for a couple of minutes. Then Sam took out a jerky treat and, giving it to Gunny, took back the rope.

A patroller standing next to Sam said, "He did all that work for a couple of minutes of play and a treat."

"He doesn't do it for the play or the treats, they're just a bonus. He does it because he's a hunter and that's what he was born to do."

As the evaluator skied up, Sam asked, "Do you want to debrief? Do you have any comments for me?"

"I only have one comment for you, and it's the only comment that matters."

"What's that?"

Raising her hand for a high-five, the evaluator said, "If I were buried in an avalanche, I'd want you and Gunny to be the ones looking for me."

♦ ♦ ♦

Snow Peak Ski Resort, Utah
Wednesday, 15 January
1045 Hours

After chatting with the ski patrollers and thanking them for their help, Sam skied slowly down to the bottom of the Timberline lift with Gunny porpoising through the fresh snow alongside him. He noticed that one of the people who had been watching the test was following them, someone he didn't recognize. When they got to the lift, the man skied alongside.

"Mr. Webber?"

"Yes."

"Hi. I'm Tom Sanders, and there's something I'd like to talk about with you. Could I ride up with you on the chair?"

"No, sorry. Gunny and I take up most of the chair, there wouldn't be room. I'll be happy to talk with you at the top or in the lodge."

"I understand. I'll meet you at the top."

Sam clipped a leash onto Gunny's harness and led him out to the lift loading area. At the "Load Here" point, they both stopped, and Gunny turned to face the chair coming up from behind. When it was close, Sam said, "Load Up!" and Gunny jumped onto the moving chair and quickly turned around and lay down next to Sam.

Sam heard the usual comments from the people waiting for the lift; "Wow! Did you see that?", or, "Hey, there's a dog on the chairlift." After doing this for almost nine years, it was no big deal for Sam and Gunny, but other people thought it was pretty cool.

After they got off the lift, Sam waited for Tom Sanders who skied up a minute later.

"What can I do for you, Mr. Sanders?"

"You're a retired Marine, right? Four years enlisted ... two in Vietnam ... sixteen as an officer?"

Who is this guy? How does he know all this? "Yes, sir. Right on all counts."

"So you know a lot about the battle for Iwo Jima, I suppose."

"Yeah, as much as your average Marine."

"Did you know that some of the Marines who were killed there were never recovered? They're still listed as, 'Missing, Presumed dead.'"

Sam thought for a second, "No, I didn't, but it doesn't surprise me. Iwo was an awful, vicious fight. No telling what might have happened. Why are you asking me?"

Sanders smiled, "How would you and Gunny like to go to Iwo Jima to help bring some of those Marines home?"

"Mr. Sanders, you have my attention. What's your plan for the rest of the day?"

"Well, besides talking to you I was hoping to take advantage of some of this great snow and do some skiing."

"You ever skied Snow Peak before?"

"No."

"OK, let's go down, I'll put Gunny up and show you around a bit. We can talk on the lifts."

"Lead the way, Marine."

♦ ♦ ♦

Ogden Valley, Utah
Wednesday, 15 January
1730 Hours

"So, before he gets here who is this guy who wants to drag you off to Iwo Jima?" Rebecca Webber asked.

Sam took a drink of beer, "Career Army, ten years in Ranger units, seems like a pretty good guy."

"How long did it take you to tell him you were the Honor Graduate of your Ranger School class?"

"About five minutes. He just said, 'Yeah, I know.' And he didn't sound too happy about it."

Rebecca chuckled, "Well the Army doesn't like to let Marines into their top school for snake eaters, and it pisses them off when a Marine gets top honors. I'm surprised he's still talking to you. Speaking of which, why is he talking to you anyway?"

"Well, like you said, he wants me and Gunny to go to Iwo Jima to look for Marines who have been missing for seventy-three years. He's with an outfit called Team Liberty, and that's what they do."

Sam was interrupted by the ringing of the doorbell, and he went to answer it.

Tom Sanders came in a minute later carrying a nice bottle of wine. "Mrs. Webber, thank you for having me to dinner on such short notice,"

"Not a problem, Mr. Sanders. After being married to Sam for forty-seven years, I'm used to it. And, my name's Rebecca."

"Thank you, Rebecca, I'm Tom."

Rebecca took a minute to examine their guest. He was tall and with a trim build that belied his almost-fifty years, and he looked like an athlete. He carried himself with a calm and confident air. His head was completely bald except for a fringe of closely shaved hair around the lower half of his scalp. His thin, ascetic face served to emphasize his magnificently broken nose

When they were all seated with a drink, Rebecca asked, "So, I understand you want to take my husband and our dog off to Iwo Jima to look for missing Marines?"

"Yes, and Sam said that there was no way he could agree to that without your permission."

"It's about time he figured that out, but I'm curious. Why him? How did you find out about him and Gunny?"

"He read the newspaper stories about that kid we found up in the Uintas last year," Sam said.

"Oh, that was so sad," Rebecca said, "That poor girl. But she'd only been dead about a month; you're talking about bodies that have been in the ground for over seventy years?"

Tom nodded, "Yes, ma'am, but I've done some research, and I've read about dogs who have found very old buried bodies."

"Is that right, Sam?"

"Yeah, we'd need to do some training, but there's plenty of old pioneer graves around here. I'm pretty sure Gunny could do it."

"OK, but what about their age? Gunny's nine and Sam's almost seventy. Will they be fit enough?"

"Well, that Uinta search they did was pretty tough," Tom said, "They were up above eleven-thousand feet on a steep, rocky slope and they did pretty well with that. A lot of what we'll be doing on Iwo will be on much easier terrain."

"I have a question," Sam said.

"Shoot"

"The Japs have Iwo now, right? We gave it back to them?"

"Yes, well, first of all, we refer to them as Japanese now, and they will be our hosts and they've been very gracious in giving us permission to conduct this search. Do you have a particular dislike for the Japanese?"

"A particular dislike? No, I don't think so. No more than anyone else who was born in 1947 and grew up listening to stories about the war in the Pacific. The Japanese weren't real popular in this country for a long time."

"I understand, but, if you come with us, you'll have to put those feelings aside."

"Yeah, Tom, I understand. I've been around the block enough times to know how to behave."

During dinner, Rebecca was mostly quiet, watching the two men. Sam didn't look much like Tom, shorter and not as lean, although thin enough, darker complexion, a full head of gray hair cut short, and a mostly intact nose. When he was speaking, Sam came across as rougher around the edges, and people often tended to underestimate his intelligence. Sam sometimes encouraged this by playing the 'good old boy' until he 'let it slip' that he had a master's degree in mathematics.

Still, anyone looking at the two of them would immediately form the same impression—military men. *They're all the same*, she thought, *somehow you just know*.

"Listening to you talk, Sam, you sound like you want to do this," Rebecca said.

"Well, yeah, I mean, it's Iwo Jima."

"And you're a Marine. Does anyone else hear the sound of distant trumpets?"

"Does that mean I can have him?"

"Yeah, what the hell. But if you get my dog hurt Mr. Sanders, you better just stay over there in the Pacific."

"Yes, ma'am."

◆ ◆ ◆

Ogden Valley, Utah
Wednesday, 15 January
1800 Hours

While The Man and Mom and the other man were eating Gunny was lying under the dinner table, waiting for someone to drop some food. Although his interest in food was always high, he was having trouble staying awake. It had been fun working with The Man to Go Find today, and even a year ago he would have still been full of energy, but lately, he was spending more and more time sleeping.

After a few minutes, Gunny's head sagged, and his eyelids drooped, and he drifted into sleep and began having his favorite dream. As usual, he dreamed of a scent. Gunny remembered every scent he had ever smelled, but this was his favorite. It was the scent of the first human hand that had held him when he was a tiny puppy. In his dream, this smell always mingled with that of his mother and brothers and sisters and made him feel good, and he slept peacefully dreaming of the night he had been born.

◆ ◆ ◆

Golden Hunters Kennels
Near Albin, Wyoming
About Nine Years Earlier
1930 Hours

Golden Hunters Wild Water Bound, Dubya to her friends, paced anxiously around the dining room of the small Wyoming ranch house. The March wind moaned outside, and Dubya was glad to be in here where it was warm. She usually didn't mind the cold, and she loved the snow, but when she was like this, it was better to be inside. Dubya could feel the puppies moving in her swollen belly, and she could tell they were almost ready to be born.

Marsha watched her dog and prepared herself for a long night. She had put the birthing pen, a child's inflatable wading pool with clean, soft towels on the bottom, in the dining room ten days ago and moved Dubya in from the kennel so she could get used to her new bed. The pool would give the new puppies room to crawl around, and the plastic sides were high and slick enough that they couldn't get out.

Nothing fancy thought Marsha, *but good working dogs don't need fancy. Not that we could afford fancy. You don't get rich breeding working dogs and running a ranch.*

Dubya walked over and put her head in Marsha's lap, and Marsha began to rub the soft fur below her ears.

"How're you doin' sweet girl? You ready for this? It's gonna go nice and easy, just like the last time. We'll get through tonight and the next eight weeks and then those puppies will go off to their new homes, and you can go back to huntin' birds."

And we can make a couple of mortgage payments.

Dubya gave a soft "woof" which could have been agreement, or a request to keep the head rub going.

Dubya, and her mate for this litter, River, were almost perfect examples of what working Golden Retrievers should be. Smaller, more compact and muscular than most Goldens, they could work in the fields all day, and their exquisite noses could detect the faintest of odors and follow it through thick brush and water to find their bird. They were both champion hunters; Dubya specialized in field trial competitions, and River was an upland bird dog.

Marsha went to the kitchen to fix herself a sandwich, and by the time she got back to the dining room, Dubya had settled herself in the birthing pen. Marsha just had time to finish eating when the first tiny, wriggling puppy emerged. In a process that would be repeated eleven more times that night, Marsha first checked to make sure the puppy's nose and mouth were clear and that it was breathing. She then quickly clamped and cut the umbilical cord and dried the new pup with a clean towel. Finally, she took a small piece of soft, colored, cotton cord and carefully tied it around the puppy's neck and gently placed the new life down next to its mother. The cords would be used to identify the puppies and gave them their puppy names.

Sometime the next morning a little male was born. He was clamped, cut, and dried, and a turquoise cord was put around his neck. Like his brothers and sisters, he was toothless, blind and deaf, and would remain so for two weeks or more. None of that mattered though, because his sense of smell, on which he would depend his whole life, was already hundreds of times better than an adult human's, and the first scent that flooded his tiny nostrils was that of a human hand. A moment later, he was placed down with his siblings next to his mother.

Turquoise Boy was five minutes old, and he had already learned to associate the smell of a human hand with warmth and safety. He was born to be a hunter, and his training had begun.

BEFORE THE BATTLE

From the Halls of Montezuma
To the Shores of Tripoli
We fight our Country's battles
In the air, on land, and sea
First to fight for right and freedom
And to keep our honor clean
We are proud to claim the title
Of United States Marine

First verse of The Marines' Hymn

Off Iwo Jima
February 19th, 1945
D-Day,
H Hour minus 4 Hours

IF *LIFE* MAGAZINE HAD PUBLISHED AN ISSUE with a cover photo of the "All-American Farm Boy of 1943" Robby Durance could have been their model. He was a young man just out of boyhood, and he had the look of someone who had grown up in the freedom of the fields and woods. He had thick, blond hair, blue eyes, and the graceful body of an athlete. His face radiated his contentment in life and his eagerness to move forward into his future.

When people back home talked about Robby, they used words like honest, hardworking, and smart. Young women tended to add handsome or good-looking. Most who knew him liked him, and he liked them.

On this morning, Robby Durance, now PFC Robert L. Durance III USMC, stared down at his metal tray where an untouched piece of steak and two eggs were getting cold.

Am I the only one here who is too damned scared to eat?

Robby looked around the troop mess deck of the attack transport where Able and Baker companies of the 1st Battalion, 25th Marines were jammed in shoulder to shoulder at the narrow tables that filled the space.

Some of the men were eating, but others were like Robby, not touching their food, or just picking at it. One old man of twenty-four, a veteran of two amphibious assaults, sat holding a cup of cold coffee staring fixedly at the wall watching a movie that only he could see.

The sound of so many nervous young men crowded together was so loud that Robby could barely hear what was being said at his table, yet he could still hear, or maybe just feel, the gut-punching rumble of the big Navy guns that had been going almost nonstop for the last three days.

Robby had heard many of the other Marines, the new guys like him who hadn't been in combat yet, talking about how there couldn't be any Japs still alive after all the shells the Navy was throwing at the island. But he had also watched the old salts, the ones who had been at Roi-Namur, or Saipan, or Tinian, or all three, and they didn't say much at all.

Robby was usually a good sleeper, and he had long ago gotten used to the cramped troop space with its tiers of bunks spaced twenty inches apart where the smell of gun oil mixed with the sweat of active young men into a unique miasma, but last night he'd tossed and turned. His mind kept going over all those things the NCOs had been drilling into his head for the past two months, what he was supposed to do and what he wasn't supposed to do. When he wasn't thinking about that, he thought about home and his family or Susan Chamblee, with her golden hair and soft, southern voice.

This morning, on what might be the last day of his life, all he could think about was Rusty.

Robby had been six when he had gotten Rusty. Rusty wasn't anything special, some Collie, mostly mutt, but the first time Robby picked Rusty up the two of them bonded in the way that only young boys and puppies can. From then on they went everywhere and did everything together. Robbie's Mom strictly forbade him from letting Rusty sleep in his bed and then pretended not to notice when he did. Rusty walked Robby to and from school each day spending the time when Robby was inside under the schoolhouse porch.

When Rusty died, Robby had to go behind the barn so the others wouldn't see him crying. It didn't make any sense for a grown man, a man who would be going to Marine Corps boot camp in less than a week, to cry over a dog.

Now Robby wished for nothing more than to have Rusty's head on his lap and to stroke his soft fur one last time.

The blare of the ship's loudspeaker suddenly cut through the mess deck din, and Robby jumped.

"Now hear this! Now hear this! All Marines report to your debark stations. I say again, all Marines report to your debark stations. On the double!"

Robby dumped his uneaten breakfast in the garbage can and headed to his berthing space to grab his rifle and gear and to get ready to go to war on the island of Iwo Jima.

TEAM LIBERTY IWO JIMA INITIAL BRIEFING

Nemo Residio
"Leave No One Behind"

Motto of the Marine Corps Personnel
Retrieval and Recovery Company

Commanding General's Conference Room
Marine Corps Base Camp Pendleton, CA
Monday, 12 June
0800 Hours

SAM WEBBER WATCHED as Tom Sanders rose from his place at the head of the conference table. Sam had been briefly introduced to the other three members of the team just a few minutes ago, and he had formed some quick initial impressions. Everyone on the team looked to be intelligent, hard-working professionals and experts in their fields. They were also a mix of very strong and very different personalities.

This is going to be interesting, he thought. *Tom's got his work cut out for him. But then, he was a Lieutenant Colonel in the Rangers, I think he can hack it.*

When he had everyone's attention, Tom began to speak.

"Lady and gentlemen, I think we can get started."

"Thank you for coming and welcome to the first full team meeting of 'Team Liberty Iwo Jima.' Today we'll be getting acquainted and starting to learn the details of the search we will begin a week from now. Dr. Jim Stewart will be doing most of the talking today, but first, let's do introductions."

"I met each of you individually when I recruited you, but I'll start anyway just to get things going."

"I'm Tom Sanders, and I'm the team leader. I'm a retired U.S. Army Lieutenant Colonel. I spent twenty-two years in the Army, about ten of those in Ranger units. This is my third deployment with Team Liberty; before this, I was the deputy team leader on two searches in Viet Nam."

"Let's go around the table. Dr. Stewart, you're up."

"Hi, I'm Dr. Jim Stewart, I'm a professor of Twentieth Century History at Brigham Young University in Provo, Utah. I'm the team historian. My job is to identify the Marines we will be looking for and the most likely search areas. I'll be assisted by two of my grad students who won't be going with us. They'll stay in Provo where they'll have access to more extensive research facilities to help me get any information I might need as we go along. I'll communicate with them via e-mail and satellite phone."

The next person at the table was an attractive woman in her early thirties with short, blond hair, icy-blue, intelligent eyes, and a severe and professional demeanor.

"I'm Dr. Alicia Phillips from the Forensic Anthropology Department at the University of Tennessee and the Tennessee State Bureau of Investigation. I'm here to examine any remains we might find to determine if they are American or Japanese and, if they are American, to try to identify them. Like Dr. Stewart, I will be assisted by two graduate students who will stay back at the University.

"I'll be bringing the full suite of equipment that I would normally take to a crime scene plus some other specialized equipment like a ground-penetrating radar system. I've had six years of experience teaching Forensic Anthropology at UT and advising law enforcement agencies across Tennessee on crime scene investigation which has included significant time in the field at crime scenes."

"Hi, I'm Steve Haney, and this is Luke."

The person to Dr. Phillips' right was a tall, athletic African-American man in his mid-twenties.

"Hi, I'm Steve Haney, and this is Luke."

As he spoke, Steve pointed to a Black Labrador Retriever lying next to him. Luke had a broad, goofy-looking grin and a rapidly wagging tail. He also had a stripe of grayish-white fur about eighteen inches long on his left side.

"Luke and I are your explosive ordnance detection team. We were a Marine special patrol dog team in Afghanistan until we got on the wrong side of a Taliban rocket-propelled grenade."

As he said this, Steve pointed to the scar on Luke's side and then reached down and rapped his right leg, which made a dead, metallic sound.

"We'll be sweeping all of the search areas to make sure that there aren't any nasty surprises out there for you."

Standing up, Tom Sanders said, "Let me interrupt for a minute here to say something you are going to hear me say a lot. No one, under any circumstances, is to go anywhere on the island until

Steve and Luke have cleared it, and I've told you it is safe to go. I need everyone to nod their head to show they understand."

Each head nodded, and Tom continued.

"I don't want to scare you, and I don't expect a problem, but this is non-negotiable. The Americans alone dropped over twenty thousand tons of explosives on Iwo, equivalent to the bombs dropped on Hiroshima and Nagasaki. Some of it didn't go off. Most of what's still there after seventy years is inert, but TNT is tricky stuff. Some of it can be highly sensitive. Steve and Luke have done this stuff before in Afghanistan and saved a bunch of lives, so they know what they're doing."

"OK," Tom continued, "Last but not least, we have the old man and his old dog."

"Screw you, Ranger," Sam said grinning, "I'm Major Sam Webber, United States Marine Corps, Retired, and this old dog lying next to me is Gunny."

Gunny lifted his head and looked up at Sam. The fur on his face and muzzle was mostly white, but his dark eyes sparkled and his lips relaxed into an easy grin.

"Gunny is a nine-year-old Golden Retriever and a search and rescue dog certified for wilderness live search and a couple of different kinds of cadaver search. Our job will be to try to locate any human remains, either on or below the surface. Gunny's done a lot of this, and he's really good. Oh, and if we happen to have an avalanche while we're on Iwo, he's certified for that too."

Sam noticed that everyone had a brief laugh at his last comment except Dr. Phillips, who had been stone-faced while he was talking.

"Just so you know," Tom said, "Sam spent twenty-four years in the Marines including two years in Vietnam as an enlisted Marine infantryman. Don't let the white in his hair or on Gunny's face fool you, they'll work the rest of us into the ground. Sam will also be my deputy team leader."

"OK, that's it for introductions. Any questions?"

"All right, let's take a coffee break, and I'll turn this over to Dr. Stewart."

♦ ♦ ♦

Commanding General's Conference Room
Marine Corps Base Camp Pendleton, CA
Monday, 12 June
0830 Hours

"Good morning, everyone. Today I hope to give you all a good background on the battle for Iwo Jima and then to focus in on the missing Marines we will be looking for. I think it's essential that we all understand as well as we can the situation we'll be facing so please don't hesitate to ask any questions you have."

Jim Stewart was an angular man in his fifties with an unruly shock of blond hair that he raked with his fingers from time to time in an unsuccessful attempt to bring it into order. He was average height and a little pudgy with pale skin that burned easily. He looked like someone who spent most of his time indoors.

Except for two years in Philadelphia, where he had done his Mormon mission, Jim had lived in and around Provo, Utah. This trip to Iwo Jima was the great adventure of his life.

"Iwo Jima was the bloodiest battle in Marine Corps history. Over sixty-eight hundred Marines and Navy Corpsmen were killed in the thirty-six days of fighting to capture an island five miles long and two miles wide. After the battle, the dead were interred in three cemeteries on the island, one for each of the Marine Divisions who fought there. Those who died aboard hospital ships were buried at sea.

"After the war, the bodies were disinterred to be returned to the U.S., and the cemeteries were closed. These remains went to either a cemetery designated by the next of kin, which could include Arlington National Cemetery, or, for those whose next of kin could not be located or who had no preference, to the National Cemetery at the Punchbowl in Hawaii.

"There were about three hundred men who remained classified as 'Missing and presumed dead.' Most of these are men whose death was so violent that no remains could be found. However, there were some whose deaths were not observed and who essentially vanished, perhaps into a cave or Japanese bunker.

"We believe there may be as many as twenty Marines whose remains exist, but were not recovered after the battle of Iwo Jima. The most famous of these is Sergeant William H. Genaust, a Marine combat correspondent who filmed the first flag raising on Suribachi and was killed there nine days later.

"Based on the research my team has done, we plan to focus our search on the remains of five Marines from the 1st squad of the 1st platoon of Baker Company, 1st Battalion, 25th Marine Regiment, which was part of the Fourth Marine Division."

"Excuse me, Doctor, may I ask a question?" Dr. Phillips said.

"Of course, please do."

"If we know that there are possibly twenty sets of remains, why are we narrowing our search to just five?"

"I can answer that," Tom said, "That was my decision. Besides the missing Marines, there are almost twenty thousand Japanese bodies still on Iwo, which makes looking for twenty Marines practically the definition of finding a needle in a haystack. And, the Japanese government has limited us to only ten days of searching. The five Marines that Jim will describe are the ones we have the most information on, and, since they were all in the same small unit and disappeared at the same time, we expect that they will be close together. Is that correct, Doctor?

"Yes, exactly. Does that answer your question, Dr. Phillips?"

"Thank you."

Stewart turned to a whiteboard behind him, "Before I get into details, here's a word on nomenclature. The 1st Battalion of the 25th Marines would be referred to as One Twenty-Five which would be written like this, '1/25'. Baker Company would be written, 'B/1/25'. So we're looking for '1st Squad, 1st Platoon B/1/25'. Got it?"

Heads nodded around the room.

"Let's start at the beginning so you can get an idea of what happened to the Marines we will be looking for. Here's the plan for the landings on D Day." Jim said, pointing to an image projected from his laptop.

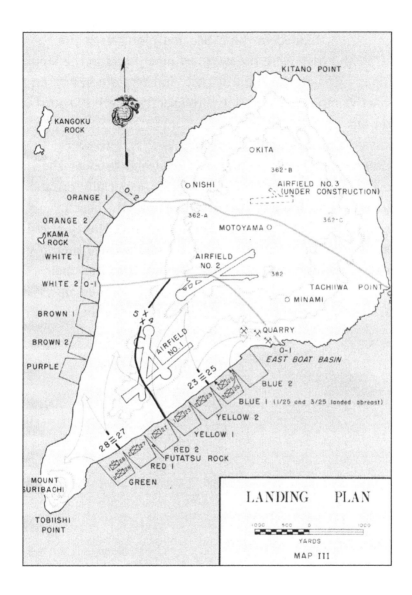

KITANO POINT

KANGOKU
ROCK

OKITA

362-B

O NISHI   AIRFIELD NO.3
                           (UNDER CONSTRUCTION)

ORANGE I

ORANGE 2   362-A
                        MOTOYAMA O   362-C
KAMA
ROCK

WHITE 1   AIRFIELD
                    NO. 2

WHITE 2 O-I   382

                                          TACHIIWA   POINT
                                      O MINAMI
BROWN 1

                              QUARRY
BROWN 2
                                  O-I
PURPLE   EAST BOAT BASIN

                    AIRFIELD
                    NO. 1
                      23 25
                              BLUE 2

                              BLUE 1 (1/25 and 3/25 landed abreast)

                    YELLOW 2

                    YELLOW 1
      28 27
                    RED 2
                  FUTATSU ROCK
                  RED 1
MOUNT
SURIBACHI   GREEN

TOBIISHI
POINT

LANDING   PLAN

1000   500   0   1000
           YARDS

MAP III

"The landings on Iwo all occurred on the eastern side of the
island from a point just north of Suribachi to a spot just east of the
current airfield, which was built on the location of Japanese Airfield
Number 2.

33

"Our unit, 1/25, landed on Blue Beach 1 along with their sister battalion 3/25 and they were the northernmost units in the landing. Baker Company was on the right of 1/25, and 1st platoon was on the right of Baker Company. We're not sure exactly where 1st squad was for the landing.

"The mission for 1/25 and 3/25 on D Day was to wheel to the right and attack northeast parallel to the beach to clear the high ground to the north of the landing beaches, especially around an old rock quarry. First, though, they had to get off the beach."

"Dr. Stewart, how tough was the landing?" Steve Haney asked.

"At first, it wasn't too bad. The Japanese had learned their lesson from previous battles like Saipan and Peleliu, and they held their fire until they had a large number of targets jammed up on the beach, and then they opened up, and it got very, very tough."

ROBBY DURANCE

Those who expect to reap the blessings of liberty must undergo the fatigues of supporting it.

Thomas Paine

Off Blue Beach 1 Iwo Jima
February 19th, 1945
D Day
H Hour minus 2 minutes

ALL RIGHT, MARINES, LOCK AND LOAD," Lieutenant Porter yelled, "We'll be on the beach in a couple of minutes. When that ramp goes down, I want this goddamn amtrac empty in ten seconds!"

It took all of Robby's concentration just to get an eight-round clip out of his ammo pouch and into his M-1. The LVT-4 was surging up and down in the surf, and the thirty Marines onboard were being thrown around like dolls. A good thing they were crammed in so tightly, it at least gave them some support.

God, don't let me screw up. Don't let me be a coward

Some part of Robby's brain congratulated him on being more scared of disgracing himself than of being hurt or dying, but that was little consolation. Scared was scared.

Robby couldn't tell what was happening beyond his field of view, which extended maybe ten feet and included only the Marines around him and the side of the amtrac. Lieutenant Porter was the only one with his head up above the thinly armored troop compartment, and he wasn't saying anything.

There had been some explosions close by, and there was a constant noise of things ripping the air above them, but Robby didn't know what any of this signified. He tried to get a sense of what was happening by looking at the veterans, but they were keeping their heads down. It was impossible to guess what they might be thinking.

The amtrac suddenly lurched upward, and the sound of the tracks changed as they began to engage on the beach. But something was wrong, the LVT wasn't moving, and the tracks were just spinning. The lieutenant was yelling something at the driver that Robby couldn't hear. Suddenly, the ramp at the rear of the amtrac lowered with a crash.

"This is as far as we're going! Get out! Get out! Move it, Marines!" Porter screamed.

Robby was caught up in the sudden rush to the rear. He ran off the side of the ramp and into a couple of feet of surf and deep, soft sand. He pitched forward and just managed to keep his rifle out of the water. Officers and NCOs were urging the men forward, but it was almost impossible to run in the fine, black, volcanic sand. With each step, Robby's foot sank in above the ankle, and the sand sifted backward taking away most of his forward progress.

When he finally got to the front of the amtrac, there was a dune of the black sand about twenty-five feet high that men were struggling to climb. The amtracs were supposed to get them to the top of this dune, but with one or two exceptions, they were stuck. Most of them were struggling to get back out into the water.

After moving only a few feet, Robby was gasping for breath. The dune was like a mountain, impossible to climb. He kept walking; up one foot, back six inches, and each step sapped more and more of his energy.

He dropped to his hands and knees and tried crawling, but it was hard trying to keep his rifle out of the gritty sand that clung to everything it touched. He finally slung the M-1 across his back and crawled to the top of the dune and collapsed.

When he got his breathing under control, he raised his head and looked around. The ground in front of him rose gradually to higher hills in the distance, featureless and black, the same sand he had just climbed through. A few Marines were starting to move inland, but many others were lying like him waiting to see what would happen. Off to his left was Suribachi, and to his right, the ground rose more steeply to broken terraces and hills.

They were supposed to move off the beach as quickly as they could, but nobody else in the squad was doing anything yet. Robby decided to wait and see what Sergeant Bilotti or Lieutenant Porter wanted him to do.

It was quieter than he had expected. He heard and saw a few explosions but nothing too close to him, and there wasn't any rifle or machine-gun fire. Maybe it really was going to be easy. Maybe the Navy had knocked out all the Japs.

Lieutenant Porter moved along the line toward Robby.

"Off the beach! Off the beach! Let's go, people, move it!"

As Porter approached, there was a noise like someone had hit a steel drum with a hammer, and Lieutenant Porter's head came apart in a hundred small pieces. He took two more steps and pitched forward, spewing a gout of blood into the black sand just a few feet from Robby.

Before Robby could comprehend what had happened, the whole world exploded around him. In an instant, he was almost deafened by cracks like the lash of a thousand whips just above his head. Seconds later explosions erupted all around him. It felt like something was pummeling every inch of his body. Men were screaming in high-pitched wails that Robby could hear even above all the other noise.

Oh, God, this is it. I'm going to die here. I'm going to die here. I want to go home!

Robby's mind, unable to cope with sights and sounds beyond anything in his wildest imagination, did as he asked and took him home.

♦ ♦ ♦

Roanoke County, Virginia
1926

When Robby was born in 1926, Cave Spring, Virginia, just south of the city of Roanoke, was a small town surrounded by mid-sized farms. The Durance farm was one of the largest in the area.

Robert Durance, Robby's great-grandfather, had come home from the Civil War in a cloud of glory. He had stood with the Virginians at First Manassas when Thomas Jackson had been named "Stonewall." Robert had been carried from the field to the bloody abattoir that was the hospital where his left arm had been amputated. He was granted a smallholding outside Cave Spring and set about establishing a homestead where he hoped to one day begin a family.

Unlike his neighbors, Robert did not believe that white men had an inherent right to own black men. However, he was a realist and understood that the only way he could hope to be a successful farmer in the South was with slave labor. He resolved that if he must be a slave owner, he would at least be a good Christian and try to treat his slaves as human beings.

He purchased two families of Negroes, four adults and five children. He would get no labor from the children, and they would just be extra mouths to feed, but he would not be responsible for breaking up these families. Then, after swearing them to silence, he made the adults a promise. If they worked faithfully with him to grow his farm, he would see that they were well fed, clothed, and housed and that he would free their children on their twenty-first birthdays.

During the hard times to come, the Durance farm always did a little better than most of the others around. When the war ended, and the slaves were freed, Robert's Negroes stayed with him, and together, they not only survived but were able to acquire additional land and slowly grow the farm. Eventually, the Durance Negroes, as they were known, became the first of their kind in Roanoke County to own their own land.

Robert's dream of a family came true in 1875 when his first son was born.

He named him Robert Lee Durance.

By the time Robby, Robert Lee Durance III, was born, his family had prospered. The secret, his father believed, was that they had never depended on tobacco alone but had always had several crops, and a herd of cattle and so weren't as harshly affected when tobacco prices went down from time to time. "You can't eat tobacco," his mother said, and she maintained a large vegetable garden. With that and the cattle, they always had plenty of food even when others were going hungry.

Despite their prosperity, the Durance family had never broken into the upper strata of society in Roanoke County. Because Robby's father and grandfather had spoken out far too often on behalf of various Negroes they thought were being mistreated, the family was viewed with suspicion. In polite society, people said that they were too friendly with the Negroes. Less politely, they were called nigger lovers.

Robby would always remember the one time his father heard him refer to one of the black men who worked on their farm as a nigger. It was the only time his father had used a belt on him, but that wasn't the worst of it. He had gone with Robby when Robby apologized to the man and then watched as Robby worked the man's share of the farm for the next week.

His family's reputation meant that Robby had to learn early to stand up for himself. It helped that Rusty was always close by. Rusty seemed to understand that Robby had to fight his own fights and, as long as it was a fair fight, he stayed out of it. But, if the other kid was too big or too nasty, or there were more kids than Robby could handle, Rusty charged in and set things right with a couple of hard nips.

Things only got serious enough for Rusty to draw blood one time when an older boy pulled a knife on Robby. It took thirty stitches to close up the wounds in the boy's hand and arm, and the doctor didn't think the hand would ever be completely right again.

The boy came from a family of white trash, or the sheriff might have taken more notice of the incident than he did. Robby's dad promised the sheriff he was going to "give that dog a beating," but somehow he never got around to it.

After that, none of the other kids wanted to give Robby any trouble.

Although Robby's family was looked on with suspicion for their political views, they were otherwise held in high regard both because of their prosperity and their heritage.

In the Shenandoah Valley of Virginia, any family that could claim to be direct descendants of a man who had served with Stonewall Jackson had an immediate claim to respectability. The fact that Robby's grandfather had fought in Cuba with Teddy Roosevelt and his dad had served with distinction in the Marine Brigade in France in World War I only enhanced their reputation.

Because of this heritage, Robby was expected to be special, and he was. Smart, hardworking, and athletically talented, Robby was also friendly and outgoing and was popular with his teachers and classmates despite his odd social views.

Cave Spring High School was far too small to compete with the other schools around in football or baseball but their basketball team, with Robby as the playmaking guard, held their own and even made it to the State quarterfinals his senior year.

In a rational world Robby would have followed in his father's and grandfather's footsteps and gone on to Washington and Lee College in nearby Lexington, but this was 1944, and the country had been at war for almost two and a half years. Upon finishing high school, Robby joined the Marines.

◆ ◆ ◆

Blue Beach 1 Iwo Jima
February 19th, 1945
D Day
H Hour plus 22 minutes

Robby felt like he was being awakened from a deep, black sleep by a sharp pain in his side.

"God Damn it, Durance!" screamed Sergeant Bilotti, jabbing him in the side again with the muzzle of his carbine. "Get your sorry ass moving! Winston's already moved out with the BAR. Get over there and start feeding him ammo or I will stick this carbine up your ass!"

Robby was suddenly flushed with a rush of shame. What was he doing? What was wrong with him? His father, his grandfather, and his great-grandfather had all fought their wars. They had passed their tests. He might die in the next minute, but he'd be damned if he'd die as a coward.

"Aye, aye sergeant," he said, and began to crawl forward, his rifle cradled in his arms.

TEAM LIBERTY IWO JIMA FINAL BRIEFING

Life is tough, but it's tougher if you're stupid.

John Wayne as Sergeant Stryker in Sands of Iwo Jima

Commanding General's Conference Room
Marine Corps Base Camp Pendleton, CA
Monday, 12 June
0900 Hours

"DR. STEWART, WHY DID THEY MAKE THAT BIG WHEEL TO THE RIGHT?" Dr. Phillips asked. "Wouldn't it have been simpler to just go straight across the island and then turn to the north?"

"Can one of our military men answer that?" asked Stewart.

"Sure," Tom said, "That's easy. If they had gone straight, they would have had an exposed flank on their right, and the Japanese could have attacked that flank or worked around and attacked from the rear. They had to clear the Japanese to their north."

"Thanks." Dr. Stewart said, "This is a key point because as a result of this wheel 1/25 ended up participating in two of the bloodiest fights on Iwo Jima, the Rock Quarry, and the Amphitheater. We'll be focusing on their battle in the Amphitheater."

"Now let's get back to where we left our squad on the beach on D Day."

"The Japanese held their fire until the first wave had landed, and the second wave was just coming ashore. Until that is, they had a lot of targets in a small area. The Marines quickly learned that the great majority of the Japanese defenders had survived the pre-invasion bombardment."

"We know that our squad suffered three casualties on D Day, two killed and one seriously wounded."

"Doctor, I'm sorry to keep interrupting, but this is all new to me," Phillips said, "How many men were in that squad?"

"During World War II a Marine rifle squad had thirteen members, a squad leader, and three, four-man fire teams. Each fire team had a team leader, a Browning Automatic Rifleman or BAR man, an assistant BAR man, and a rifleman." Stewart replied.

"They suffered almost twenty-five percent casualties on the first day?" Phillips asked. "Why weren't they taken off the line?"

"If you're referring to the maxim that a military unit is usually considered to be ineffective once it has suffered more than ten percent casualties—it's called being decimated—then, you're right, they should have been replaced. However, that rule didn't hold on Iwo Jima where many units fought on after having received thirty, forty, or, in a few cases, fifty percent casualties."

"My God, it must have been horrible," Phillips said.

"Yes, it was. You and I can't imagine what it was like. Perhaps one of our combat veterans could give us some idea?"

Stewart looked at Sam, Tom, and Steve in turn. They each just shook their head.

"In any event," Stewart continued "progress on D day was less than planned, but it was sufficient to allow the following waves to land and be established ashore."

"Now I don't intend to give you a day by day accounting of what happened to the Marines for whom we are searching. However, I do want to talk for a moment about the night of D day because it illustrates a critical point that differentiates Iwo Jima from many other battles in the Pacific.

"On that first night, Marine units all along the line stopped and made sure they were tied in with units on both flanks, even if that meant retreating a short distance. Well before dark, Marines began digging defensive positions. This was done in anticipation of a Banzai counterattack."

Dr. Phillips raised her hand, "Once again I need some help. I've heard the term 'Banzai,' but I don't know what it means. Could you explain?"

"Certainly."

"The Code of Bushido, the unwritten code of the Samurai, is roughly comparable to the European code of chivalry. Under Bushido, Banzai was considered to be a form of honorable suicide and was originally a way to die with glory if a battle was lost. However, by World War II, the leaders of the Japanese Army believed that their soldiers were physically and morally superior to their enemies. They thought that if they launched them in a mighty blow against the enemy at a time when he was most vulnerable, victory would be assured. The Banzai charge, they believed, was unstoppable, and, in the early days of the war when fighting against poorly trained and equipped troops, they were correct.

"The first time the Japanese Army tried a Banzai attack against U.S. Marines was at the battle of the Tenaru River on Guadalcanal in

1942. The Japanese Ichiki Regiment attacked at night with about nine hundred fifty men against about four hundred Marines. Before the battle, Colonel Ichiki was so confident of winning that he filled in his diary for the next day with the words, 'Enjoyed the fruits of victory.'

"The Marines killed Colonel Ichiki and over eight hundred of his men and lost fewer than thirty of their own.

"The same futile waste of life was repeated over and over on islands across the Pacific. The Japanese were slow to change their tactics because to do so would mean that they had to admit that they were wrong, which would have been a loss of face for the Army's leaders.

"So, the Marines had gotten used to having to repel a Banzai attack in the early stages of an island invasion. In fact, they quickly saw that these attacks played into their hands. Every major attack the Japanese launched against Marines who were supported by artillery and naval gunfire was repulsed with heavy losses to the attackers. As far as the Marines were concerned, every Japanese soldier they killed in a Banzai attack was one less that they had to dig out of a cave or bunker.

"That all changed on Iwo Jima. The Japanese commander, General Kuribayashi, knew that victory in the war was no longer possible. The only thing he could do was kill as many Americans as possible, and hope that America would tire of the fighting and offer terms for peace that Japan could accept. Kuribayashi was also one of the generals who understood the futility of the Banzai charge. He determined that the best way to kill Americans was to wage a defensive battle where his troops always had the advantage of fighting from heavily fortified, interconnected positions and the Americans were the ones who had to fight in the open with little cover or concealment.

"Kuribayashi was also able to largely negate the American advantage in firepower by digging deeply and cleverly. Iwo Jima was literally honeycombed with bunkers and caves connected by miles of tunnels. If one position was taken, the surviving Japanese could escape through these tunnels and continue the fight, often from positions to the rear of the attacking Americans.

"This brings us back to the night of D Day. There was no Banzai attack that night. Instead, the exhausted Marines were subjected to constant bombardment from artillery and mortars, sniper fire, and small isolated attacks. The next morning the Marines had to continue the offensive against Japanese defenders who had gotten at least some rest after the D Day fighting.

"This was the pattern that would be repeated over and over for the next thirty-five days."

"My God, how did they do it?"

"I don't know, Doctor," Stewart said, "Perhaps Mr. Webber can help us understand."

Sam was about to shake his head again, then looked thoughtful for a moment. "They did it because they were Marines. I know it sounds trite, but that's the only answer. Iwo Jima may have been the Marines' toughest battle, but it was not an isolated incident. Belleau Wood, Tarawa, Chosin Reservoir, I can name a dozen others. Somehow the Marines have found a way to make a man more afraid of letting down his buddies and his unit than he is of dying. Every Marine feels that he—excuse me, he or she—has a responsibility to uphold the honor and traditions of the Corps. I can't explain it any better than that."

"I think Sam has it exactly right," Tom said, "Remember Napoleon said that, '... in war, the moral is to the physical as three is to one.' What he meant was that intangibles like unit loyalty, what the Marines call *esprit de corps*, and a will to fight are more important than numbers or firepower. I hate to admit it, but the Marines do the moral part of war better than anyone else."

"Thank you," Stewart said, "I think as we all learn more about this battle we'll begin to understand what Sam and Tom are talking about.

"OK, let's take a short break, and when we start again, I'll explain exactly whom we are searching for and where we'll be working."

♦ ♦ ♦

Commanding General's Conference Room
Marine Corps Base Camp Pendleton, CA
Monday, 12 June
0930 Hours

Sam Webber got a cup of coffee and walked over to Dr. Phillips.

"Dr. Phillips, I'm looking forward to working with you on this search."

Phillips' reply was cold and distant. "Mr. Webber, I appreciate that, however, I don't see what you and your dog have to offer. Furthermore, I am concerned that your dog may destroy evidence or compromise a crime scene."

"Well, Doctor, this ain't our first rodeo. Gunny and I've been on over fifty searches, and I think we've been a big help in several cases. We've worked with CSI teams before, and no one has complained yet."

"Be that as it may, Mr. Webber, I don't have any plans to use your dog, and I want him kept well clear of my search area."

"Excuse me, Dr. Phillips," Tom said as he walked over, "I couldn't help but overhear, and I have to make a comment. You haven't worked with dogs before, but I have, both in combat and on our Team Liberty searches in Vietnam. I can tell you that they are a valuable tool, especially when we have to search large areas like we do on Iwo. I think you'll find that Gunny will be a big help."

"Mr. Sanders, I am sure that dogs have their uses, but a rigorous forensic investigation is not the place for a dog or an untrained person for that matter. That's why we mark off our search areas with crime scene tape."

Tom had known that Alicia Phillips was going to be challenging to deal with the first time he had met her, but she was a brilliant forensic anthropologist, and he was lucky to get her on this search. Fortunately, twenty-two years in the Army had taught him how to deal with difficult people.

"Dr. Phillips, the way I see things working is that Sam and Gunny will search an area that you and Dr. Stewart designate. If Gunny finds something or shows interest in a particular spot, then you move in to do your detailed search, and Sam and Gunny will get out of your way."

"I have serious concerns that ..."

"Good, then that's settled," Tom said, "Let's get back to the meeting. Dr. Stewart has a lot more information for us."

As the rest of the team moved back to the conference table, Alicia Phillips stood rooted in place with a shocked expression on her face.

♦ ♦ ♦

Commanding General's Conference Room
Marine Corps Base Camp Pendleton, CA
Monday, 12 June

0945 Hours

"OK, everyone ready to start again?" asked Stewart. When he had everyone's attention, he continued.

"I'll skip ahead now to March 1st, 1945. Our squad has been in almost continuous combat for ten days, although they did get a couple of days back off the line in reserve.

"This map shows the situation at that time.

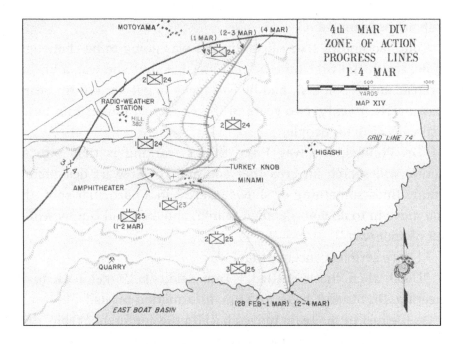

"Although there's no scale on this map, what it shows is that 1/25 moved about two thousand meters, maybe a mile and a quarter, in ten days. Most of you could walk that far in thirty minutes or so. That should give you an idea of how difficult the fighting was here.

"Look at the center of the map. There's our unit, 1/25, and that arrow is pointing right to where we will be doing our search, the area known as the Amphitheater. The Amphitheater was a part of a Japanese defensive belt that also included the hill named Turkey Knob and Hill 382. This whole system was named the Meat Grinder by the Marines. Taking the Meat Grinder cost more American lives than Suribachi or any other position on Iwo Jima."

Stewart paused to let that sink in.

"By the time they got to the Amphitheater, our squad was down from thirteen men to only five. Since they had received four replacements during these ten days, that means that they had taken twelve casualties, almost one hundred percent of their original number."

The team went utterly silent.

"I've put together some charts that summarize what happened to the members of the squad from D Day to D +10.

"The first chart is the original squad roster on D Day.

Squad Leader –   **Sergeant Joe Billotti**

1st Fire Team

Team Leader	**CPL Jeff Hanks**
BAR	**PFC Ken Roberts**
Asst. BAR	**PFC Gerry Jones**
Rifleman	**PFC Steve Simms**

2nd Fire Team

Team Leader	**CPL Aaron Moses**
BAR	**PFC Donald Winston**

Asst. BAR	**PFC Robert Durance**
Rifleman	**PFC Edward Hobbs**

3rd Fire Team

Team Leader	**CPL Ernesto DeSilva**
BAR	**PFC James Franklin**
Asst. BAR	**PFC Sam Cottrell**
Rifleman	**PVT Larry Lawrence**

"This next chart shows the squad's attrition and replacements from D day through D +5. If you're not familiar with the terminology, KIA is 'Killed in Action,' WIA is 'Wounded in Action,' and MIA is 'Missing in Action.'

D-Day: **PFC Winston KIA, CPL DeSilva, and PFC Franklin WIA**

D +2 **PFC Cottrell KIA**

D + 4 **PFC Roberts KIA, PFC Jones WIA**

D + 5 **SGT Billotti KIA**
Replacements: CPL Ron Sullivan, PFC Heinrich Kohl, PFC Richard Schultz, PVT Simon Laskey

"This is what the squad looked like after it was reorganized on D +5.

Squad Leader	**CPL Jeff Hanks**

1st Fire Team

Team Leader	CPL Ron Sullivan
BAR	PFC Steve Simms
Rifleman	PFC Heinrich Kohl

2nd Fire Team

Team Leader	CPL Aaron Moses
BAR	PFC Edward Hobbs
Rifleman	PFC Richard Schultz

3rd Fire Team

Team Leader	PFC Robert Durance
BAR	PVT Larry Lawrence
Rifleman	PVT Simon Laskey

"And, finally, this is the attrition up through D + 10.

D + 7:	PFC Simms KIA
D + 8	CPL Sullivan KIA, CPL Moses WIA
D +9	PFC Schultz KIA, PFC Kohl WIA
D + 10	CPL Hanks, PFC Durance, PVT Hobbs, PVT Lawrence, PVT Laskey MIA

"Those men who all went missing on D +10, March 1st,, 1945, are the men we will be looking for."

"Dr. Stewart, were those types of casualties common?" Phillips asked.

"There were seventy-two thousand Marines and Navy Hospital Corpsmen in the landing force. They sustained twenty-six thousand casualties, which equates to thirty-five percent. Included in that total of seventy-two thousand were all of the support personnel, the mechanics and cooks and truck drivers. Although no one was ever safe on Iwo Jima and many of those in support roles were killed or wounded it stands to reason that the casualty rate was much higher among the infantry units that were on the front line day in and day out.

"To give you an example, Easy Company, 2nd Battalion, 28th Marines, the unit that raised the flag over Suribachi, took eighty-four percent casualties, including replacements, over the course of the battle.

"The statistics don't tell the whole story, however. When B/1/25 made their attack on D +10, the Commanding Officer of 1/25 was Captain James C. Headley, and he had been the commander since D +3. A battalion is typically commanded by a Lieutenant Colonel, an officer two ranks higher.

"In fact, of the original twenty-four battalion commanders on D Day, only seven were still alive and in command at the battle's end.

"I think we can see that, although our squad may have suffered more than usual, their situation was not out of the ordinary for Iwo Jima."

"So, what did they face at the Amphitheater?" Stewart posed.

"On D +10 Baker Company was assigned the task of assaulting the Amphitheater in coordination with attacks by the other companies of 1/25 across the top of the Amphitheater and toward the Turkey Knob. At the same time the 1st Battalion, 24th Marines were hitting hill 382. In other words, it was a full out attempt to take the Meat Grinder."

"The Amphitheater was a daunting objective. About three hundred yards across and two hundred yards from front to back it formed a U-shaped bowl with steeply sloped ridges all the way around. The face of the ridges was a mixture of soft sand and jumbles of rocks ranging from the size of your fist to the size of a small truck. Those ridges went up approximately 120 feet from the floor of the Amphitheater, and they were filled with bunkers, caves and fighting positions all designed to be mutually supporting. Furthermore, many of the positions were connected by tunnels deep inside the ridges."

Phillips asked. "What does mutually supporting mean?"

"Good question. Essentially it means that no one position could be attacked without coming under fire from one or more other positions."

"That must have been tough."

"It was, and especially so since the Japanese were masters at designing these positions. The Marines made no grand charge or single overwhelming attack here. Being entrenched up on the ridge, the Japanese had the upper hand both literally and figuratively. The Marines' only choice was to whittle away at the Japanese positions one at a time, which was very costly both in terms of time and lives.

"To give you an idea of just how tough a position the Amphitheater was, I'll show you one last slide.

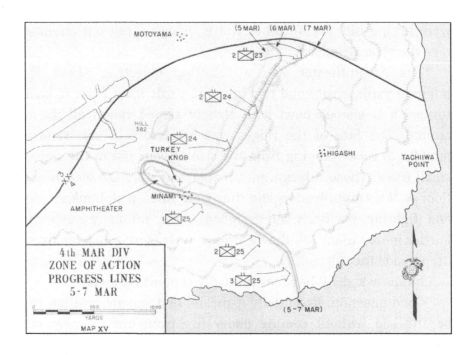

"As you can see, this shows the Fourth Marine Division's lines on March 5th through the 7th or D+14 to D+16. Although the Division had made significant progress elsewhere, the Amphitheater and Turkey Knob had still not been taken almost a week after Baker Company's initial assault, as shown by that deep bulge in the lines. In fact, these were among the last major positions to be secured before the end of the battle."

"Wow, I never knew that," Sam said, "I guess like most people I'd always assumed that Suribachi was the toughest objective."

"Doctor, perhaps you could explain just how they would have attacked those positions," Phillips said, "That might give us an idea of the most likely places to find the missing men."

"Dr. Phillips, Baker Company was pinned down and unable to advance before they got within a hundred yards of the ridges where most of the bunkers were and, if I understand correctly, they needed to get much closer than that to mount a successful attack. Is that correct, Tom?"

"Don't ask me, Rangers don't do bunkers, we're light infantry. We leave that kind of heavy lifting to the Marines. Maybe one of our Jarheads can answer you."

"I can tell you how we'd do it today," Steve Haney said, "We'd back off a few hundred yards and paint the bunker with a laser and call in Marine Air with a five hundred pound PGM or a Hellfire missile and then go in and pick up the pieces. They didn't have that luxury on Iwo."

"What's a PGM, what's a Hellfire?"

"Dr. Phillips, a PGM is a Precision Guided Munition, a laser-guided bomb. A Hellfire is an anti-tank missile with about thirty pounds of explosives in its warhead, and it is also laser-guided," Steve replied.

"What did they do on Iwo Jima?"

"Clearing a bunker on Iwo meant getting up close and personal with the guys you were trying to kill," Sam said, "It meant a guy carrying twenty gallons of napalm in two tanks on his back had to get within twenty-five yards of the bunker with his flamethrower and hose it down, and then another guy had to get right up next to the bunker to throw in a twenty-pound satchel charge. Meanwhile, all those Japanese in their supporting bunkers were trying to kill them."

"That must have been incredibly dangerous!" Phillips said.

"Yeah, the only guy on Iwo with a shorter life expectancy than a flame gunner was an infantry Second Lieutenant," Sam said.

"Does that answer your question, Dr. Phillips?" Jim asked.

"Yes, thank you."

"So, what do we know about our five Marines at the Amphitheater?" Sam Webber asked.

"We know they were there, and we know they went missing. Exactly where they were and how they went missing is a mystery, especially since the ground there was so flat and featureless. You'd think that it would be impossible for five men to just disappear in a place like that. We know that 1st Platoon was on the right flank of Baker Company, and we believe 1st Squad was on the right of the platoon.

"Lieutenant Porter, the platoon commander, was the first person in Baker Company to be killed on D day. Staff Sergeant Cron took over, and he was still the platoon commander when they went into the Amphitheater. According to his statement taken after the battle, the platoon was under heavy fire and pinned down for most of the time they were in the Amphitheater, and the squads became jumbled together as individuals sought cover or tried to find useful firing positions.

"Although we know that 1st Platoon was on the right, we don't know how large a front they had to cover because we don't know if Baker Company attacked with two platoons abreast or all three platoons abreast. Doctrine would call for two platoons in the front and one in reserve but, because of the large number of casualties most units suffered, there often weren't enough men in a unit to do things the way they wanted."

"Why isn't more information available?" Dr. Phillips asked.

"Let me take a shot at answering that," Sam said, "I'm guessing that after the first day at the Amphitheater Baker Company was down to sixty or seventy percent of personnel. Is that about right Dr. Stewart?"

"Actually, they were a little under sixty percent."

"OK, that makes it even worse. So, after the attack on the Amphitheater, they got back off the line to an area that was only slightly safer than where they had just been, but where there were still mortar and artillery rounds landing from time to time. They had wounded to take care of. They needed an ammo resupply. They needed chow. The company commander had to go to the battalion CP to get his orders for the next day, and the company XO, if they even had one, had to get the company dug in and prepared for the night and a possible counterattack. And remember, we're talking about guys who are physically and mentally exhausted after ten days of combat who have just seen a bunch of their friends killed and maimed. It's not surprising that no one took the time to type up a nice, neat report in triplicate with all the details about the unfortunate disappearance of 1st Squad."

"Sounds like you're speaking from experience, Sam," Tom said.

"Yeah," Sam replied.

"You're certainly right about the lack of any detailed reports of the battle, Mr. Webber. What my team has been able to find are a few scraps of handwritten notes dated from D +10 and some typewritten notes of interviews with survivors taken almost four weeks later after the end of the battle, plus a few letters that were donated to the Marine Corps Historical Branch many years later."

"Lady and gentlemen," Tom Sanders interjected, "The Commanding General is going to want his conference room back in a few minutes so let me summarize what we've learned and where we go from here.

"First, I'd like to thank Dr. Stewart for that excellent historical background. I think it's given us all a better understanding of what we will be facing on Iwo.

"The bottom line is that our squad went missing while their platoon and the rest of Baker Company was pinned down in the low, open area of the Amphitheater. Since we're pretty sure they never made it up to the ridges to attack the bunkers and pillboxes there, it makes sense that we will initially focus our search on the right half of the open ground of the Amphitheater. We won't know exactly where our search area will be until Dr.'s Stewart and

Phillips get a chance to look at the area first hand. We need to do that as soon as we get on the ground so we can start searching no later than our third or fourth day on the island.

"So" he continued "If no one has any major questions, I think that's as far as we can go today. Everyone has the schedule for tomorrow. Please don't be late. I'll see you all on the bus."

ROBBY D+2 TO D+5

"The raising of that flag on Suribachi means a Marine Corps for the next five hundred years."

Secretary of the Navy James V. Forrestal to Major General Holland M. Smith off Iwo Jima on D+4

Iwo Jima: Near the Rock Quarry
24 February, 1945
D +5
0700 hours

AFTER FIVE DAYS THAT BLURRED TOGETHER in Robby's mind like a barely remembered bad dream, Baker Company and the rest of 1/25 had been pulled off the line into regimental reserve. They were only a few hundred yards from the non-stop fighting on the front line at the Rock Quarry, but it felt almost peaceful here. Robby was in a foxhole that someone else had dug, a real foxhole, reinforced with sandbags and deep enough that he could get below ground level and be safe from almost anything but a direct hit from a mortar or artillery round. No one was telling him to get up and run through Jap fire or lay down a base of fire for some other poor bastard.

Robby lay back against the soft, sandy wall of the foxhole. The gritty volcanic sand clinging to the sweat on his skin made him look almost black. The only part of him that was reasonably clean was the Browning Automatic Rifle laying across his chest to keep it out of the sand. He couldn't remember the last time he'd slept for more than a few minutes at a time. There were explosions, some of them nearby, but he didn't even blink. He had learned to gauge to within a few feet what was dangerous and what could be ignored. He was eating "Ham and Lima Beans" from a C-ration can. Robby was one of the few who liked what most Marines referred to as "Ham and Motherfuckers."

For the first time in five days, he didn't feel like he was about to die at any minute.

An unusual commotion just outside the foxhole jerked him into full alert, and he grabbed his BAR. Before he could get his weapon up something big and black came over the side of the hole and landed in his lap. The next thing he knew, he was looking into the muzzle of a large Doberman Pinscher who immediately started licking him in the face.

"Duke, Duke, what the hell are you doin'?" yelled a Marine standing above Robby. "Knock it off! Sit! Sit!"

The dog reluctantly sat back, his bright eyes still focused on Robby.

"Damn, Marine, I'm sorry. I don't know what got into him. He usually don't pay any attention to strangers. He didn't hurt you, did he?"

"No, it's OK; he's fine. He was just being friendly."

"Yeah, that's his problem; he's too damn friendly. Whoever heard of a friendly war dog?"

"Well, if you don't want him, I'll take him."

"Naw, he's a good dog. He's saved my ass a couple of times, and not just me either. Still, I don't know why he came running over to you like that, he's never done that before."

"He just knows when he's found somebody who likes dogs. Here, Duke, you want the rest of my chow?"

Duke quickly licked the remaining food out of the can that Robby held out to him.

"You're lucky to have him."

"Yeah, I know it. Hey, we gotta get going. C'mon Duke, we got a war to fight."

"Good luck to you and Duke."

"Yeah, Semper Fi, Mac."[1]

As Robby watched the dog walk away, he realized that he hadn't felt this good in a long time.

"Hey, Durance! Where you at?"

"Over here in the hole."

Corporal Jeff Hanks slid into the hole next to Robby.

"Billotti's dead," Hanks said.

"Shit! I was afraid of that."

"Yeah, all that time out in front leadin' us up against all them bunkers and some fuckin' Jap shoots him in the back when we're headin' to the rear."

"What are we going to do?"

"With Bilotti gettin' it today that makes seven casualties and gets us down to six guys. I just got told we're getting four replacements and one of them's a corporal. I'll take over the squad, and we'll make three, three-man fire teams. Moses will have one, the new corporal will have one, and you'll have one."

---

[1] Semper Fidelis, the motto of the Marine Corps, is Latin for "Always Faithful". Shortened to Semper Fi it has become an all-purpose form of greeting among Marines.

"Me? I'm just a PFC!"

"Yeah, well, for a rebel shit-kicker you ain't a bad Marine. You're definitely the best of the sorry lot we got left. Anyway, the other new guys are Privates or PFCs, so you get one of them plus that shitbird, Lawrence. I'll let you know when they get here."

As Hanks left the hole, Robby shook his head in disbelief. He had no idea how he had kept himself alive for five days, and now he was going to be responsible for two others. How could he do it?

After Sergeant Bilotti had snapped him out of his fearful trance back on the beach, they had moved forward to find PFC Frank Winston, the 2nd Team's BAR man. Robby had a knapsack full of BAR magazines, and his job was to keep Winston supplied with ammo and to spot targets for him. They found Winston about fifty yards forward. He was in a prone position behind his BAR, and there was a small pile of empty cartridge cases to his right. He looked normal in every respect except for the large, black stain in the middle of his back.

Bilotti rolled Winston over and confirmed that he was dead. He had been shot at the base of his throat, and the bullet had exited between his shoulder blades. His eyes were open and unblinking, staring at the sky.

"All right, Durance, you got the BAR," Bilotti said, "Get in that crater over there, and I'll find Moses and Hobbs and send them over. Turn the ammo over to Hobbs, he'll be your A-gunner."

Robby grabbed the BAR, and his stomach lurched as he saw that most of the stock was covered with Winston's blood. Swallowing hard to keep from throwing up he began crawling to the crater twenty yards away.

That had been bad, but it wasn't the worst. The worst was D +3, or was it D +4? It must have been D +3, that was the first day at the Rock Quarry. The squad was attacking a small hill just outside the quarry. It was an obvious spot for a bunker, but they weren't getting any fire from there. First fire team with Corporal Hanks in charge was in front and almost at the base of the hill when Jones and Roberts disappeared in an orange-black cloud. When the smoke had dissipated, Robby could see Roberts lying in a heap and Jones sitting, looking down to where two fountains of blood shot out from the stumps where his legs had been blown off just below the hips. Jones sat there, not screaming, not doing anything, just watching the river of blood from his femoral arteries slow and then stop. Then, he just toppled over.

The Japs had suckered them in. They had left a prominent position unmanned and had put a minefield in front of it. It had taken them an hour to get to Roberts with Corporal Hanks slowly crawling toward him and probing for mines with his bayonet. Amazingly, Roberts was still alive when they dragged him back, but he looked awful. No one knew if he had made it back to the ship.

Robby remembered that D+4 was the day they saw the flag. It was late morning or early afternoon, and they were waiting to be sent back into the Rock Quarry. He had heard a new sound, and at first, he couldn't figure out what it was, and then he realized that it was ships' whistles, a lot of them. Then he heard cheering. It was as if the battle had stopped for a minute. Marines were yelling, and a few were even standing up and pointing toward Suribachi. After squinting, he finally saw a flash of colors that stood out against the dull, dark landscape. It was a flag, an American flag, and it was waving up on top of Suribachi!

That had been a really good feeling, but it hadn't lasted long. An hour later they were back in the Rock Quarry fighting for their lives.

And now, somehow, Robby had to act like a fire team leader and try to keep two other Marines alive. Once again, he thought about his ancestors and what they had done. Could this be any worse than Belleau Wood, or San Juan Hill or Manassas? Robby didn't know, but he did know that he had no choice. He had to live up to his legacy. He couldn't let the others down; neither his fore-bearers nor his fellow Marines. Robby would do what he had to do.

He closed his eyes for a second and thought about Duke, the war dog. Then his thoughts drifted to Rusty as they had so often lately. For a moment, his face relaxed, and he smiled a tired smile.

"Durance! Get over here and draw chow for your team. We gotta get everyone fed and dug in before dark."

"On the way," he replied and dragged himself back to the war.

SAM WEBBER

We gotta get outta this place
If it's the last thing we ever do
We gotta get outta this place
'Cause girl, there's a better life for me and
you

We Gotta Get Outta this Place, The Animals,
1965
Unofficial anthem of U.S. troops in Vietnam

Above the Pacific, West of Los Angeles
Tuesday 13 June

LADIES AND GENTLEMEN THIS IS YOUR PILOT. We have leveled off at our cruising altitude of thirty-eight thousand feet, and everything looks good, so I'll turn off the seatbelt sign. We're on track for an on-time arrival in Oahu."

"While I've got a moment I'd like to make a couple of announcements. As usual on this route, we have some servicemen and women on their way to duty stations on Hawaii and points beyond. I would like to welcome them aboard and thank them for their service."

A round of applause rippled through the 777 Dreamliner.

"I would also like to recognize another special group. You may have noticed that we have a couple of four-legged passengers in the cabin. They and their human teammates are part of an organization called Team Liberty, and they're on their way to the island of Iwo Jima to search for the remains of Marines who have been missing since 1945. We wish them the best of luck."

"I'll bet Dr. Phillips just loves it that the dogs get top billing." Sam Webber said to Steve Haney after another round of applause died away.

"Yeah, she sure has a thing about our dogs. Why do you think that is?"

Sam and Steve were seated in the back of the plane in a row of three seats with the middle seat empty, the only vacant seat in the cabin. Gunny and Luke were curled up companionably at their feet.

"All I know is what Tom Sanders told me," Sam replied. "She's a brilliant scientist, and she's used to getting her own way. She's wound up pretty tight, but I think she's basically a good person. Once she's figured out that we're really on her side, I think she'll loosen up."

"I hope so; she's starting to get on my nerves."

"Yeah, I know, but I'm pretty sure we're going to need her expertise."

"Well, I won't need her to help me and Luke find explosives, so she's all yours. You two make a cute couple anyway."

Sam smiled. He really liked this young man. Reclining his seat back the inch or two that it allowed, he thought back to another young man from a long time ago.

♦ ♦ ♦

Archbishop John Carroll High School
Washington, D.C.
June, 1965

The day after graduation, Sam was back at school looking for Brother Francis, his history teacher and mentor, and the one person he could rely on for good advice. He found him in the library.

"Good morning, Sam. My fine Augustinian nose tells me you did some celebrating last night."

"What? Oh, yeah, sorry, Brother. Dickie Smith had a party at his house. We got a little wild, but nothing I need to go to confession for or anything."

"I'm sure the Lord will forgive a little youthful exuberance and, after all, you had something to celebrate. Eighth in your class, not bad."

"Thank you, Brother. Of course, there were only sixty guys in the class, so it's not that big a deal."

"Big enough of a deal to get you into Notre Dame!"

"Well, getting in and going are two different things. You know I don't have the money for Notre Dame. I couldn't have stayed here if you hadn't gotten me that scholarship."

"Your father still refuses to help?"

"That bast... sorry. No, he never even replied to my last letter."

"There are other schools. If you had a job on campus ..."

"Brother Francis to be honest, I'm not sure I want to go to school right now. I want to do something different."

"You know that if you don't go to school, you'll be subject to the draft. Do you want to go into the Army?"

"The Army? No, Brother, that's the last thing I want."

"Then what? You have far too much talent and energy to let go to waste. It would be, literally, a sin."

"Brother, I haven't told anyone else this, I'm thinking about joining the Marines."

Brother Francis sat back with a sad half-smile on his face and looked at Sam for a long moment.

"Why?"

"You should know, Brother. You were a Marine"

"I was a Marine a long time ago, in 1942. It was a different time, a different war."

"Yes, but, you always told us how proud you were and all the things it meant to you. I guess I just want something to be proud of."

"Sam, you have so much to be proud of; you're a fine young man. I know it's been tough since your Dad left and I know your Mom hasn't always been there for you, but please don't make a hasty decision that you might regret. This war we have now is terrible, and the Marines will be right in the worst of it. This could be a life or death decision."

"Brother, you fought on Guadalcanal. You got malaria so bad you were in the hospital for months. Right?"

"Yes, it was while I was in the hospital that I got my calling to serve Christ."

"I'll just ask you one question. If you had it to do all over again, would you still join the Marines?"

Brother Francis reluctantly nodded his head.

Two days later Sam went to the Marine Corps recruiting station and signed up.

◆ ◆ ◆

Parris Island, South Carolina
August, 1965

Sam thought he knew all about the Marines. He had read Leon Uris' *Battle Cry* and Richard Tregaskis' *Guadalcanal Diary* and watched *Sands of Iwo Jima* a dozen times, but when the bus rolled up outside the receiving barracks at Marine Corps Recruit Depot, Parris Island, South Carolina it was like he had been transported to another universe.

The next eight weeks seemed like eight years. Boot camp, usually a twelve-week course, had recently been shortened to eight weeks to feed the increasing demands of the war in Viet Nam. The drill instructors, DI's, seemed to think that it was their sacred duty to cram twelve weeks of misery into only eight.

Of all the many things Sam learned at boot camp, two lessons stuck out above the others.

The first was that he could do more and endure more than he ever imagined. Time and again, he would reach the edge of exhaustion and find that, with a little encouragement from a DI screaming in his ear, he could somehow keep going.

The second, the more surprising, was that he really liked this shit. Even though he hated almost every moment, he found that each day brought some small set of accomplishments that he could take pride in. He liked it that the DI's never called them Marines. It was always private, or recruit, or shithead, or something worse, but never Marines. That title had to be earned, and he was determined to earn it.

By the time his platoon graduated, Sam had earned the title Marine and had been named the Honor Graduate of his platoon, which brought with it a dress blue uniform and promotion to PFC.

Then, along with most of the rest of the platoon, he was off to Camp Geiger, North Carolina for advanced infantry training.

At Geiger, they spent six more weeks almost continuously in the field. Here they learned how to survive and how to kill in combat. There were classes on mines and booby traps and how to avoid them, and on ambushes, how to set them, and how to fight your way out of them. Patrolling, map reading, communications, first aid were all covered. They fired every weapon found in a Marine infantry battalion, and they threw hand grenades and crawled under barbed wire with live machine-gun bullets snapping by just inches over their heads.

The classes that Sam enjoyed most were the ones that hadn't changed since the Marines had first come to these lowland pine forests on the coast of North Carolina in 1942. They learned how to climb down a net on the side of a ship into a landing craft—always grip the vertical strands of rope, never the horizontal, or the guy above you will step on your hand. How to debark a landing craft on the beach—always go off the side of the ramp so that if the boat surges forward with a wave, you won't get your leg pinned under the ramp—and many other skills that gave Sam and the others a connection to the Marines who had been here before.

Sam's favorite class was "The Marine Rifle Squad in the Attack of a Fortified Position." Here, they learned how the Marines had taken all those bunkers and pillboxes on Tarawa and Peleliu and Iwo Jima.

The secret was the Four B's: Blind 'em, Burn 'em, Blast 'em, and Bury 'em.

The class was a live-fire exercise. Sam was selected to be the flamethrower gunner. Although he was a little nervous about carrying twenty gallons of napalm and a tank of high-pressure air while his buddies were firing live rounds just a few feet away, he was also thrilled to be living all those scenes from *Sands of Iwo Jima* he had watched so many times.

After two of his squadmates had thrown smoke grenades to the front of the concrete bunker—Blind 'em—Sam had moved with one fire team to a position on the left of the bunker and about fifty yards away while the rest of the squad laid down a base of fire.

Then Sam, with an instructor alongside him, moved to a position about twenty-five yards from the bunker. As bullets smacked into the concrete in front of him, Sam braced himself to fire. A flamethrower has a hell of a kick and, if you're not careful, it can knock you over backward with flame spewing out the nozzle, which would be a very bad thing.

Sam squeezed the trigger releasing a stream of napalm and a second later cranked the igniter at the nozzle with his left hand. The napalm exploded into a flame that covered the front of the bunker—Burn 'em. Sam was so astonished at what he had done that the instructor had to smack him twice on the helmet to get him to release the trigger and stop the river of fire.

As Sam retreated, another Marine ran up close to the bunker and threw a satchel charge against the front—Blast 'em. Sam just had time to get to cover before the two pounds of TNT exploded. In combat, they would have used ten or twenty pounds of TNT, but two was impressive enough. They also would have used a long pole to push the charge into the bunker through a firing port. However, this bunker had to train many more squads of Marines, so they weren't supposed to actually destroy it. For the same reason, they didn't bring up a bulldozer tank to bury the bunker.

As Sam's squad left the training area, the next squad got into place for their turn at playing John Wayne.

As they strutted away full of high spirits, their senior instructor brought them back to earth.

"You Marines think you're hot shit, doncha? Well, let's go back and run that exercise again with a couple of machine-guns and a buncha gooks shootin' back atcha. Think you'd like that you buncha miserable fuckin' boots?"

A week after the bunker exercise, they finished their training and got their orders. Sam and most of the others would be taking ten days leave and then heading to the Third Marine Division in Vietnam.

Before they would be allowed in public on their own as Marines for the first time they had to undergo scrutiny from the Battalion Sergeant Major to ensure that they would not embarrass his Marine Corps by being anything less than perfectly squared away.

The Sergeant Major walked the ranks with the Company 1st Sergeant behind him as Sam, and the others stood at Attention in their Winter Service Alpha uniforms. The Sergeant Major had rows of ribbons covering his chest that indicated service in combat in WWII, Korea, and Vietnam. The hash marks on his sleeve showed he had spent over thirty years as a Marine.

When he had finished his inspection, he told the 1st Sergeant to give the detail "At Ease."

"You Marines are all going to Vietnam, is that right?"

"YES, SERGEANT MAJOR!" came the reply from a hundred throats.

"Well, it ain't much of a war, but it's the only fucking war we got. I expect you Marines to uphold the honor and traditions of our Corps and the Third Marine Division and, if you don't, you better hope you get killed because if I get ahold of you, I'm gonna unscrew your head and shit down your neck. Do you understand?"

"YES, SERGEANT MAJOR!"

"All right. Good luck, Marines. Dismissed."

◆ ◆ ◆

Danang, Republic of Vietnam
February, 1966

Sam had turned nineteen years old in January when he left home for Vietnam. He was glad to be on his way. As expected, his father was nowhere to be found, and his mother was off in her own world where there wasn't much room for him. She even forgot it was his birthday.

Before he headed to the war, there was more training. Sam spent three weeks at Camp Las Pulgas, part of Camp Pendleton between L.A. and San Diego. There the focus was on those things he would need to know to stay alive in Vietnam, mainly patrolling and mines and booby traps.

The highlight of his time in California came one evening when he had a little free time and was strolling through mainside at Pendleton and saw a theater marquee that proclaimed,

Free Concert Tonight!
L/Cpls. Don and Phil Everly, USMC
2000 to 2200

I'll be damned. I didn't know the Everly Brothers were Marines.[2]

The theater was jammed to overflowing, and the Everly Brothers played every song they knew until the Base Commander finally chased them off stage sometime after midnight. It was the best concert Sam would ever see.

A week later he staggered off a C-141 at Kadena Air Force Base in Okinawa after a brutal fourteen hours spent in canvas seats on the flight from Hawaii. The next three days were mostly standing in line to fill out forms, get shots, or draw new gear. He and the other

---

[2] The Everly Brothers enlisted in the Marine Corps Reserve at the height of their recording career in October, 1961. Had they not enlisted they would have been drafted into the Army as Elvis Presley was. They went through boot camp and basic infantry training like any Marine and spent six months on active duty.

hundred or so Marines who filled up the C-130 before dawn on the fourth day were glad to be finally going somewhere to do something.

He was assigned to the 2nd Battalion, 9th Marines who were based about ten miles south of Danang near Hill 55 along the bed of an old French railroad. The railroad had once connected Danang and Saigon, four hundred miles to the south, but the VC, and the Viet Minh before them, had blown up the tracks so many times it had been abandoned, and the rails ripped up and smelted down.

Once at 2/9 he had been further assigned to the 3rd platoon of Echo Company as an assistant automatic rifleman. He had drawn his gear and been issued a well-used M-14 rifle which had a couple of large gouges in its wooden stock and some foul-smelling substance embedded in its flash suppressor.

He later learned that the previous owner of his rifle had been killed by a mine two days before and that the gouges were from pieces of shrapnel and the foul-smelling substance was human flesh.

Welcome to Viet-fucking-Nam.

Things had not gotten appreciably better from that point.

2/9's mission was a simple restatement of the traditional mission of any Marine infantry unit, "To locate, close with, and destroy the enemy by fire and maneuver." The enemy referred to was the 2nd North Vietnamese Army Division that operated in the Quang Nam and Quang Tin provinces south and west of Danang supported by main force and provisional units of the Viet Cong.

After Sam had been in-country about a month, he went on his first company-size sweep. After three days of slogging through dried out rice paddies in brutal one hundred degree-plus heat while the VC harassed them with sniper fire and booby traps, Sam and the rest of Echo Company were exhausted. In the late afternoon, they staggered into the shade of trees around a small village south of the

American base at Hill 55. As luck would have it, Sam's squad was assigned to run an ambush patrol fifteen-hundred yards outside the company's lines that night. Sam didn't see how he could drag his tired, dehydrated body another ten feet, but when his squad leader, Sergeant Garcia, passed the word to "saddle-up," he got his gear, checked his rifle and got into line.

There was no moon that night, and the clouds had moved in to obscure the stars as the squad left the perimeter. It was too dark to maintain any sort of regular interval between individuals, so half the time the Marines were holding on to the man ahead to avoid being separated. Sam was walking in about the middle of the column just behind one of the platoon corpsmen, Doc Sampson, who had volunteered to accompany the squad. Doc may have been a trained medical technician and dedicated to saving lives, but he was neither a pacifist nor a fool. In addition to the .45 caliber pistol most of the corpsmen carried, Sampson also had a big 12 gauge shotgun loaded with buckshot.

Despite the darkness, the squad moved steadily, if slowly, across the dried-out rice paddies. They were about two hundred yards outside of the company perimeter when a strange, helmeted figure ghosted out of the blackness and started talking to Doc Sampson in Vietnamese! He had mistaken the patrol for one of his squads and was probably trying to find out why it was heading in the wrong direction. He learned just how wrong he was when Doc stuck the shotgun muzzle in his chest and pulled the trigger. The blast of the 12 gauge shattered the quiet and was the start of an almost continuous din that would not end until just before dawn. When Doc shot the NVA soldier, Sam's immediate reaction was to flatten to the ground. All he wanted to do was to curl into a little ball and hope no one would see him. But the excited chatter of Vietnamese voices on all sides convinced Sam and the others that they needed to be someplace else in a hurry.

Sergeant Garcia took control and got everyone moving toward a small hamlet a couple hundred yards away. If they could get there and find some cover they might be able to keep themselves alive long enough to figure out what to do next. Fortunately, the VC were even more confused than Sam and the rest of the squad. The Marines managed to half-crawl, half-run almost one hundred yards before anyone started shooting at them. The VC knew they were somewhere nearby, but they couldn't see in the dark any better than the Marines could. None of the shots came close.

Before the squad could get to cover they heard the THUNK, THUNK, THUNK of mortar rounds being fired from the vicinity of the company perimeter. A few seconds later, the same sound came from somewhere in front of them, and there were no friendlies in that direction. So there they were, disorganized and separated in the middle of no-man's land with an all-out battle about to erupt all around them.

Before anyone could decide what to do, the illumination rounds from the company's mortars turned the night to day and left them fully exposed in the open rice paddy. This left no choice but to find some cover—fast. At least the illumination showed them the hamlet they had been heading toward, and they started moving in that direction.

Somehow Sam ended up in the lead, and he moved as quickly as he could in a high crawl on his knees and elbows. Sam was so intent on getting to cover that he literally crawled right into a camouflaged trench line that stretched along the edge of the hamlet. In the next few seconds Sampson and the others tumbled down from the flare-lit paddy, and after some initial confusion and a near knife fight, the squad settled in to catch its breath and decide what to do next.

Sergeant Garcia took a quick headcount and found that, miraculously, the squad was all present and unhurt. All around them, the sounds of a major fight were building to a deafening roar. To the rear, back at the company perimeter, it sounded like every Marine with a weapon was firing as fast as he could pull the trigger. Rifle and machine-gun fire was punctuated by the explosions of grenades and Claymore mines. Mortars and artillery were starting to fall on preplanned targets. Tracers from friendly fire zipped by close over Sam's head. They were safe in the trench for the moment, but that could change very quickly.

Garcia started setting the squad up in a defensive position. The trench ran along the edge of the hamlet for twenty yards or so and then angled sharply in the direction from which they could hear the VC mortars being fired. At the point where the trench turned, there was a small clump of bamboo whose branches hung over the trench and partly hid it from view. This is where Sam ended up, on the far right of the squad position. Garcia wanted someone in place to look down the trench and give an early warning of any approaching enemy. To do this meant Sam had to leave the relative safety of the trench and crawl into the bamboo. There was a small depression that, if he lay very flat, let him get his body below ground level and provided some measure of protection.

As soon as Garcia had everyone in position, he got on the radio. Sam could hear him telling the company commander their situation and describing his best guess at where the VC mortars were located. After a little while, Sam could tell that he had changed frequencies and was talking on an artillery fire control net. Within a few minutes, the first spotting rounds started landing near their positions.

Sam was amazed at how calm Garcia's voice was. Here they were, surrounded by God knows how many VC, hopelessly cut off from any support, and Garcia sounded like he was on a training exercise at Camp Pendleton. He slowly worked the artillery in until rounds were falling seventy-five to one-hundred yards from their position, and then Garcia told them to 'fire for effect.' In less than a minute the squad was surrounded by explosions. Sam tried to burrow himself into his little depression. He didn't know how long he lay there like that. Long enough that he was almost entirely covered with leaves and branches cut off of the bamboo above him by the artillery fragments.

After an eternity, the volume of fire started to slacken. Evidently, the VC mortars had completed their mission or had been silenced by Garcia's artillery, and the Marines back at the company perimeter had defeated the VC assault. Sporadic fire continued, and occasionally built to a heavy exchange, but the fight was over. Unbelievably, none of Sam's squad were hurt even though some of the artillery had landed less than fifty yards away. Then, as they were about to start congratulating themselves, they heard the sound of Vietnamese voices from just in front of Sam's position.

There was a narrow trail running along the top of the trench, and it was apparent that eight or ten VC were walking toward them down it. They couldn't tell how many there were, but it didn't matter. They were still in the middle of a large number of the enemy, and, if discovered, wouldn't last long. Garcia crawled up next to Sam so he could look down the trail. He had the detonator from a Claymore mine in his hand. It was too dark to see anything, but it was clear that the VC had no idea the squad was close by because they were talking in normal voices, and Sam could hear them clearly. They were moving slowly down the trail directly toward the squad's position. If they got close enough to see them, Garcia would have to use the Claymore and they'd have to try to fight their way out.

Garcia stopped breathing and was about to fire the Claymore. Sam buried his head as far into the ground as he could and waited for the pound of C-4 explosive in the Claymore to go off just a few feet away. Nothing happened. Sam wanted to scream at Garcia,

"Fire the damn thing and get it over with!" but he couldn't speak. Then Garcia relaxed slightly and laid the Claymore detonator down. It was then that Sam noticed that the sound of the VC voices was receding. They had turned around. For some unknown reason the VC had turned around, and Garcia wasn't going to have to start a firefight in the middle of an enemy battalion. That was when Sam pissed on himself.

They stayed there in that trench for the rest of the night. Occasionally, an artillery round would land nearby, or there would be a burst of fire from back at the perimeter, but it was almost peaceful compared to what had just happened.

At first light, the squad slowly crept out of the trench and retraced its steps back to the rest of the company. The rice paddies were littered with bodies and pieces of bodies. Echo Company was credited with killing 150 VC that night. That figure may not have been accurate, but there were an awful lot of bodies, and the VC didn't usually leave many bodies behind. There had been ten Marines killed and about twenty wounded. When they got back to the company area, it was as though they'd entered some strange, slow-motion world. Everyone moved as though they were walking through thick syrup.

And they still had three more days to go on their sweep.

For Sam, the rest of the time in Echo Company was day after day of patrols and sweeps. Even when the company was at a base camp, squads and platoons were sent continuously out on security and ambush patrols.

Every few days, something would happen; a Marine killed or wounded by a sniper, three or four Marines injured by a mine, four or five wounded or killed in a thirty-minute firefight. Added to the combat losses were the victims of heat exhaustion, or malaria, or any number of other diseases.

After four months, despite the lack of significant head-to-head fights, Sam could look around and see only four or five others who had been in the 3rd platoon when he had joined it. Some of the missing faces were Marines whose thirteen-month tour of duty had ended and who had gone home. The rest had been killed or wounded, often by one of the thousands of mines and booby traps strewn throughout 2/9's operating area.

One day in early June, the 3rd platoon left their base camp and crossed the Ai Nhia River on the pontoon bridge that replaced the railroad bridge that had been destroyed years before. They were to conduct a routine security patrol several kilometers to the hamlet of Phoung Luc.

In 1966 a fully-manned Marine rifle platoon would comprise forty-seven Marines and two Corpsmen. On this day there were only thirty-one Marines and two Corpsmen in 3rd platoon, and this number included two, three-man M-60 machine gun teams attached to them from the weapons platoon. This meant that 3rd platoon was at slightly more than half strength.

Sam had been promoted to Lance Corporal and was a fire team leader in 1st squad. His fire team had only three Marines instead of four, and Sam was doing double duty as the squad grenadier, so he carried an M-79 40 mm grenade launcher [3] instead of an M-14.

The platoon commander, Second Lieutenant Selfridge, had been moved up to replace the company executive officer who had been wounded the previous week. The platoon was now led by Staff Sergeant Connors who was new to Viet Nam, and this was his first combat patrol.

The platoon moved across the dry rice paddies south of the Ai Nhia and into the tiny hamlet of Bich Nam. On the eastern side of

---

[3] The M-79 was known as the "blooper" for the noise it made when fired. It could fire out to about three hundred yards and, even though the 40mm high explosive round was not large, it was an effective anti-personnel weapon.

Bich Nam, they began to deploy on line to prepare to cross the three hundred yards of dry rice paddies to the next hamlet.

This was the same tactic that 3rd platoon had used the last time they had run this patrol a week or so before, but Staff Sergeant Connors didn't know that.

The VC, however, did.

Emplaced about six feet off the ground in a banana tree on the eastern side of Bich Nam was a Soviet MON-100 anti-personnel mine. This mine had been made in Russia and sent by ship to the North Vietnamese port of Haiphong and then transported down the Ho Chi Minh trail to South Vietnam. It contained almost five pounds of explosive and was designed to shoot 450 steel rod fragments out to a range of one hundred meters. It was intended for use against massed attacks of hundreds of troops, and on this day it was going to be used against a depleted rifle platoon.

The 2nd and 3rd squads of 3rd platoon had gotten online, and Sam's 1st squad was just coming up to them when the VC veteran crouching in a camouflaged hole twenty yards away connected two wires to an old radio battery and set off the MON-100 detonator.

The mine went off with a blast that overwhelmed the senses. The carnage was horrific.

The four or five Marines closest to the mine were literally blown apart. Others lost limbs or were shredded with shrapnel. Staff Sergeant Connors lost both legs, and his radioman was killed and the radio destroyed. At the end of the line farthest from the mine, one Marine was killed by a single piece of shrapnel that pierced his skull and went into his brain stem.

There were no casualties in 1st squad, but they were now faced with dealing with the aftermath. The only thing that saved them that day was Sergeant Garcia. His calm assurance kept Sam and the rest of the squad from panicking while he took control of the situation.

Garcia was carrying a PRC-6 radio, an old piece of shit that only the Marines still used, but which amazingly worked well enough to cover the short distance back to the base camp. He alerted the company to the situation and got medevac choppers on the way and requested that a reaction team be dispatched to help.

The first priority was security. The VC might follow up the mine with a ground attack. Garcia sent Sam and his team plus an M-60 team out into the rice paddy to set up a defensive position while the rest of the squad and the one remaining Corpsman tried to do what they could for the wounded.

Two hours later the eleven survivors of 3rd platoon limped back into the base camp area. Twenty-two Marines and one Corpsman had been killed or wounded in a single mine blast.

That evening Sam sat on the edge of his foxhole and tried to think about his future. He had been in Vietnam for four months, and almost everyone he had met when he first joined 3rd Platoon was dead or wounded, and he had nine more fucking months to go.

Future? He had no future.

◆ ◆ ◆

Near Hill 55 South of Danang
June, 1966

Sam stayed at the Echo Company base camp for the next week while 3rd Platoon was reconstituted. There was a new lieutenant who looked about twenty years younger than Sam felt and a new platoon sergeant who looked like he might know what he was doing.

There were twenty new guys straight from boot camp and infantry training regiment that Sam wanted nothing to do with. He could tell just by looking that half of them would be gone in a couple of weeks, and he couldn't take losing any more friends.

Echo Company had been alerted for a company sweep in two days when the new platoon sergeant pulled Sam aside.

"Webber I've been watching you the last couple of days, and you're beginning to scare me. I understand why you're shook up, but I'm worried about how you're gonna function when we get back out in the bush."

"You're worried? Shit, Staff Sergeant, I'm scared to death!"

"Yeah, well, I can't blame you, but I think we gotta do something. You willing to listen to an idea that might help."

"Sure. What is it?"

"Echo Company just got tagged to provide four Marines for some new outfit that's standing up. Something called the Combined Action Program. I don't know nothin' about it, but the Marines are supposed to be combat veterans and volunteers. You're a vet for sure. Do you want to volunteer?"

"Can it be any worse than what I'm doing now?"

"I don't know, but it'll at least get you a few days back in the rear while they do all the paperwork and you'll miss this next op."

"Hell yes, sign me up. Thanks, Staff Sergeant."

A week later, Sam knew he had made the right choice. By this time, he had learned that the Combined Action Program was an idea the Marines had come up with to fight the VC at the local level. The concept was to put a squad of Marines and a Navy Corpsman in a village where they would live full-time and establish a village defense unit with a platoon of the local Vietnamese militia called the Popular Forces or PF's.

The combined Marine and PF force was called a Combined Action Platoon or CAP. Their mission was to provide security for the villagers so that they could return to living something like a normal life. The thinking was that if the villagers felt secure and safe, they would be more likely to support the government and less likely to support the VC. It was also thought that these small platoon outposts scattered around major US bases would provide security and free up more Marines to take the fight to the VC and NVA in the hinterlands.

Sam had been around long enough to see some of the problems in this logic. The CAPs were small and lightly armed, and the PFs weren't the best soldiers that South Vietnam had to offer. It could get pretty scary running a patrol with just two Marines and four poorly trained and ill-equipped Vietnamese.

However, he decided he would worry about that later because he had gotten lucky. He was assigned to a CAP in a village in East Danang that was situated about halfway between two major bases, Camp Tien Sha, a Navy logistics base at the mouth of Danang harbor, to the north, and the Marine Air Group 16 and China Beach complex to the south.

In other words, he was going to be a long way from the killing fields down around Hill 55. He might get shot at a few times, and you always had to be aware of booby traps, but his chances of surviving the next nine months had grown significantly.

In the next eight months, Sam was promoted twice, the primary requirements for promotion in Marine infantry units in Vietnam being a pulse and having most of your major body parts. Now Sergeant Webber, Sam faced a decision.

He was now the CAP squad leader for a CAP near the China Beach Naval Hospital. It was a little more active area but quiet and safe compared to his time in 2/9. He was short of his twentieth birthday and in charge of a squad of Marines and about forty PFs. He was responsible for the safety of a village of about one thousand people and for securing the western approaches to the hospital complex.

He found that he enjoyed the challenge of this much authority and responsibility.

What would he do now? His tour would be over in a month, and he could go home, but go home to what? He hadn't gotten a letter from his mother in a couple of months, and the girls he corresponded with were only friends. Back in The World, he would be just another junior sergeant in some unit that spent its time training to do what he'd been doing for the last year, and he would have a good chance of being sent back to Vietnam before his enlistment was over.

His other option was to extend his tour in Vietnam for six months. If he did that the Marine Corps would fly him home at no expense and he would be given thirty days leave that would not count against the leave he had accrued in the last year. When he checked into this option, he learned that his commanding officer would be happy to have him for six more months but that he wouldn't be able to come back to the same CAP because his replacement had already been selected and they couldn't leave the CAP without a leader for thirty days. Chances were that his next CAP would be in a significantly more active area.

Sam decided the hell with it. He'd rather be in a CAP doing something he considered important and challenging than be a stateside Marine in the middle of a war. If that meant he had to go back to being shot at on a regular basis, he figured he could deal with it.

Sam's leave at home went quickly. He spent some time with friends from school, got caught up on sleep, and regained most of the weight he'd lost. Thanks primarily to the lowering of sexual mores in this era of Peace and Love, he even managed to get laid a few times despite his short haircut. The most memorable moment, however, was the evening he spent with Brother Francis.

Brother Francis had insisted on taking him out to dinner, and they went to *The Tombs* near Georgetown University. They ate burgers, drank a couple of beers and talked about things of little consequence until their table was cleared and a young waitress appeared with a tray on which sat a bottle of twelve-year-old *Jamison's Irish Whiskey*, a pitcher of water and two glasses.

Then, in a ceremony as ancient as recorded history, the old veteran filled two glasses with warm, amber liquid and, raising his own glass in a toast, said to the new warrior, "OK, Marine, tell me about Vietnam."

For the first time, Sam was able to talk about what had happened in the past thirteen months, even that day when his platoon was destroyed by the mine. The relief of being able to tell someone who understood and would not judge was immense. Just as importantly, when he and Brother Francis staggered together out to the cab after the bar had closed, Sam had been accepted into a brotherhood whose rite of initiation was facing death in combat.

♦ ♦ ♦

Danang, Vietnam
May, 1967

Sam returned to Vietnam in early May of 1967. He reported-in to the Headquarters of the 2nd Combined Action Group and was ushered into the office of the new Commanding Officer, Lieutenant Colonel Cooper.

Cooper told him to take a seat and got him a cup of coffee and welcomed him back. They talked for a few minutes, and Sam understood that Cooper was sizing him up for something. Finally, Cooper was satisfied, and they got down to business.

"Sergeant Webber, I know you expect to go back out in the field as a CAP squad leader, but I have something different in mind for you. You want to listen to what I'm thinking?"

"Yes, Sir"

Oh shit, he's being way too nice to me. I don't think I'm going to like this.

"I've got sergeants and staff sergeants in charge of all my CAPs right now. They're all good Marines, but a bunch of them are new to the program. I've also got a bunch of new, junior Marines in the field, because, well frankly, we've been taking a lot of casualties lately. What I need are people who can go out and train these new guys. People who've seen it all, the combat side and the civic action side. People like you. What do you think?"

He seems like a good guy, but I'm guessing I don't have much choice.

"Aye, aye, Sir. Whatever you need."

"Good. You'll report to your former company commander, Captain Rogers. He's heading up what we're calling the CAP Mobile Training Team. You'll travel from CAP to CAP spending a few days at each assessing their strong points and weak points and helping them to get up to speed. Got it?"

"Yes, Sir"

"This is important. You do a good job for me here, and I'll see you get a fitness report that makes you sound like John Wayne."

Sam stood, came to Attention in front of Lieutenant Colonel Cooper's desk, said, "Aye, aye, Sir," did a sharp about-face, and marched out of the office.

Sam soon learned that he would be the junior man on the team. Captain Rogers and Gunnery Sergeant Johnson were in charge, and they would focus on helping the CAP Marines learn how to work, train, and fight alongside their PF counterparts. A lot of their time would be spent educating the Marines on the culture and history of Vietnam to help them better understand why the PFs often acted in ways that the Marines found inexplicable, if not bizarre.

That left Sam and Staff Sergeant Reynolds to focus on tactical training that included everything from setting up the CAP's defensive perimeter to planning and conducting the joint Marine and PF patrols.

The next five months went by quickly. Sam's work was interesting and with just enough combat action to keep him on his toes. He was in some fights, including one night attack against the CAP where the team was staying, but compared to his time in 2/9, it was pretty tame.

As his second tour was coming to a close, he was called back to the CAG Headquarters to meet with Lieutenant Colonel Cooper. Cooper politely asked him to have a seat and then handed him a canteen cup half-filled with a dark liquid that smelled suspiciously like good bourbon whiskey.

"Webber you've done a good job just as I expected. Captain Rogers has spoken very highly of you. I promised you a good fitness report, and you'll get that plus an extra ribbon or two to wear home."

"Thank you, Sir."

"You've done your part and a lot more. You certainly deserve a trip home and a nice, easy duty station, but I wonder if you'd be interested in listening to a little idea I have?"

This guy missed his calling. He should be selling used cars.

"Of course, Sir."

"Take a look at the map here."

The entire wall behind Cooper's desk was covered by a 1:50,000 scale map of the 2nd CAG Area of Operations that stretched from Phu Bai in the north to Chu Lai in the south.

"You ever been down to An Hoa?"

"No, Sir."

Walking to the map, Cooper pointed to a tiny speck down in the far southwestern corner of the CAG's area. It was a long, long way from anywhere except the mountains that rose higher and higher to the west toward the Laotian border.

"You ever heard of the Arizona Territory?"

Oh, shit!

"Yes, Sir. Everybody knows about the Arizona."

The Arizona Territory, so-called because of its complete lawlessness, was a desolate place of deserted villages and overgrown rice fields that had been home to major elements of VC and NVA for years. The South Vietnamese Army never went there, and even the Marines seldom ventured into the Arizona with less than a battalion.

"I've got a CAP, November 3, that sits right here just across the Thu Bon River from the Arizona and about fifteen hundred yards from the An Hoa combat base. I gotta tell you it's a bad place, but it's critical. We must maintain our position in the An Hoa basin or the gooks will just move in from the Arizona and take over."

"Now my problem is that I'm going to lose my squad leader down there in a little over a month. He's a good man, and he's doing a good job, but he's got a wife and new baby, and it's time for him to go home. I need someone I can count on down there, and you've shown me that you can do the job."

"I know I'm asking a lot, but here's what I'll do. If you agree to extend for another six months, I'll send you home tomorrow, a month early, for your thirty days leave. And, you come back and give me three good months at November 3, and I'll find someone to replace you and either send you home or give you a job as an instructor here, your call."

"What do you think?"

"Sir, I've been in-country for eighteen months, and I've hardly gotten a scratch. My luck is bound to run out. I'd have to be crazy to volunteer to go to a place like An Hoa."

"Yep. Only a crazy man would do something like that. A crazy man or a good Marine NCO looking for a real challenge and a chance to do something important."

You son of a bitch.

"Sir, can I have a couple of days to think about it?"

"Sure. Look, here's fifty MPC.[4] We'll get you a ride over to China Beach, and they'll put you up in the in-country R&R center.[5] Get a good meal, get a shower, get drunk, whatever. Come back in two days and give me your answer. Whatever your answer is, I'll still give you that fitness report and I'll get you out of here a month early. Deal?"

"Aye, aye, Sir."

Maybe he's not such a son of a bitch after all. He knows I'm going to say yes and he's giving me two days of free R&R, and that fifty MPC came out of his own pocket.

♦ ♦ ♦

CAP November 3
Near An Hoa, South Vietnam
February, 1968

---

[4] Military Payment Currency. In an effort to control the currency black market, all U.S. troops in-country were paid in MPC script instead of dollars.

[5] China Beach east of Danang was home to, among other things like the Naval Hospital, a Rest and Recreation center where Marines could get a break from the field for a couple of days.

When Sam had arrived at November 3 in October, he was pleased to find that he had inherited not only a good squad of Marines and a good Corpsman but also a pretty good platoon of PFs. In a short while, he became confident that November 3 would be able to accomplish its mission of protecting the village of Phu Da and destroying the local VC infrastructure. There were plenty of large, main-force VC and NVA units in his area but, for the most part, that wasn't his problem. The 2nd Battalion, Fifth Marines was stationed at An Hoa, and they were the ones who went toe to toe with the bad guys bringing with them the full Marine combined arms package of infantry, armor, artillery, and Marine Air.

By February, 1968 Sam was well into his fourth month as the squad leader of November 3. Although the Colonel had promised to relieve him after three months, that plan, along with many others, had gone out the window when the NVA and VC had started the buildup to the Tet Offensive more than a month earlier.

Fighting throughout Vietnam had been intensifying since December, but the North Vietnamese had managed to convince General Westmorland and his staff at Military Assistance Command Vietnam that their main effort would be against the Marine base at Khe Sanh. In early January Westmorland started moving units around to reinforce the bases in the north just below the DMZ. One of the units that was moved was 2/5, and they were replaced with a Vietnamese battalion with a very poor combat reputation. The Vietnamese commander decided that his mission was strictly to protect the airfield at An Hoa and that there was no need for his troops to venture outside the base.

Now instead of fighting small VC units under the protective umbrella of 2/5's aggressive patrolling and combat sweeps November 3 was on its own in a very dangerous place. To add insult to injury, the South Vietnamese Province Chief decided that Phu Da had become too risky and ordered that the villagers be moved to a tent camp near the District Headquarters at Duc Duc for "temporary security."

Evidently, no one at MACV thought that the big attack that they were preparing for might come somewhere other than the northern bases. Therefore, General Westmorland was surprised on January 31st, the first day of Tet, when the VC and NVA attacked cities, villages, and military positions across the country.

While General Westmorland may have been fooled by the NVA, the Marines at November 3 had known something was coming for a while. Combat action throughout the An Hoa Basin increased steadily during November, December, and January. Almost every patrol from November 3 encountered at least some sniper or harassing fire, and several patrols got into big enough fights that they had to call for mortars or artillery from An Hoa to help them break contact.

In one incident, a group of thirty or so VC snuck into the village of Phu Da while another VC unit kept the Marines and PFs pinned down in November 3 with machine guns and mortars. The VC worked their way through the village savagely and indiscriminately beating old men, women, and children. The next morning Sam had to call for emergency medevacs for over twenty of the villagers.

Sam and his Marines were angry and frustrated at their inability to protect the people who were depending on them. They started working on plans for getting some pay-back and giving the villagers the security they needed.

In early February the Tet Offensive was raging across the country, but there had been no significant attacks in the An Hoa area. One day, as the regular day patrol was returning, a group of U.S. Army advisors attached to the Vietnamese battalion was at November 3 to get a look at the area. They were standing around near the bunker on the corner of the compound facing the southern edge of Phu Da, which was about seventy-five yards away.

Suddenly, there were two explosions followed by a hail of small arms fire. One of the soldiers went down with an AK-47 round through his chest. Everyone else took cover and started returning fire into the ville as the Corpsman went to work on the wounded man. As the Marines and PFs poured covering fire into Phu Da, the visiting soldiers hustled their comrade into their jeep and took off at high speed toward An Hoa. The firefight continued for several more minutes with the NVA employing rocket-propelled grenades and 60mm mortars in addition to a large volume of small arms fire. The firing slowly slackened, but the Marines and PFs could not expose themselves inside the compound without drawing a burst of fire.

The NVA had followed the patrol into Phu Da and had taken cover in the bomb shelters that were a part of almost every house in Vietnam. They had opened fire with an RPG, which explained the two explosions that had started the action. Although the firing had died down, it was evident that a large enemy force was entrenched less than one hundred yards from Sam's defensive perimeter. It was unlikely that the NVA would mount an attack during daylight, but they had to be driven out of the village before dark, or November 3 would be in serious trouble. Sam got on the radio and called for help.

The response from the Marine staff that remained at An Hoa was not encouraging, but it was better than nothing. The Vietnamese were unable, or unwilling, to come to November 3's aid, but two Marine tanks were on their way. The firepower of the tanks would be a welcome addition, but the terrain around Phu Da was broken and overgrown, ideal for infantry with anti-tank weapons. Nonetheless, Sam was glad to hear the rumble of the approaching M48 tanks about an hour later. A plan was quickly worked out that called for the machineguns on the tanks to clear any NVA to the front while the CAP Marines and PFs protected the flanks and rear of the tanks and rooted out any NVA who may have stayed behind in one of the bomb shelters.

The plan worked well, probably because the NVA decided not to try to take on the tanks in the daylight. The village was cleared with only token resistance from the NVA. A grenade was thrown into each bomb shelter to ensure that no NVA was overlooked.

When the sweep of the village was completed, the Gunnery Sergeant who had led the section of tanks came over with bad news. An Hoa was anticipating an attack, and the tanks had to return immediately. As the tanks prepared to leave, Sam took stock of their situation.

It would be impossible to defend both the village and November 3 with the number of people Sam had, but if he let the VC and NVA back into the village, they would have a perfect position to launch an attack at a time of their choosing. No one doubted that the enemy intended to try to take out November 3 that night The PF leader wanted to take his chances inside the perimeter and rely on the artillery at An Hoa to thwart any attack, but Sam was uncomfortable with the idea of letting the NVA in so close. Besides, if the enemy coordinated his attack on November 3 with an attack on An Hoa, the artillery might be too busy defending itself to help them. Sam decided on a desperate measure, they would try to ambush the enemy's attack force before it could get into position.

The plan Sam devised was simple but risky because it required him to split his small force and could succeed only if the enemy attacked from the village. If the VC and NVA came from another direction, they might be able to overwhelm the compound before the ambush team could get back to help. The PFs adamantly refused to have any part in the ambush so they would man the perimeter with only five Marines in the compound at critical points. It wasn't so much that the PFs were afraid, although they were, but that they thought the Marines were crazy to try to take on a large and heavily armed force with so few people. Sam agreed that the PFs were probably right, but he still believed that the ambush offered their best chance of making it through the night. Also, November 3 had a few scores to settle.

Sam planned that the Marines and PFs would move back to the compound and, along the way, six Marines and the Corpsman would drop out of the column, hopefully without being detected, and would hide in the village until dark. Once it was dark, the ambush team would move into three positions along the two major trails through the village.

The first position was at the point where the two trails joined about one hundred yards from November 3's outer perimeter. The other ambush positions were about twenty-five to fifty yards away along each path. The center position had an M-60 machine gun and everyone else, including the Corpsman, had M16s. To even the odds a bit, each position would set up two Claymore mines. The killing zone was designated as the area between the two trails and inside the three positions. With almost no formal tactical training but a lot of combat experience, Sam had come up with a plan for a classic V-shaped ambush. Now all he had to do was to make it work.

About an hour before dark, the Marines and PFs made a big show of forming into a tactical column and moving back toward the CAP compound. The seven volunteers for the ambush mixed themselves into the center of the group. As they passed one of the hooches near the middle of the village, each of the ambush team members ducked quickly through the back door and settled down inside to wait for darkness. After forty-five minutes, Sam decided it was dark enough, and the three teams started moving as quietly as possible to their assigned positions. Sam took two Marines and set up on the westernmost trail in the direction he thought as the most likely approach for the NVA.

By the time everyone was in place, it was very, very dark. There was no moon, and the stars were hidden by overcast. Under the trees in the village, visibility was limited to no more than a few feet. The darkness caused a few problems, particularly when the Marines tried to set up their Claymores. It was only because they were on familiar ground that they were able to get the Claymores oriented in the right direction. Because of the darkness, Sam ended up setting up one of his Claymores much closer to his position than he intended.

Once everything was in place, the teams settled down to wait. Experience had taught Sam that ambushes were ninety-nine percent waiting and one percent violence and terror, but this one was going to be different.

Sam's team detected the enemy first. They couldn't see them or hear them—they *felt* them moving past, not on the trail, but filtering through the houses and underbrush between the two trails. It was impossible to know how many there were. With no clear targets, Sam's team held their fire.

Only a couple of minutes later the quiet was shattered by a long burst of fire from the M-60 at the base of the V and the roar of a Claymore. The enemy responded almost immediately with an RPG and automatic weapons. An intense firefight raged for several minutes then suddenly diminished as the NVA pulled back.

Two almost simultaneous explosions indicated that they had pulled back right into the ambush team on the eastern trail who had fired their Claymores. Two of the three ambush teams were now pouring fire into the killing zone as fast as they could. The pitch-black night was filled with the roar of weapons from both sides and the screams of the wounded.

Sam's team on the western trail still had not gotten off a shot since they had spent the whole battle trying to avoid being hit by stray bullets and Claymore pellets from squadmates. Now, as the volume of fire started to die down for the second time, there was movement directly in front of them. It was too dark to see, but there were definitely people milling around right in front of one of Sam's Claymores! Then someone in the group started talking rapidly and loudly in Vietnamese.

What was probably a discourse on the ineptitude of NVA lieutenants was cut short by the blast of Sam's first Claymore. The other two Marines joined in with automatic rifle fire. The NVA must have been standing practically on top of the Claymore when it went off. It was later discovered that some of the steel pellets had gone entirely through one of the soldiers and still had enough velocity to go through the metal sides of the RPG he was carrying on his back.

Wounded NVA were moaning and crying just in front of Sam. To make sure they were out of the fight, he threw a fragmentation grenade toward the sound. That did the job.

Before he could fire the second Claymore, a dark figure suddenly loomed up only to be cut down by a quick burst of fire. At this point, Sam figured it was time to head back to the compound before the NVA recovered from their shock. He told the other two Marines he would fire the second Claymore to cover their exit. With his head up out of the hole to make sure his Marines were clear he stroked the second mine's firing mechanism, and this was the Claymore he had inadvertently set up only about ten feet away. It was just sheer luck that Sam didn't catch a face full of fragments from the Claymore's backblast, but the concussion almost knocked him out.

Woozy and disoriented, Sam staggered as quickly as he could back toward November 3. The other Marines were waiting a short distance down the trail, and they helped him back in.

Once in the compound, a quick count showed that everyone had made it back safely and that only one Marine would require a medevac for a shrapnel wound. In the meantime, the artillery at An

Hoa was firing prearranged concentrations on likely enemy avenues of retreat from the village.

The next day Sam escorted several members of An Hoa's intelligence staff through the ambush area. According to their analysis, the experts were able to tell Sam that November 3 had fought a company of NVA reinforced with local VC units, at least 150 men. They gave November 3 credit for twelve confirmed kills and an unknown number of wounded. The numbers weren't significant. What mattered was that they had stopped the NVA from taking their CAP and, with 2/5 due back soon, it looked like they had survived the Tet offensive.

That afternoon over a couple of warm beers, Sam and the rest of the squad all agreed that it had been a pretty good little ambush.

Sam had been feeling crappy since the ambush, but it was the next day that it really hit him. That morning Sam felt like he'd gone ten rounds with Mohamed Ali, every inch of his body hurt. When he took his morning piss, it came out dark red. He was on his way to ask the Corpsman for some aspirin when everything started spinning around him, and the ground came up toward his face very fast.

He woke up to the sound of the medevac chopper landing. He didn't know what was happening, but he could tell by the look on everyone's face that he would never be back to November 3.

♦ ♦ ♦

Above the Pacific, Near Honolulu
Tuesday 13 June

Sam awoke with a start as his ears popped from the pressure as the 777 began its descent into Oahu. His face was covered with sweat, and his shirt was clammy.

"Hey, Sam, are you OK?"

Sam took a couple of deep breaths to calm himself before trying to answer.

"Yeah, Steve, I'm good. Just a bad dream."

"One of those ones that feature a lot of loud noises and screaming?"

"Yeah. You get 'em too?"

"Yeah. Do they ever stop?"

"Well, evidently not, although it's been a good while since the last time I had one of these."

"Is there anything you can do about it?"

"Finding a good woman was a big help to me."

"You're not just talking about sex, are you?"

"No, no. What I mean is that it helps to have someone you trust enough to be able to talk about what hurts. If that person happens to be someone you enjoy going to bed with, that's a bonus. I'm guessing you're having a hard time finding anyone at school who understands what you've been through."

"Yeah, there are a few vets at UVA, and I've gone to some meetings, but I just haven't met anyone I really feel like talking to. Does that make sense?"

"Sure, a lot of this shit gets buried pretty deep inside, and you don't just open up to anyone, vet or not."

"Yeah, it sucks."

"I'll tell you what. Let's see if the two of us can get together with Tom one night and drink a few beers and tell a few lies and see what happens."

"OK, I think I'd like that. Thanks, Marine."

THE GHOST

Death is no more than passing from one
room into another

Helen Keller

Iwo Jima: Team Liberty Base Camp
Thursday, 22 June
The Night before Search Day 1
2000 Hours

IT WAS EARLY IN THE EVENING, and most of the team was over in the dining hut making their plans for the next day, but Gunny was sleeping near The Man's bed. He wasn't an old dog, but he wasn't a puppy either and all the traveling he had been doing, especially the long flights, had exhausted him.

As tired as he was, he should have been sleeping soundly, but tonight his sleep was fitful and disturbed. His body and legs twitched, his tongue hung loosely from his open mouth, and he whined softly from time to time.

Many would think he dreamed of chasing rabbits, but dogs don't dream like that. A dog's senses of smell and hearing are much more acute than his vision, so his dreams are dreams of odors and scents and sounds with only a rare image. The odors he dreams are those that are important to him; food of all types, of course, yet there are many odors that have meaning for dogs.

Tonight Gunny dreamed of an odor, a smell so faint most humans could not detect it, the scent of Old Bone, a dry, musty smell of decay. It wasn't the smell of Old Bone that disturbed him. Old Bone was a good smell. It was a smell he searched for when The Man told him it was 'Time to Go to Work' and then to 'Look Close and Adios.' When he found Old Bone, he got a treat, and The Man told him he was a Good Dog.

What bothered him was what he was seeing and hearing. For once, an image was central to his dream. It was the image of a man dressed in green, but it was faint and indistinct. It was not a man that he knew. The man himself did not scare Gunny. What scared him was that the man did not have any human scent. The few times that he saw the image of a man in his dreams, he always smelled their scent. When he saw this man, all he could smell was Old Bone.

And then there was the sound the man made. The man spoke, but it was not a sound Gunny knew; it was not a sound The Man made to him. It was this sound that made him whine each time the man spoke. The sound was, "Please, Please."

♦ ♦ ♦

Iwo Jima: Team Liberty Base Camp
Thursday, 22 June
The Night before Search Day 1
2000 Hours

On the other side of the hut, Luke was also dreaming of a strange man dressed in green, but his experience was different from Gunny's.

Luke could also smell the Old Bone, but it was not a special odor for him since he had never been trained to find Old Bone. It was new and interesting, but neither good nor bad. He also thought it was strange that the man smelled like Old Bone and not like a man, but his training and combat experience had taught him to expect strange things, so he wasn't disturbed the way Gunny was.

He did catch a slight whiff of an odor he had been trained to find, but it was very faint, and, when it got no stronger, he ignored it.

The man in green was also making sounds to Luke. "Help him, help him." Luke didn't know what those sounds meant and, after puzzling over it for a few minutes, he rolled over and went back to a dreamless sleep.

♦ ♦ ♦

Iwo Jima: Team Liberty Base Camp
Thursday, 22 June
The Night before Search Day 1
2130 Hours

By the time the team meeting had finished, and Sam and Steve had gotten to the hut, both dogs had settled down and were sound asleep.

Like Gunny, Sam was feeling every one of his almost seventy years. Just getting here and getting ready to start searching had been tough, and this was the easy part.

They had only spent one day in Hawaii and then it was a long, long flight from there to Okinawa on an Air Force C-17. It wasn't nearly as pleasant as their commercial flight to Oahu. Still, it was a hell of a lot better than it had been on a C-141 fifty-one years before.

They had spent three days on Okinawa adjusting to their jet lag and being briefed by everyone from the Commanding General of the Third Marine Division to some wienies from the State Department. Most of the briefings were on what to do and what not to do on Iwo Jima to avoid pissing off the Japanese. Sam really didn't care whether he pissed off the Japanese or not, so he used the briefing time to catch up on his sleep.

The last leg was on a Marine C-130 to Iwo. On approach, the pilot made a circle of the island to give the team an overall perspective. After all these months of anticipation, it was a sobering sight. It was almost impossible to believe that twenty-six thousand men had died on this tiny speck in the middle of the ocean.

When they arrived, they were welcomed by Commander Matsuyama, the officer in charge of the Japanese Maritime Self Defense Force detachment on Iwo. He was the man in charge of the whole island. The Commander spoke to them through an interpreter. To Sam, the "welcome" was somewhat less than cordial. Matsuyama made it clear that he viewed their presence as an unwanted intrusion on what he referred to several times as "this sacred shrine of the Japanese nation."

Fuck him, Sam thought. *You don't want us intruding, then next time don't lose the fucking war.*

The three days since their arrival had been busy, but it had all been preparation work; it was necessary stuff, just not very exciting.

They had settled into their base camp, a small compound of three Quonset huts situated on the eastern side of the Japanese airbase not far from the ridge above the Amphitheater. One hut was the barracks for the male team members with the two dog teams in one half and Jim Stewart and Tom Sanders in the other. A communal bath and shower separated the two halves. Another identical hut housed Dr. Phillips in one half and her CSI lab in the other half. The last hut was the dining facility, which also served as the team's meeting area.

Meals were prepared in the Japanese officer's mess and sent over to the dining hut in vacuum containers. Some of the team had a bit of trouble getting used to a Japanese diet, but Sam was enjoying it. A refrigerator in the dining facility contained Japanese beer, soft drinks, and sake that the team members could purchase by signing a chit on the honor system.

The technical team, Dr. Stewart and Dr. Phillips, had been the busiest. They were responsible for locating, mapping, and setting up the search area. Steve Haney and Luke had been working too; going out ahead of everyone else and checking for unexploded ordnance. For Sam and Gunny, it had mainly been training and getting Gunny acclimated to this strange, new environment.

Now they were finally ready to go, and Sam's only thought was to get some sleep so he'd be able to work his assigned search area tomorrow. He said goodnight to Steve and crawled into bed and was asleep almost immediately.

The dream started sometime in the early morning hours. Sam suddenly found himself back in Vietnam, pinned down in an open field. Automatic and semi-automatic fire cracked around him, and mortars landed nearby. It wasn't heavy fire, but it was enough to keep him on his belly. As the dream became clearer, he saw he wasn't in a field after all; he was on a beach, and the sand was black and gritty.

Just like the sand here on Iwo.

He lifted his head. There were other Marines all around him; most were lying low, and a few were moving forward in short bounds. For some strange reason, they were wearing old-style uniforms and carrying M-1s and BARs.

An officer was moving along the beach toward Sam.

Porter. That's Lieutenant Porter. How do I know that?

A second later, Lieutenant Porter's head shattered into pieces, and the world around Sam exploded with more violent noise than he had ever heard before.

Oh shit! I'm not in Vietnam, I'm on the beach on Iwo Jima, and I am in a world of hurt!

Sam jolted awake with his heart pounding and looked around. The hut was quiet except for the low snores of the two dogs. Steve was asleep, but not peacefully. Something was bothering him, too.

I hope he's not having a dream like mine.

♦ ♦ ♦

Iwo Jima: Team Liberty Base Camp
Thursday, 22 June
The Night before Search Day 1
2230 Hours

Steve had been dreaming of home, of when he was a boy on the farm, and it was a good dream and peaceful.

But suddenly someone was poking him in the side with something hard and yelling at him. Steve tried to ignore it, but it was persistent. His dream of home faded quickly, and he awoke to the sound of screams and explosions and someone yelling angrily in his ear.

."....or I'll jam this carbine up your ass!"

I won't be a coward, I won't be a coward.

"Aye, aye, sergeant."

As Steve began to crawl forward through the black, gritty sand, he thought, *Billotti, that's Sergeant Billotti. He's going to get shot in the back in a few days.*

Steve didn't awaken, his dream just faded, and he had no memory of how the rest of the night passed.

♦ ♦ ♦

Iwo Jima: Team Liberty Base Camp
Thursday, 22 June
The Night before Search Day 1
2300 Hours

Alicia Phillips had been upset since the meetings back in California and that plus her anxiety about the search starting tomorrow was keeping her awake. This search was the type of thing that could make or break her reputation, and it bothered her that she didn't have control over what was happening. In particular, she didn't have control over the dogs.

She wasn't too worried about the bomb dog. She could understand what he was going to do and recognized the need. Plus, she didn't think that he would cause much of a problem. But that damned search dog! She didn't see what good he would do, and there was a good chance he would do something stupid and contaminate the search scene. If that happened and some remains were missed or misidentified it wouldn't be the dog they'd blame, it would be her.

It wasn't that she didn't like dogs; she'd had dogs growing up, and they were fine—as pets, but she couldn't convince Tom Sanders that the dog would be a liability in a forensic search.

Sanders listened to Webber more than her, and that was another thing that angered her. They were both nice enough men on their own, but together, they were bull-headed about how this search was going to be done, and Alicia was not used to being told "No."

With all these thoughts going through her mind, there was no way she would be able to sleep, so she decided to walk around the base camp area and try to settle down. Up here on the airfield, there was a breeze that dispelled the worst of the smell of sulfur and the night was quite pleasant. She was just beginning to relax and enjoy herself when she saw the figure of a man approaching.

Nobody told me the Japanese had sentries out, but this guy's definitely carrying a gun.

The moon was past full but still bright, and as the man approached, she could see him more clearly. He was large for a Japanese, and he seemed to be carrying more equipment than she would expect of a sentry. He was wearing a helmet, and he had a large rifle with what looked like a bayonet attached slung over his shoulder.

A moment later, the hairs on her arms and the back of her neck went erect as she recognized that what she was seeing was something out of a World War II newsreel. It was a man dressed in the green combat fatigues of a Marine complete to the cloth camouflaged cover on his helmet. She could see the belt and suspenders that held ammunition pouches and grenades. As he came closer, slowly trudging along like someone who was infinitely tired, she could see that his face was almost black with dirt.

"Hey! Hello! Who are you? Hello!"

The man did not respond, did not even turn his head in her direction, but kept slowly moving, looking straight ahead.

As the man passed her about ten feet away, Alicia suddenly felt as though she had been plunged into an icy bath, and she cringed away from him suddenly frightened.

As the man passed, her temperature returned to normal, and she regained her senses.

This has to be some sort of a joke those guys are playing on me. Typical frat house hazing. Well, let's see how far they'll take it.

Alicia turned to follow the man who was heading toward the airfield fence beyond which was the steep slope leading down into the Amphitheater. She watched him approach the fence and then... he was on the other side!

How in the hell did they do that? They must have cut a hole in the fence. That's carrying things too far, we'll get in trouble with the Japanese.

When she got to the fence, she couldn't find any sign of a hole or evidence that the fence had been disturbed in any way.

As she watched, the man approached the drop off into the Amphitheater. It wasn't vertical, but it was a lot steeper than anyone could just walk down, especially at night. The man just kept walking and slowly disappeared from sight. Alicia could not hear any sounds; no one was sliding, and no rocks were falling. The night was completely quiet.

Walking back to her hut, she realized that her explanation for what had happened didn't hold water. No one knew that she would be out walking; she hadn't known herself. And what about that icy chill?

What in the hell just happened???

◆ ◆ ◆

Iwo Jima: Team Liberty Base Camp
Friday, 23 June
Search Day 1
0515 Hours

Tom seldom dreamt, but shortly before dawn, he found himself crawling with another man beside him, both of them struggling to keep their rifles out of the black, gritty sand.

Huh! That's an M-1. Why am I carrying an M-1? And that's Billotti, Sergeant Billotti.

As if someone had suddenly twisted heaven's volume knob, Tom was engulfed by the sounds of the most violent battle he had ever experienced.

Shit! This is Iwo Jima. What the hell am I doing here?

He and Billotti crawled up to a third man.

That's Winston. Oh God, look at all the blood. Poor bastard.

Billotti was yelling something he could barely hear,"... you got the BAR. Get in that crater over there, and I'll find Moses and Hobbs and send them over. Turn the ammo over to Hobbs, he'll be your A-gunner."

Tom nodded dully and reached for the blood-covered BAR. As he began to crawl forward, the dream faded.

On the other side of the hut, Jim Stewart had spent the night in undisturbed sleep.

JOE JENNINGS

SEARCH DAY ONE

Place names which pass into history often identify locations so unrewarding that only war could have rendered them memorable: Dunkirk and Alamein, Corregidor and Imphal, Anzio and Bastogne. Yet even in such company, Iwo Jima was striking in its wretchedness.

Max Hastings in "Retribution, The Battle for Japan, 1944 – 1945"

Iwo Jima: Team Liberty Base Camp
Friday, 23 June
Search Day 1
0700 Hours

JIM WAS SURPRISED TO BE THE FIRST ONE in for breakfast. He was not a morning person; he always tried to arrange his academic schedule to never have a class before ten, and so he was usually the last one up and the last one to the dining hut.

This morning he was excited to be starting their search, and he'd had no trouble getting up. It was odd that the others hadn't gotten

112

to the bathroom before him, but he supposed that everyone had a lazy morning now and then.

What bothered him was the appearance of the rest of the team as they straggled in. They looked tired and edgy, almost as if they were hungover. Jim himself didn't drink, but he knew plenty of otherwise good Mormons who did, and what the consequences looked like. That wasn't the explanation though since the others had only had one or two beers the night before.

When he asked each one if they were all right, he got four variations of, "Yeah, sure, fine."

Something happened last night that nobody wants to talk about. I wonder what it was.

The meal was passed mostly in silence until Tom said, "OK, Search Day One. Let's get going and get ourselves off to a good start!"

That lifted everyone's mood, and the team left to get their gear ready.

♦ ♦ ♦

Iwo Jima: Amphitheater Search Area
Friday, 23 June
Search Day 1
0800 Hours

"Gunny! Look close ... Adios!"

As Gunny in his orange search harness moved off into the black sand and sparse, knee-high brush Sam Webber thought, *And so begins day one in the ninth circle of hell.*

It was easy to think of hell in this place. The utter barrenness, the steam rising from vents in the earth, the almost total lack of shade, and, of course, the constant, sometimes overpowering, stench of sulfur. This was a punishing land, a land that resented the intrusion of humans and threw up obstacles to everything they tried to do.

Sam had been surprised to find that most of Iwo was heavily, almost lushly, vegetated. All the photos he had seen had shown barren rock and sand, but, of course, those photos had been taken after tens of thousands of tons of explosives had pummeled the island reducing it to a wasteland. Now, nature had healed many of the scars of war, and Iwo was beginning to look like any other island in this part of the Pacific.

However, some places still looked as though they had never recovered from the battle; one was Suribachi, another was here in front of the Amphitheater. It was as though the bloodiest places were the ones that still looked like they did seventy years ago.

After his dream last night he could easily imagine what it must have been like to be pinned down here on this flat expanse of dark sand and jagged rock when even the few low bushes here today did not exist.

In spite of his gloomy thoughts, Sam was glad to finally be doing what he had come here to do, search with his dog to find the remains of missing Marines. Judging by the way Gunny had disappeared, he was ready to go too.

Twenty-three inches tall and weighing sixty-seven pounds Gunny was right at the average size for a working Golden Retriever. His smaller size and lighter frame allowed him to cover large distances in rough terrain where a typical pet Golden would rapidly founder and tire. Even as a nine-year-old he was agile enough to scramble up almost sheer rock to get his nose into the wind, or to crawl under logs and deadfall following a scent.

Gunny's size and appearance did have some drawbacks, however. With a luxurious, wavy golden coat draped across his trim frame, people often assumed he was a female. More to the point on this particular day, a two-foot-tall dog could disappear into two-foot-tall brush pretty quickly.

Sam glanced down at the screen of his GPS system. Gunny, with his GPS collar, was about twenty yards away to the northeast and he walked off in that direction to start their search.

Today's plan, as formulated by Jim Stewart and Alicia Phillips, was to do a detailed search of an area about one hundred yards on a side that started about fifty yards outside the entrance to the Amphitheater. This area had subsequently been sub-divided into ten-yard squares with carefully placed flags.

Sam planned to start with a hasty search of the overall area to be followed by detailed searches of each sub-area. Sam began to walk a rough grid pattern from south to north and Gunny generally worked out in front of him with many small excursions to one side or another to check an odor or to get a whiff of a breeze.

Ideally, Sam would work his pattern across the prevailing wind to give Gunny the best chance to pick up a scent. But here in the Amphitheater, the wind swirled around the ridges and up and down the gullies with little or no pattern. So, Sam just picked a direction to work and left it to Gunny to sort it all out.

♦ ♦ ♦

Iwo Jima: Amphitheater Search Area
Friday, 23 June
Search Day 1
0805 Hours

The last week had not been much fun for Gunny. Too much time indoors and way, way too much time on airplanes. Gunny didn't like airplanes. Helicopters were fun because you could look out the window and see where you were going and when you landed, it was always 'Time to Go to Work.' Airplanes meant long hours with nothing to do and even worse, nothing to eat. Not a Golden Retriever's idea of a good time.

But now it was finally 'Time to Go to Work,' and Gunny knew that this was a 'Real Search.' For days he had been watching The Man and the other people, and he heard the pitch and cadence of their speech getting higher and faster, and there was that particular smell that humans had when they got excited. It all meant that this was something important, not just training.

Gunny was happy. He was doing what he loved to do more than anything else, hunting with The Man. Now he had to find the Old Bone, and it was hard with all the other new smells especially the smell that was like the stick that The Man used to make fire. That smell was everywhere, and he didn't like it, but he could sort it out and ignore it, at least while he was working.

As he worked through the brush, he began to hear something very faintly, a sound that made him uneasy. It sounded like...yes, there it was, the sound from his dream, "Please, Please." It was coming from ahead and off to his right. He turned his head toward the sound, and as he did, there was the lightest breath of wind, and on that wind was the faint scent of Old Bone.

Gunny turned into the wind and lifted his head to get his nose as high as possible. His tail came up with excitement, and he started to move into the wind alternately sniffing the air and then the branches of the brush for every scent molecule he could find. He zig-zagged right and left, searching for the edges of the scent cone as it narrowed toward the source. As he moved, the scent became slightly stronger, and he began to move more quickly.

♦ ♦ ♦

Iwo Jima: Amphitheater Search Area
Friday, 23 June
Search Day 1
0805 Hours

"Webber! What the hell is your dog doing?" Dr. Phillips cried. "Get him back here, he's outside the grid. We don't have time for his damn silly games. We've got work to do!"

Sam only half heard her, all of his attention was on Gunny. He had seen the head snap, and the tail come up, and he watched as Gunny left the grid heading down into a shallow gully. Gunny certainly looked like he was in scent, but was it possible for him to smell seventy-year-old bone fragments from that far away?

Dr. Phillips is right, I should follow the plan. There's a lot of work to do, and we're just getting started. Besides, it won't make my life any easier if I piss her any off more than she already is.

Sam opened his mouth and was about to call Gunny off and put him back to work in the grid when he remembered the three things that every search dog handler absolutely had to do:

Trust Your Dog, Trust Your Dog, and Trust Your Dog

Ignoring the rising volume of Dr. Phillip's cries, Sam followed his dog down into the gully.

♦ ♦ ♦

Iwo Jima: Amphitheater Search Area
Friday, 23 June
Search Day 1
0805 Hours

Damn it, damn it, damn it! I told them over and over that dog would be more trouble than he's worth, but nobody listens, and nobody understands.

Alicia Phillips drew a couple of deep breaths and tried to calm herself back into professional mode. Once she did that she took a minute to review and assess what had just happened.

She had explained in every way she could the importance of scientific rigor in a search of this kind. Even a moment of carelessness or a single wrong move could lead to evidence being lost or compromised. She wasn't surprised that the three military men didn't listen. Those three were typically bull-headed. She was somewhat surprised that she couldn't get Dr. Stewart on her side, although he was a historian, not a scientist.

Alicia could not remember a time when science and scientific methods and procedures had not been important to her. She also could remember only a few times when she wasn't able to convince people to see things her way. She had always been strong-willed.

♦ ♦ ♦

Chevy Chase, Maryland
June, 2003

"Tennessee? Tennessee? You're not going to Tennessee!"

"Yes, Father, I am."

"No, you're going to Hopkins just like your Mom and I."

"And Grandfather and Great Grandfather, etcetera, etcetera, ad nauseum. I think it's time some of the family fortune went elsewhere."

"Gloria, talk some sense into this girl."

"Your Dad is right, Dear. Hopkins is much the finer school if you plan to have the successful career in medicine you've always wanted."

"No, that's what you and Father have always wanted. That's not what I plan to do."

"That's nonsense. And stop saying 'Father'and 'Mother.' You always get formal when you're trying to have your way."

"Yes, Father, you've seen through me again. I suppose it's that sharp intellect of yours that's made you such a successful surgeon."

"No, I am a successful surgeon and your Mother...Mom is a successful gynecologist because we went to a first-class school, not some football factory in the middle of nowhere."

"Football factory? This from the man who was MVP on the lacrosse team for three years? Pots calling kettles black, Father."

At the mention of his lacrosse career, Alicia watched her father grow slightly taller and smile with a faraway look in his eye. *Sometimes this is just too easy to be any fun*, she thought.

"For heaven's sake, Alicia, what do you mean you don't want to be a doctor? Medicine is in your blood."

"No, Mother, science is in my blood, not medicine. And, don't worry, I plan to go to medical school, I just don't plan to be a doctor."

"Why wouldn't you want to be a doctor?"

"Father, how many times have I watched you and Mother agonize over some difficult case, or about having to give someone a poor prognosis, or about some child you couldn't save? That's not for me. I want the intellectual challenge of medicine without all the anguish of having to deal with sick people. I plan to work on patients who are already dead."

"What? You're going to be a pathologist? A medical examiner?"

"Yes, Father. That or a forensic anthropologist, and Tennessee is the best place for me to do that. Tennessee has a Body Farm, Hopkins doesn't."[6]

"Well, it's out of the question. You won't get one penny from me to go to Tennessee."

"OK, Father, if that's the way you want it, but the letter I received today informed me that the University of Tennessee would be happy to grant the valedictorian of the National Cathedral School entrance into their pre-med program with a full scholarship. And, since you were so sweet to put that lovely little car you bought me in my own name, it looks like all I'll need is money for gas and the occasional beer, which I'm sure I can find a part-time job to cover."

"Well, I won't permit it."

"Too late, Daddy, I already mailed back my acceptance. I'm eighteen, and in Tennessee, I'm pretty sure that's about five years past legal adulthood. So, come here and give me a big hug and tell me how happy you are for me."

Seven years later, Alicia graduated from the University of Tennessee with a Ph.D. in Forensic Anthropology. She was

---

[6] The Anthropological Research Facility (ARF), commonly called the Body Farm, at the University of Tennessee was the first of its kind in the nation. Inside its two acre fenced area donated bodies are left to decompose in a natural setting where they are studied by faculty and students who collect data relevant to the human decomposition process. This data is used by Crime Scene Investigators and anthropologists around the world.

immediately hired by the Tennessee State Bureau of Investigation as a crime scene investigator.

During her time in pre-med and in the anthropology department, one thing was emphasized to her over and over, and that was the need for full scientific rigor in everything she did. She was trained to be precise and thorough because the slightest flaw in an examination or investigation could doom an otherwise airtight case in a court of law, or lead to a series of incorrect conclusions in an anthropological study.

Not only did this make sense to Alicia, but it also appealed to her essential nature. She fully believed that the scientific method, if rigorously applied with intelligence and hard work, could eventually get to the bottom of any problem.

At no time in all her studies had anyone ever said anything about dogs as anything other than research subjects.

◆ ◆ ◆

Iwo Jima: Amphitheater Search Area
Friday, 23 June
Search Day 1
0810 Hours

Dr. Phillips gradually became aware of a sound she had not heard earlier—it was a dog barking somewhere in the gully about seventy yards north of her. She decided she had better get down there and see what they were doing and if she could convince them to get back to work.

The barking stopped, but she had a fix on it and started in that direction. She soon saw the faint trace of the path the dog and

Webber had made and followed that into a shallow gully. Once she got down into the ditch, she could see Webber about thirty yards in front of her—no sign of the damn dog, though. As she got closer, she finally saw the dog sitting in a small area where the brush was a little sparser than it was elsewhere.

"OK," she asked. "What the hell is he doing?"

"That's what we in K9 search and rescue call a final alert or indication", Sam said with more than just a hint of a smile. "Gunny's found something for you."

"What has he found? I don't see anything."

"Gunny! Show me!"

At Sam's command, Gunny stepped forward and lowered his nose to touch what looked like a thin, fan-shaped, dark brown rock.

"What? A rock? He found a rock? What the...Oh my god! That's an ilium, a human ilium!"

"If by ilium you mean the same thing as a pelvis then, yes Doctor, Gunny has found a human ilium."

Dr. Phillips looked at Gunny, who raised his head and looked directly at her. His lower lip relaxed, and his upper lip curled slightly into what could only be described as a self-satisfied grin.

Well, I'll be damned, she thought.

STEVE AND LUKE

And once by God, I was a Marine!

--Actor Lee Marvin, circa 1967, about serving in WW II

Amphitheater Search Area, Iwo Jima
Friday, 23 June
Search Day 1

SAM AND DR. PHILLIPS WERE STARING INTENTLY at the small piece of bone protruding out of the black sand, and they were startled to hear a loud voice just above them.

"OK, folks, what have we got here?" Tom Sanders asked.

"Well, Tom, it looks like Gunny has found an ilium," Sam said.

"Is that the same thing as a pelvis?"

"No." Dr. Phillips said somewhat testily, "It is not the same thing as a pelvis. The ilium is the large bone of the pelvic girdle."

"OK, ilium then," Tom said, "What does it tell us?"

"Right now, not much. All I can say for sure is that this is a human bone. It will take some work before I can estimate how long it's been in the ground. The ilium is very useful in determining sex, I'm pretty sure this is a male, but it is not much help in determining race. I really need more bone. A skull would be nice."

"Well, we'll work on finding you a skull then," Tom said then turned to look behind, "But before we do anything else; Steve, you and Luke have swept this gully, right?"

"Yes, sir," Steve Haney replied. "You said to sweep the search area plus at least fifty yards all the way around. Luke and I have been all the way to where this gully starts up the ridge. I marked the far limit with that orange flag."

Tom Sanders' greatest fear was that one of his team members would be seriously injured or killed by a seventy-year-old unexploded bomb. For that reason, he had insisted that a trained Military Working Dog explosive detection team, like the ones he had worked with in Iraq and Afghanistan, be assigned to Team Liberty.

Sanders had contacted Ted Rogers, who had been one of the dog handlers supporting his Ranger Company in Iraq in 2005, and asked for help in finding a dog team for the Iwo Jima mission. Rogers was now the Sergeant Major of the Inter-Service Advanced Skills K9 (ISAK) Course at Yuma, Arizona. Within a week Rogers had replied that he thought he had what Sanders was looking for.

◆ ◆ ◆

Lackland Air Force Base, Texas
October, 2010

From the time Marine Corporal Steve Haney first reported-in to Lackland Air Force Base in Texas, [7] there was little doubt in anyone's mind that he would be an outstanding dog handler. The athletic twenty-one-year-old had already done a tour in Afghanistan as a combat infantryman and performed well enough to be meritoriously promoted to his current rank and assigned as a squad leader, usually a job for a sergeant. He was smart, well-spoken, and highly motivated.

The training staff was not so sure about the Military Working Dog assigned to Haney.

Luke, whose official MWD name was L-149, had been born at Lackland and he was bred for the work he would do. Luke was a Labrador Retriever, and his sleek, coal-black fur was just a couple of shades darker than his new handler's skin. Luke was two years old. He was muscular and strong, and there was no doubt about his physical ability, it was his attitude that had the training cadre concerned.

Luke went through life with a wagging tail and an open-mouthed grin on his face. The initial impression most people had of Luke was, "Nice dog, but dumb as a box of rocks." Luke's desire to be everyone's friend had gotten him in trouble a few months earlier when he tried to get friendly with a Texas rattlesnake. Luke had seen his mistake at the last second and jumped away quickly enough that he only got a glancing hit, but even a little bit of snake venom had caused a wound that hurt for a week and taught Luke a valuable lesson.

Luke and Steve were slated to train as a special patrol dog team. Their job would be to walk ahead of a Marine patrol with Luke working off-leash to detect and warn of ambushes and IEDs. This was one of the most demanding jobs for an MWD team, and they

---

[7] The Air Force runs the Military Working Dog program for all the Services. The 341st Training Squadron at Lackland Air Force Base in Texas is where all new handlers go to be paired with a dog and receive their basic training from instructors from all the Service Branches.

had to be fully focused on the mission at all times or lives could be lost. The question was whether happy-go-lucky Luke was the right dog for this mission.

From the first time, they met, Steve Haney never had any doubts about Luke, because Steve knew as much, if not more, than his instructors about Labrador Retrievers.

For that, Steve had an old slave named Toby to thank.

◆ ◆ ◆

Live Oak Farm, Virginia
1980

Live Oak Farm had once been a medium-sized plantation owned by a man named Lucius Haney who raised mainly tobacco and cotton and owned about fifty slaves. One of the slaves had been named Toby, and he was the same age as old man Haney's son Albert. Toby was brought to the main house when he was a baby and grew up with Albert, and the two became close friends.

It was one of the many incongruities of the slave system that relationships like Albert and Toby's were common. Often these relationships would last a lifetime with the young white boy becoming the master and the young slave becoming a butler or valet. However, Albert and Toby's upbringing differed from the norm in one crucial aspect that would make all the difference.

Toby was given an education.

Although Virginia law prohibited slaves from meeting for the purpose of receiving an education, it said nothing about individual slaves being educated alongside white children. It was not uncommon for a few slaves to be given enough training to allow them to manage household affairs or conduct some business on behalf of the master.

It is not known why Lucius Haney allowed Toby to attend lessons with Albert's tutor. Did he intend for Toby to become a head butler, or did he just assume that Toby would not be capable of learning anything? Whatever the intent, the reality was that Toby and Albert were both bright, eager students who took delight in trying to outdo each other in their lessons. By the time the Civil War started, Toby knew as much about running Live Oak as Albert, and they both knew more than Albert's father.

Much of Virginia was devastated by the war, and Live Oak was not spared. Haney's wife died of consumption in the first year of the war. Both armies demanded food and fodder and never paid for it except with worthless script. When Toby brought Albert's body home after the battle of Sharpsburg, Lucius Haney could not bear this final blow. He became a recluse in his home and left the running of Live Oak to Toby.

Somehow Toby held Live Oak together. He kept a tobacco crop planted in the main field for show and then had his fellow slaves plant food crops in small plots hidden in the thick woods. He traded vegetables for chickens whose coops were also kept hidden. Most importantly, he convinced many of the slaves that the safest place for them was at Live Oak, and he promised them that one day they would all be free.

When the war ended Toby retrieved the silver and other valuables that he had hidden, and, by carefully selling it off piece by piece, he was able to amass enough money to form a corporation and hire a white man to be the figurehead. Shortly before he died, Lucius Haney sold Live Oak to the Haney Corporation for one dollar.

The Haney Negroes now owned Live Oak.

Over the years, many of Live Oak's original slaves left but Toby and his family stayed and adopted Haney as their last name in

Albert's memory. Toby always insisted that his children and their children, male and female, receive the best possible education, regardless of the cost. He reasoned that this was the only way that a black family would be able to not only coexist but also compete with the rest of the farms in central Virginia that were almost exclusively owned by whites.

In 1980 when Steve Haney's father, Richard, took over Live Oak Farm from his father it was a prosperous dairy business. However, Richard Haney knew that no matter how thriving a farm might be, it never hurt to have as many streams of income as possible for when times were bad. So, he started thinking about dogs.

The Haneys had been using dogs for hunting for generations, and there were always dogs around, in kennels, in the house and generally underfoot wherever you went. When Steve was born, many of the dogs were Labs, good, strong, working-line dogs who could hunt birds in the fields all day or break the ice in a pond to retrieve a duck.

As a graduate of the University of Virginia, Richard Haney was a curious and well-read man and he began to wonder if there was money in hunting dogs. He soon determined that a well-run breeding and training program could be a profitable sideline for the farm. It had the added benefit of giving his three young sons something useful to do.

When Steve reported to Lackland, he had already spent most of his life working and playing with Labrador Retrievers.

♦ ♦ ♦

Marine Corps Air Station, Yuma, Arizona
January, 2011

Surprising everyone except Steve, Luke showed that he had an on/off switch. When Luke's harness went on his mouth closed, the grin disappeared, and the tail stopped wagging. His full attention was on Steve, and his response to Steve's commands was instantaneous.

As the training exercises became more and more difficult, Luke became more and more focused and intense. But no matter how hard the work or how the long the day, when Steve took off his harness and told him "Free dog!" Luke went right back to being just good old Luke.

After eight weeks of basic skills training at Lackland Steve and Luke, the honor graduates, went to Yuma, Arizona for the ISAK course. If Lackland was where they got their undergraduate degree, then Yuma was where they would get their Masters and Ph.D.

All of the instructors at Yuma were combat veteran dog handlers. They understood the responsibility the dog team carried on its shoulders, and they were determined that no team was going to leave Yuma until they were ready for a combat deployment.

Steve and Luke learned to detect both explosives and ambushes in all types of terrain, in buildings, and along water-filled ditches, and with explosive simulators and smoke grenades going off around them. They worked in the heat of the day and in the surprisingly cold desert nights.

Steve was forced to endure long periods without food or sleep, but he always carried extra rations for Luke. And water! Steve carried two one-hundred-ounce Camelbaks and still found that he sometimes had to go thirsty to make sure that Luke had enough.

Steve learned how to watch his dog—really watch his dog. He learned every nuance of Luke's behavior. At the same time, Luke was learning how to work with Steve. Eventually, the two of them shared a form of extra-sensory communication.

Luke always looked at Steve a second before Steve needed to give him a hand signal, and Steve always knew Luke had found his target before Luke gave his final alert indication.

When they graduated with top honors, which included a promotion to sergeant for Steve, they were ready to go to war.

◆ ◆ ◆

Camp Leatherneck
Helmand Province, Afghanistan
June, 2011

Steve and Luke deployed to Camp Leatherneck in the Helmand Province of southern Afghanistan in mid-2011. From there they were assigned out to various Marine units for periods of a couple of days to three weeks at a time.

They did a lot of work with MARSOC, the Marine special operations units, conducting nighttime raids to kill or capture Taliban leaders. They also worked with regular Marine infantry units patrolling into Taliban strongholds in an attempt to loosen the Taliban's hold on the local populace. In each case, Steve and Luke were out front, with Luke working whatever breeze there was to detect the scent of explosives or Taliban insurgents.

It was dangerous work and critically important. It didn't take long for Steve and Luke to gain the confidence of their fellow Marines, and they were often requested when a particularly dangerous mission came up.

Steve's tour was up in early-2012. He was due to go home, and shortly after that, his enlistment would be up, and he would be going to the University of Virginia.

The idea of leaving Luke, of having Luke going out on patrols with another handler was weighing heavily on Steve's mind. It was silly, wasn't it, to put a dog ahead of what he wanted for the rest of his life? Yet, the more he thought about it, the less silly it seemed.

One day about a month before he was due to go home, Steve walked into the Sergeant Major's office and signed his reenlistment papers and extended his tour in Afghanistan for an extra six months.

Steve never regretted his decision. He and Luke were a team. He was going to do everything he could to keep them together, and in a few years, when Luke was ready to retire, Steve would adopt him, and the two of them would go to college together.

Five months later, everything was on track. In a couple of months, Steve and Luke would be heading to the Marine Corps Air Station at Cherry Point, North Carolina, where they would become part of the base security unit. This promised to be almost a vacation after a year on patrol in Afghanistan. The level of Taliban activity in Helmand was much lower than it had been when they arrived, and the last two months of their tour looked to be relatively easy.

On the day that changed everything, Steve and Luke were leading a routine patrol into a village north of Camp Leatherneck. This particular village had not caused much trouble in the past, and everything looked peaceful.

Steve was almost on autopilot when he noticed a change in Luke's behavior. Luke had stopped moving from side to side in front of Steve and moved to the center of the dirt road leading to the village. Luke's normal gait had slowed and changed to something almost like a stalk.

Steve had just noticed that there were no villagers visible and that it was unnaturally quiet when Luke came to a full stop and emitted a low, rumbling growl from deep in his chest. This was not one of Luke's usual alerts, but something was wrong.

Steve quickly raised his left arm, fist clenched, above his head and the rest of the patrol immediately dropped to the ground and moved into defensive positions. A second later, a Taliban gunner one hundred yards away launched his rocket-propelled grenade.

In his after-action report, the lieutenant who led the patrol credited Steve and Luke with keeping his Marines from walking into a well-planned Taliban trap. If they had gone another twenty or thirty yards, they would have been caught in the kill zone of an L-shaped ambush.

When Steve's signal had sent the patrol to cover, the Taliban RPG gunner had gotten nervous and had initiated the ambush early. The Marines had reacted as they were trained and quickly established fire superiority over the enemy and then attacked up the long axis of the L routing the Taliban who fled, leaving five of their dead behind.

The only Marine casualties came from the first RPG round. The rocket-propelled grenade landed between Steve and Luke, and Steve felt a blow like someone had just swung a baseball bat into his shin and he knew right away that his right leg was gone. He looked down, and there was nothing below the knee. He then immediately forgot about his leg because above the roar of gunfire and explosions, he could hear his dog screaming. Steve started crawling to Luke.

Luke lay on his right side, exposing a large gash in his left flank from which the blood flowed rapidly. Steve had almost reached Luke when one of the two Navy Corpsmen attached to the patrol grabbed him and held him back.

When Steve kept trying to break away and get to Luke, the Corpsman said, "Easy sergeant. Doc Johnson will take care of your dog. If I don't stop the bleeding from your leg, you're gonna die. Let us do our job!"

Despite the snap of high-velocity bullets just inches overhead, both Corpsmen focused on their patients. Steve's bleeding was quickly stopped with a tourniquet and pressure bandage.

Luke's injury was more difficult. He was bleeding badly from the gash along his side, and Doc Johnson could clearly hear a bubbling, wheezing sound. Luke had a sucking chest wound, which meant that his lung function was compromised. Doc had to stop the bleeding and seal up the chest or Luke wouldn't survive.

Doc Johnson called to his partner, "Hey, Johnny, if your guy is stable, I could use some help over here."

Johnny Edwards stabbed Steve in the thigh with a morphine syrette and crawled across to where Bill Johnson was working on Luke.

"Johnny, if you can get this chest sealed I'll dump some Quick Clot into this wound and see if I can get the bleeding to stop."

In any other circumstance, a medical responder would never leave a severely injured human to help take care of a dog, but this was different. Luke wasn't just a dog. As far as the Corpsmen were concerned, Luke was a Marine, and right now he was the one that needed the most help.

At first, Luke was frightened by the strange men kneeling over him, but he quickly understood that they were trying to help, and he lay back and relaxed. Whenever Johnson or Edwards got close enough, Luke would raise his head and lick their face or hands to let them know he appreciated what they were doing.

In a few minutes, the two Corpsmen had Luke's chest sealed and his bleeding under control. Before Steve was knocked out by the morphine, he showed Johnson where to find the vein in Luke's foreleg so they could get him on an IV. Doc Edwards then got Steve's IV started.

By the time the two wounded Marines were stable, the firefight was almost over, and a med-evac helo was on its way in.

As he was being carried to the landing zone, Steve kept calling for Luke. He was afraid that Luke wouldn't get on the helo with him. "Don't worry about your dog, sergeant." the lieutenant said, "You guys saved our ass. We'll get him on that med-evac if we have to do it at gunpoint!"

As it turned out, there was no problem getting Luke on the helo. The Air Force med-evac crew had been in Afghanistan long enough to know how vital these patrol dogs were. Luke was treated exactly like a wounded Marine on the fifteen-minute flight to the trauma center at Camp Leatherneck.

Two teams were waiting for the helo when it landed, a doctor and a trauma nurse and two Corpsmen for Steve and a veterinarian and two veterinary technicians for Luke. Their stay at Leatherneck was just long enough to get some meds into them and ensure that they were stable and then they were on another helo for the flight to the more extensive facilities at Kabul. Two days later they were on their way to Ramstein, Germany and then home.

Home meant two different places for Steve and Luke. Steve was sent to Bethesda Naval Hospital outside Washington, D.C., where he would spend three months undergoing rehabilitation and being fitted for his prostheses.

Luke went back to Lackland; not only because it has the best military veterinary facilities in the country, but because that was where Luke would be evaluated for his possible return to duty, if not as a patrol dog, then in some other capacity. The U. S. Government spends a lot of money on a Military Working Dog, and it likes to see a full return on its investment.

Steve spent his first two weeks at Bethesda worrying. He didn't worry about himself, he was getting the best care possible and that he would soon be back, if not to one hundred percent, then to something close to it. He worried about Luke.

How would he feel if he never saw Luke again? That was a real possibility if Luke was returned to duty and deployed with another handler. Steve's concern for Luke was so strong that it almost took his mind off the pain of physical therapy.

Steve was in the PT room when he got the bad news/good news. They had found tiny pieces of metal and dirt along with part of a rib embedded in Luke's left lung and had to remove almost thirty percent of the lung tissue. The good news was that Luke would be medically retired, was available for adoption, and Steve's name was on the top of the adoption candidate list. Did Steve want him?

Steve's official adoption request was in the mail in less than two hours.

Steve could have stayed in the Marines on limited duty, possibly as an instructor at Lackland. It was tempting, Steve loved being a Marine, but he decided it was time to move on. He and Luke were heading to the University of Virginia.

◆ ◆ ◆

University of Virginia
Charlottesville, Virginia
April

When Tom Sanders first met Steve and Luke on the Grounds of the University of Virginia, he wasn't sure he liked what he saw.

Steve was almost defiantly wearing shorts, which clearly showed that his right leg from just below the knee was fabricated from carbon fiber and metal alloy. Luke, whose black fur was marred along his left side by a jagged patch of grayish, almost white fur eighteen inches long, looked about as smart as a box of rocks.

After they had introduced themselves, Tom asked Steve if there was someplace where they could talk.

"Have you ever had a tour of Thomas Jefferson's 'Academical Village'?" Steve replied.

"I don't even know what that is," Tom said.

"That's what Thomas Jefferson called the University he founded. Mr. Jefferson was very proud of his school. In fact, the epitaph on his grave says that he was the author of the Declaration of Independence and of the Statute of Virginia for religious freedom and Father of the University of Virginia. It doesn't mention that he was President of the United States."

"So, let's take a walk."

Tom quickly noticed that Steve walked like an athlete with no hint of a limp and that Luke, who was not on a leash despite several signs that indicated that he should be, walked calmly alongside Steve in a perfect "Heel." He also noticed that many of the people they passed, including some attractive young women, waved and said, "Hi Steve. Hi Luke."

Tom started the conversation by asking Steve about what he was studying.

"I'm getting a dual major in history and political science," Steve replied.

"Interesting, what led you to that?" Tom asked.

"Well, I've been in a war and been shot up, and I thought I'd like to understand 'Why' a little better. I mean, I know why I was there, I'm a Marine, and that's what we do, but I want to know why there are wars in the first place and what, if anything, we've learned from them."

Tom nodded in reply. He had picked up on Steve's use of the present tense when describing his status as a Marine. "Once a Marine, always a Marine." The damned Jarheads really believe that shit, but he was smiling at the thought.

As they continued their walk, Steve explained that he was keeping in shape by working out with the Naval ROTC students at the University. The Marine Officer Instructor assigned to UVA liked to have Steve and Luke participate in their unit runs. He said that it was motivational for his officer candidates.

Steve added that he and Luke had even been able to keep up with their detection skills by volunteering with the Charlottesville Police Department's K9 team. He would like to get some refresher work at Yuma before they had to do anything for real, but he was confident that he and Luke could do whatever Tom needed.

"What about Luke?" Tom asked. "I understand he lost a big chunk of lung."

"Luke's smarter than he looks. He figured out that he can still do everything he did before if he just slows down a little. He'll be fine."

They walked on in silence for a couple of minutes.

"So, just what is it you need us to do?" Steve asked.

Tom stopped and looked Steve in the eyes for a long moment and made a decision.

"Well, Marine, how would you like to go to Iwo Jima?"

"Would a Muslim like to go to Mecca?" Steve replied. "Sure."

"OK, let's find someplace where we can sit down and have a beer, and I'll start at the beginning."

◆ ◆ ◆

"The Corner"
Charlottesville, Virginia
April

Steve took Tom to the *Virginian*, a bar across the street from the University that had been selling beer and crab cake sandwiches to UVA students since 1923. It was mid-afternoon, and the place was almost empty, so they were able to get a booth in the back where they could talk.

Tom was only a little surprised to see that the bartender and waitress didn't blink an eye when Luke walked in with them and curled up under their table.

"I want you to hear the full story before you commit to anything," Tom said after they had ordered their food and a beer. "Feel free to ask any questions you have."

"OK, shoot."

"What do you know about Team Liberty?" Tom asked.

"Aren't they the ones that have been going around to Normandy and Bastogne and places like that to look for MIAs from World War Two?" Steve replied.

"That's them, but they've done a lot more than that. Did you hear about what they did at Peleliu?"

"Oh yeah, didn't they find a bunch of guys from the First Marine Division that were never recovered after the battle?"

"Yes, over thirty Marines who had been lost in the caves and ravines in the Umurbrogol. It was a hell of a job. But Team Liberty is not only interested in World War Two but in recovering the missing from all of our wars. Let me tell you the full story."

"Team Liberty was started in the early nineties by a group of retired General Officers from all of the services. These were men and women who had been in one or more wars and who knew what it was like to have people they were responsible for go missing in action."

"These officers believed that the United States in general and the Joint POW/MIA Accounting Command, called JPAC, in particular, were not doing all that could be done to find, identify and repatriate the remains of missing US servicemen and women."

"They thought they could do a better job, so they formed a non-profit organization named Team Liberty and found funding for it, mostly from other retired senior officers, and started looking."

"They soon learned that it was a harder job than they had thought. It turns out that there are about eighty-three thousand Americans still missing from World War Two and later conflicts. Many of these had gone down at sea on ships or planes and would never be found, but many others were lost on land. Just trying to figure out the best places to search and to prioritize their efforts was a huge task in itself. They quickly understood that they were going to need professional help, and they set out to find the best people they could."

Tom took a sip of beer and asked, "With me so far?"

"Yes, Sir, but what kind of expert help did they need? I mean, who's an expert at finding missing soldiers?"

"Maybe the easiest way to explain it is to tell you about the team that will be going to Iwo Jima. Team Liberty Iwo Jima is the formal name, and it is the beneficiary of almost twenty-five years of experience, and, in my humble opinion, is the best team that has been fielded so far."

"OK, go ahead."

"I'll start with myself. As a team leader, I am the least specialized of all of the team members. I'm basically responsible for everything from making decisions about where to search to making sure everyone stays safe and gets fed on time."

"So, this is like a full-time job for you?"

"For me, yes. The rest of the team are part-timers like you will be if you sign on. Before you ask, yes we get paid, not a lot, but enough. You would get about what you got as a Marine sergeant plus your hazardous duty pay and a little extra for bringing Luke."

"OK, go on."

"Since the Japanese government tries to limit the number of people on Iwo Jima, our team is smaller than others, and I don't have a deputy. Another team member will be dual-hatted in that job."

"Do you have someone in mind? I mean, how many people have signed up for this?"

"I do have a deputy team leader, and I have candidates in line for the rest of the positions, but I haven't gotten a firm commitment from them all yet. I hope to have the team finalized by next week."

"OK."

"The next person will be our team historian. This will be someone with detailed knowledge of WWII in the Pacific and the battle for Iwo Jima in particular. His job will be to identify the most likely locations to search for missing Marines."

"All right, that makes sense."

"The next team member will be our forensic anthropologist."

"Forensic anthropologist? What's that for?"

"Well, remember we're looking for guys who have been dead for over seventy years, and there is only a handful of them on the same island as about twenty thousand dead Japanese. When we find something, it's likely to be fragmented and deteriorated. We need to be able to determine if the remains we find are American or Japanese, and we need to make sure we collect all the data we can to aid in the final identification of the remains. That's what forensic anthropologists do. It's a lot like a crime scene investigation, and we will essentially have the capability of a full CSI team with us."

"OK, so what do we do if we discover remains that aɪ Japanese?"

"We treat those remains with the same respect we would an American, and we turn them over to the Japanese military on Iwo Jima along with all associated data and evidence."

"So, the Japanese have Iwo Jima now?"

"That's right. We returned Iwo to them in 1968. It is now governed as a prefecture of Tokyo. The Japanese Maritime Self Defense Force runs an airbase there, and there are several hundred Japanese soldiers engaged in explosive ordnance disposal and the search for missing Japanese soldiers. There are no civilians on the island."

"Our last guy is the deputy team leader, and he is both one of your fellow Marines and a fellow dog handler. Sam Webber is a retired Major and a Vietnam vet so he's our oldest team member. He was an enlisted Marine in Vietnam, and he's seen as much or more combat as you and I put together. His dog is a Golden Retriever named Gunny."

"Great name for a dog, but why do you need two dog teams?"

"Sam and Gunny are members of a K9 Search and Rescue team, and they are certified for avalanche and wilderness live find and land and water cadaver search. In preparation for this mission, they have been focusing their training on what Sam calls Human Remains Detection, HRD, which is finding small pieces of human remains, especially very old bones. Their job will be to do detailed searches of the areas identified by our historian to either find actual remains or, at least to help narrow the search."

"That sounds interesting. I can't wait to watch them work."

"That sounds like you're ready to sign up."

"Yes, Sir, I am. When do you plan to go?"

ve a couple of academics involved we've scheduled

ie summer. That also gets us the best weather on

"I'm due to graduate in early June. Will that work?"

"Yes, no problem. So, you're in?"

"Yes, sir."

"OK, that's going to piss the Japanese off. They don't want any dogs on Iwo at all. They're really touchy about that place."

"Well, we're really touchy about places like Gettysburg, so I guess that makes sense."

"Roger that, Marine. Welcome aboard."

THE GHOST II

*Histories are more full of examples of the
fidelity of dogs than of friends.*

--Alexander Pope

Iwo Jima: Amphitheater Search Area
Friday, 23 June
Search Day 1

GUNNY'S FIND OF THE ILIUM was just the start of a long day. Sam
offered to have Gunny do a detailed search in the area around the
bone, and, to his surprise, Dr. Phillips quickly accepted. While
Gunny was working, she started to plan for finding whatever
remains might be in the area.

It had taken Gunny about twenty minutes to "Look Close" at an
area ten yards on each side of the partially exposed bone. He went
to final alert on one small fragment of bone and sniffed and pawed
at the dirt in three other places, which Sam explained meant that
there was something there but not enough to trigger a final alert.

Sam carefully marked all four spots with small green flags signifying a dog find.

Then, while Dr. Phillips began the long process of documenting the site and preparing it for investigation, Sam and Gunny went back to continue their search of the original grid. It was slow, tedious work and Gunny needed frequent rests in the heat—a dog that's panting is a dog that isn't using his nose. They got through about a quarter of the area.

Eight long, hot hours later they were back at the team's base camp. Gunny had found nothing more of interest, on the other hand, Dr. Phillips, using a ground-penetrating radar system, had detected several buried anomalies that she was anxious to get out and investigate. Two of these anomalies were directly under green flags.

Sam was sitting at a picnic table outside the Quonset hut that served as their kitchen and dining area admiring the view out over the ocean and finishing his bottle of Kirin Ichiban beer when Alicia Phillips placed another bottle of beer in front of him and sat down across the table with her own beer.

"Mr. Webber, I never got a chance to say thanks for the job you and your dog did this morning. It was very helpful."

Sam took a sip of his fresh beer and said, "Dr. Phillips you are very welcome, but don't you think it's time we started using first names, and, by the way, the dog's name is Gunny."

"You're right, of course ... Sam. I guess I've been pretty distant. It's just that I've never worked with a dog team before and I didn't understand what they can do."

"Would it help if I gave you a little background on our capabilities? We've got about fifteen minutes before the team meeting, I can give you a quick overview."

"Yes, and maybe you could start by telling me what Adios means."

"Why Dr. Phillips I'm surprised that you don't know that Adios is Spanish for 'farewell," Sam said with a grin.

"Thank you for the Spanish lesson, but what I meant, as you very well know, is what does it mean to the ... uh, Gunny."

"Let me start from the beginning and see if I can explain. Gunny and I are certified as a team for both live find and cadaver search. When I want Gunny to find the scent of a live human, either in a wilderness or an avalanche search I give him his live find command which is 'Go Find.' Now it gets a bit tricky here because you often don't know if your missing person is alive or dead, so Gunny is trained to alert to either live scent or cadaver scent when I tell him to 'Go Find.'"

"Am I making sense so far?"

"Yes, so I assume that 'Adios' is his cadaver search command, but why use that?"

"Sometimes when we're searching for someone we know or presume is deceased there are friends and family of the victim either observing or participating in the search, so I use a command that has no meaning in that context. Gunny doesn't care, and 'Adios' sounds a lot better than 'Go find the dead guy.'"

Alicia smiled. "OK, so what about 'Look Close'?"

"When I talk about cadaver search I'm generally speaking of whole bodies or large parts of dismembered bodies. In other words, enough decomposed or decomposing material that Gunny would be able to get its scent from more than just a few feet away. I use the term human remains detection, or HRD, when I'm talking about much smaller pieces or older, completely decomposed pieces, especially bone."

"Like what we're looking for here?" Alicia asked.

"Right, and "Look Close," tells Gunny what to look for. For the last couple of months, he and I have focused our training on tiny pieces of material and very old bodies."

"Where do you find old bodies to train with?"

"Where we live in northern Utah is within a couple of hour's drive of several of the old pioneer trails. There are graves all along those trails, and many of those graves have been located and marked by history buffs who study the western migrations of the 19th century. We go out and train dogs on those old gravesites."

"But those graves are over one hundred fifty years old!"

"Yep."

"How is that possible? How do you know the dogs aren't just finding old animal bones or something?"

"The grave locations are pretty well documented, so we know what's there, and we know if the dog is alerting at the right spot."

"Sam, how much do you know about the process of decomposition of the human body?"

"Well, I read this interesting paper on the chemical compounds that are developed at different stages of decomposition. I think some student at Tennessee wrote it."

"You read my Ph.D. thesis??"

"Yes, Ma'am. It was pretty interesting."

"I'm impressed, but then you know that the amounts of chemicals that exist at the final stages of skeletonization are tiny, only trace amounts."

"Yes, and those trace amounts are well within a dog's capabilities according to a study of canine olfaction done by Penn State University."

"Really? I haven't seen that study."

"It was done as a part of a study for the Department of Defense that was looking at the feasibility of developing a robotic sensor for drugs and explosives that would have the same capabilities as a dog."

"What did they conclude?"

"Well, they didn't come right out and say it, but the bottom line was that the Pentagon should get more dogs."

"OK, but there's still one thing I don't understand. Gunny was at least fifty yards away from that ilium when he turned and went off the search grid. How is it possible that he got the smell of such a small piece of very old bone from that far away?"

"He was closer to sixty yards away, I measured it. And I've been asking myself the same question for the last few hours. Normally he would have had to be a lot closer, ten feet or less, to pick up a scent like that. You saw how he had to be within a few feet of that other piece of bone he found, that's more typical."

"How do you explain it?"

"Right now, I can't."

♦ ♦ ♦

Team Liberty Base Camp, Iwo Jima
Friday, 23 June
Search Day 1
1830 Hours

While Alicia and Sam were talking, Gunny was sleeping under the table. It had been a long day for an old dog, but Gunny felt good. He had found the Old Bone, and The Man had told him that he was a Good Dog and he had gotten more treats than usual.

He was dreaming again about the other man, the one that had scared him before. It was still strange that he couldn't smell the man's scent, and the Old Bone smell that came from him was different from the Old Bone he had found that morning. Gunny could see him a little better now, and he looked just like a normal man, dressed all in green, so he didn't seem as threatening. The sound the man was making now wasn't scary, it was like sounds The Man made to him.

"Good boy, Good boy." the man said.

Gunny was confused. He thought that the man was friendly, and now he was making sounds that Gunny understood, and that made him feel good. But Gunny relied on scent, and he had never smelled a man that smelled like Old Bone. He thought that this was a Good Man, but he couldn't be sure yet.

He also didn't understand why his dreams were changing. Why did he keep seeing this man? Did the man want something? What could it be? Gunny didn't like not being able to understand. Usually, things were simple for him, good smell, bad smell, good taste, bad taste, friendly, not-friendly. What was happening in his dreams was new and a little disturbing. So, Gunny did what he usually did when he couldn't understand something; he ignored it and let himself drift deeper into sleep. If he was meant to understand it, he would when the time was right.

◆ ◆ ◆

Team Liberty Base Camp, Iwo Jima
Friday, 23 June
Search Day 1
2000 Hours

"OK everyone, let's settle down and get this meeting started. It's been a long day, and tomorrow will be the same. I'm sure you all want to get some sleep."

"For our first day of actual searching, we've done pretty well. Alicia, would you like to recap what happened?"

"Sure, Tom. Thanks to Sam and Gunny, we've found two pieces of bone, and one of them is what appears to be a portion of a human pelvis. I've left it in the ground until I can make a proper recovery, but I should have it out and back to our field lab here tomorrow. I also have some indications that there may be additional bone in the same area and I'll be working to extract that tomorrow also."

Tom had noticed Alicia's use of Sam and Gunny's names and thought with a smile, *I love it when a team comes together.*

"Any idea what that bone indicates?" Jim Stewart asked.

"All we know now is that it is human bone and probably male. Judging simply by the size of the bone it could be American, or it could just be a large Japanese. We need more bone."

"And as I told Alicia, we're going to work on that. That's why I want to discuss our plan for tomorrow," Tom said, "Although it's great that we found that bone, we don't know if it has anything to do with one of our missing Marines and we didn't get a lot of our area searched today. I'm hoping that some of you have some ideas for how we can do better tomorrow."

"I'll be busy excavating the area we marked off today and trying to get more information about our initial find," Alicia said, "Maybe we can get Sam and Gunny to do an expanded search around today's find."

Sam joined in, "I think that's a good idea and we'll plan to do that first thing in the morning. We should be able to work around you and not disturb your investigation, Alicia."

Sam continued, "I also have some thoughts on how we might restructure our search."

"Great," Tom said, "Let's hear it."

"If it's all right, I'd rather do that tomorrow morning when we get to the search area. I think we need to be able to look at the ground to see if my idea makes any sense."

"OK. It sounds like we have a lot to do in the morning so we'd better get an early start. I'll lay on chow for 0600, and we'll plan to be at the Amphitheater by 0700. Will that work?"

No one objected, so Tom ended the meeting, and everyone went off to get ready for the next day.

BAKER COMPANY AT THE AMPHITHEATER

We few, we happy few, we band of brothers;
For he today that sheds his blood with me
Shall be my brother

Henry V, Act IV Scene iii

Iwo Jima
Near The Amphitheater
1 March, 1945
D+10
0700 Hours

ROBBY SAT IN A SMALL HUDDLE at the bottom of a large shell crater with the rest of the squad while Corporal Hanks briefed them on the plan for today's attack.

The last four days they had been mainly in support and reserve, and that hadn't been too bad, but that was only relative to the first five days. They'd had a chance to get caught up on some essentials like eating and sleeping, if hash out of a can and a couple of hours of fitful dozing could be considered eating and sleeping. Even though it had been relatively quiet, three of the four replacements had been injured and were gone, and Corporal Moses was dead just because they were in the wrong place when a Jap mortar or artillery round came down.

Listening to Corporal Hanks, Robby understood that their little vacation was over. Baker Company was moving up to attack a position Hanks was calling the Amphitheater. The rest of the Battalion was attacking as well. The plan was to take the main Jap positions in the Meat Grinder.

Now there's a name to inspire confidence. "Meat Grinder," whose brilliant idea was that?

Hanks said that all three platoons would attack online because there weren't enough men left to keep a platoon in reserve. 1st Platoon would be on the right of the Company, and 1st Squad would be on the right of the Platoon. The Company would have two tanks attached for the attack, and they would be the reserve to be put in wherever the company commander thought best once the fighting started.

The good news, such as it was, was that the company would have fire support from a battery of 155mm howitzers and another battery of 105's. The bad news was because of the way the ridges in the Amphitheater curved around, it was going to be difficult for the artillery to hit anything but the part of the ridge that would be to their immediate front. 1st Platoon would have to clear the Jap positions on the right flank of the Amphitheater the hard way. They would have a flamethrower team attached to them to help with that.

With the squad down to only five men, it was essentially just a large fire team, so Robby was no longer a fire team leader. He carried a BAR again, one of two in the squad. Corporal Hanks was the squad leader and Hobbs, Lawrence, and Laskey were the rest. Hobbs carried the other BAR.

Robby was glad to carry the BAR. A lot of Marines didn't like it because it weighed twenty pounds with a full magazine and had a hell of a kick, especially when it was on "fast rate" automatic and pumping out six hundred .30-06 rounds a minute. It also tended to draw a lot of attention from all the small brown men who were trying to kill them. Robby liked it because it was solid and dependable and it just fit him, so he was confident that he could hit whatever he was aiming at. With such a small squad there were no A-gunners to carry extra ammo so Robby loaded himself down with as many twenty round magazines as he could beg, borrow or steal.

"OK, that's it," Hanks said, "Durance, if anything happens to me you've got the squad." Robby was too tired to be surprised, he just nodded.

The briefing had lasted less than five minutes—there wasn't much to say. They all knew what to do and what to expect. It was going to be a bitch, and Robby could feel his gut beginning to churn with fear. He started silently repeating his mantra, *I won't be a coward. I won't be a coward.*

The flame gunner and his A-gunner came over and introduced themselves. Robby didn't get their names, he didn't want to. If there was anyone on Iwo with a shorter life expectancy than an infantryman it was a flame gunner. One way or another, he would probably never see these two again, and the less he knew about them, the better.

They would be moving out at 0830 and had to cross the Line of Departure, the LOD, right at 0900 because that was when the artillery would commence firing. The LOD was a cart track about two hundred yards from the mouth of the Amphitheater. Once the artillery started firing, Baker Company had to keep moving to stay as close to the exploding shells as they could. This wasn't in the book, and it wasn't how they trained, but it was how they had learned to stay alive on Iwo. It was better to take a chance on an artillery round landing short than it was to give the Japs any time to recover from the shelling and get their guns in place.

Robby had acquired a real prize, a can of Del Monte peaches. He had to decide whether to eat them now or save them until after the attack on the Amphitheater. He would be hungry and thirsty after the fight, and the sweet juice would taste good, but with an infantryman's fatalism, Robby knew that he might not be alive after the battle. He pulled the can from his pack and got ready to eat.

As soon as he pulled the peaches out, four pairs of eyes locked onto the can. Canned peaches were just about as good as it got for an infantry Marine on Iwo. He wanted those peaches for himself, but some things are more important than peaches.

He sawed off the lid of the can with his K-Bar knife and scooped out one slice of peach and took a gulp of syrup and then passed the peaches around the rest of the squad. Corporal Hanks took a slice on his spoon and raised it in a small salute to Robby, "Semper Fi, Rob." Hanks then passed it to Lawrence, Laskey, and Hobbs and each man gave the same salute.

I guess that's what Semper Fi really means.

♦ ♦ ♦

Iwo Jima
Near the Amphitheater Line of Departure
1 March 1945
D +10
0859 Hours

Baker Company had moved the three hundred or so yards to the LOD in a loose column formation. Although they were not under direct fire, there were still rounds of all sizes passing just overhead or exploding nearby, so they walked hunched over to be closer to the ground if something came too close. As they came within sight of the dirt track that was the LOD, a hand signal was passed down the column, and the Company began to move onto a line facing the Amphitheater.

The movement of Baker Company would have failed a test at any tactical training school in the States. It looked more like a shambling mob of bums than a Marine rifle company—unless, that is, you watched it through the eyes of someone who had been fighting on Iwo Jima for the last ten days. Then you would notice that each man was covered by at least one other man every step of the way and that the automatic weapons, the BARs, and machine guns, were covered by two or more men. You would see that there were weapons pointed outward every few degrees all the way around and that each squad or fire team was moving from one covered position to another without any signals being given.

After ten days in the harsh school of Iwo Jima, Baker Company had become one of the finest infantry companies in the world. But that wouldn't be enough.

As they crossed the LOD, the first artillery rounds rumbled overhead like the thunder of a train when you're standing under the El in New York City. As the artillery began to impact two hundred yards to their front, right at the mouth of the Amphitheater, the Marines picked up their pace. The idea was to hug the artillery like you would your best girl and take a chance you might get slapped.

When they got within one hundred yards of where the shells were landing, they began to hear shrapnel whistling close by. True to the plan, the artillery lifted just at this moment and began to impact along the slopes of the ridges.

The Japanese had not opened fire, but no one in Baker Company was fooled. They had danced this dance before, and they'd find out just how much of a bitch this was going to be when the artillery stopped, which it did a minute later as the lead Marines came to the entrance of the bowl of the Amphitheater.

Robby and the 1st squad were moving below a steep slope that rose up to their right. It was unnaturally quiet as though everyone on the island was holding their breath for what would happen next. Robby continued to move, his eyes alternately scanning the slopes of the ridge for any sign of Japs and then looking at the flat, open ground around him for holes, rocks, any kind of cover. There wasn't much.

A single shot rang out, and the flame gunner walking to Robby's rear fell in an inert lump, instantly dead. Robby just had time to think, p*oor bastard*, when, with a great ripping noise, automatic weapons opened up all around the slopes of the Amphitheater, and the air was suddenly filled with white and green tracers. Robby and everyone else in Baker Company hit the deck.

After the initial storm, the rate of fire fell off significantly. The Marines had seen this before too. Maybe the Japs were conserving their ammo or trying to entice the Marines to attack. It made no difference anyway, the fire was still too heavy for the Marines to do anything but get as flat as they could and hope for the best. There was no thought of continuing the attack. The only question was how many of them would make it out of there alive.

The two M-4 Sherman tanks assigned to the company moved forward firing canister rounds from their main guns because they couldn't see the Jap positions well enough to use their high explosive shells. Their co-axial 30 caliber machine guns were firing as fast as possible and, in an incredible show of courage, both tank commanders were fully exposed atop their turrets firing their .50 caliber machine guns.

Maybe those guys will be able to make the Japs hunker down enough that we can get out of here

A second later that hope was dashed when, with an ear-splitting crack, a high-velocity anti-tank round hit the nearest tank, and the ten-ton turret was blown off the chassis to land twenty yards away, crushing the tank commander beneath it. Robby could hear the other three crewmen trapped inside the burning hulk screaming as they burned.

The second tank continued firing for another few seconds, but after a near miss from the anti-tank gun, it pivoted around to retreat. Before it had gone more than a few feet, it was hit in the engine compartment and came to an immediate stop and started to burn. This crew was luckier than the other. They bailed out and ran for their lives to the rear.

Robby was horrified by what he had seen, but he had no idea what he could do. Bullets were snapping just inches over his head at supersonic speed. To lift up, to do anything, was certain death. And then, above the roar and screams, he heard Corporal Hanks voice.

"First squad, over here! Move toward me! There's cover!"

Robby lifted his head just far enough to see Hanks about twenty yards ahead and to his right waving his arm. He couldn't see any sign of cover, but it didn't matter. Move or stay, he would probably get shot either way. Might as well die trying.

Robby started low crawling. When there was a brief lull, he would push up to his hands and knees and scurry forward a few feet. It took forever, but he was soon alongside Hanks.

"Down there! That little gully. You'll have cover. Get down there, and I'll send the rest of the squad."

Robby quickly crawled a few feet forward and then found himself sliding down to the bottom of what looked like a dry creek bed. As he lay there gasping for breath, bullets still snapped above him, but now they were feet away instead of inches. He felt almost safe.

Over the next minute, the three Privates crawled and rolled down beside him. Now only Hanks was left out in the open, and he started to move the last few feet into the gully, but all of his waving and yelling had attracted attention.

Before he could get over the edge of the gully, the same sniper who had killed the flame gunner shot Hanks in the left side of his chest just below the armpit and tumbled him into the gully alongside Robby. Before the blood in his lungs filled his mouth, Hanks spoke his last words.

"You... you've got the squad."

Robby watched as the life went out of Hank's eyes. He had never been so alone in his life.

"Jesus, Durance let's get the hell out of here before that sniper kills all of us" yelled Lawrence.

Robby just looked at him. Didn't he care about Hanks? Couldn't he take a moment to remember him? Hanks was a good guy, a good Marine. But now what?

With a shock, Robby realized that he was the one who had to make that decision. He was the squad leader. It wasn't much of a squad, just four guys, but that didn't matter. He had to decide what to do with them.

Robby took a quick look around. This gully ran south to north along the base of the right-hand side of the Amphitheater. It didn't take long to figure out that he only had two options. If he headed south and they stayed low there was a good chance they could get far enough back to be out of the worst of it and maybe make it to the rear. To head north in the direction of the attack seemed pointless.

Then Robby focused on the screams he had heard ever since the Japs opened up. Cries for "Corpsman up!" "Help me, help me!" and

GHOSTS OF IWO JIMA

the keening wails of the severely injured. Could he go back and leave the rest of the Company, his friends, out there in that hell?

"C'mon Durance, let's go," Lawrence said, "That way, down the gully, we'll be safe. We can get out of here!"

Robby looked at Lawrence and then at Laskey and Hobbs. He looked up at the slope rising above them. He was about to make a decision that would define the rest of his life, however long or short that might be.

"No, we're not going back. There's a heavy machine guy just up that slope that's tearing our guys to pieces. I can't go back and leave those guys out there without trying to do something."

"I'm just a PFC, but I'm the squad leader, and I say we're going up there after that gun. I can't make you go but, if you don't and I don't get killed I'll make sure everyone in the Company knows you ran out on them!"

"Jesus, Durance, you're nuts."

"Yeah, maybe I am, Lawrence, but I'd rather be nuts than be a coward. I'm heading up this gully. Follow me or run— your choice."

Robby turned and began to crawl up the gully. Hobbs and Laskey followed immediately. Lawrence watched them go and started to turn in the other direction but stopped. With a muttered curse, he hurried to catch up with the others.

159

SEARCH DAY TWO

*Nothing except a battle lost can be half so
melancholy as a battle won*

Duke of Wellington

Iwo Jima: Amphitheater Search Area
Saturday 24 June
Search Day 2
0715 Hours

THE TEAM GATHERED NEAR where Sam and Gunny had started their search the day before.

"What do we see here?" Sam asked. "Try to imagine it as it was on 1 March, 1945 when it would have been even more barren than it is now. Tom, Steve, I want you especially to look at this not as an area to be searched, but as an objective your company has been tasked to seize."

After thinking for a moment, Tom said, "It would have been scary as hell. The Japanese were dug into those ridges and, even if all the vegetation were gone, as it probably was, their positions would have been nearly impossible to see. The farther we moved into the Amphitheater, the worse it would get because then the Japanese could hit us from three sides. We would have to clear the ridges on either side before we could hope to clear the ridge in the front."

"Yeah," agreed Steve, "Scary. And there's no cover. It's flat as a table, and even the scrub brush that's here now would have been blasted away."

"There would have been some cover," Jim Stewart said, "Remember that this area was heavily shelled before the Marines attacked. There would have been shell craters all over. You can still see those faint depressions that were the largest craters."

"True," Tom said, "But those craters would have only provided minimal cover. The Japanese were up high enough that they were shooting down. If you were in a part of a crater that gave you some protection that also meant that you couldn't return fire at the guys shooting at you."

"OK," Sam said, "That agrees with what I'm thinking. Jim, can you tell us what you know about the disposition of Baker Company when they began their attack?"

"Well, as I said back at Camp Pendleton, we don't know anything for sure. The information I've gathered is from bits and pieces of after-action reports, survivor interviews, and a few letters that the company commander wrote to his wife. We think that the company attacked with all three platoons abreast. Normally they would have attacked with only two platoons forward and one in reserve, but the company was so depleted that they simply didn't have enough men to do that. They had two M-4 Sherman tanks supporting them, and that's the only reason they were able to make any progress at all."

"How much difference did those tanks make?" Sam asked.

"They were very helpful in the initial assault, but once they got into the bowl of the Amphitheater itself, they were taken under fire by what was probably a Type 1 47mm anti-tank gun dug in on the right side of the bowl. Both tanks were lost rather quickly, and that's when the attack bogged down."

"And how far in do you think they made it?" Sam asked.

"I don't think they made it more than halfway to the ridge to our front. Maybe about to the end of our first one hundred yard search area here and then they were pinned down."

"How did they get out?" Alicia asked.

"They were able to get the 81mm mortars from 1/25 to fire a bunch of smoke rounds, which gave them enough concealment to make a fighting withdrawal."

"And how many casualties did they take?"

"We know that pretty well from the unit diaries. They had twelve Marines killed and eighteen wounded, and when they got back to the battalion area, they learned that one whole squad, the five Marines we are searching for, was missing."

"So the attack failed?" Tom asked.

"Yes, and remember what I said back at Pendleton that the Amphitheater was one of the last positions taken before the island was declared secure and even then it took two or three companies plus a couple of flame tanks to finish the fight.

"What's a flame tank?" Alicia asked.

"It was an M-4 Sherman tank modified by removing the main gun and replacing it with a long nozzle and large tanks of napalm and high-pressure CO_2. It could shoot gallons of flaming napalm about one hundred yards. It was very effective against bunkers and pillboxes, but also vulnerable because it had to get so close. They couldn't bring a flame tank in until they were sure they had cleared the anti-tank guns."

"This is a fascinating discussion, everyone," Tom said, "Right now though, I'd like to get back to Sam to see what he has in mind."

"Thanks, Tom. Here's what I'm thinking. We've talked about what we can see here but who can tell me what we can't see?"

There was silence for a moment, and then Alicia said, "We can't see where Gunny found the bone."

"Bingo. In fact, you can't see any part of that gully when you're standing here and if you were down on your belly getting shot at you certainly wouldn't be able to see it. I have two big questions. The first is where was our squad during the attack, and the second is would that gully have been here in 1945?"

"I think I see what you're getting at, Sam" Jim Stewart said, "Staff Sergeant Cron, the acting platoon commander, was debriefed pretty extensively after the attack when it was learned that an entire squad was missing. He stated that 1st Platoon had been on the right of Baker Company and that 1st Squad had been on the right of the platoon, which would put them closest to where the gully is now. However, remember that everything got pretty mixed up down here and we can't be sure where they might have ended up."

"I can answer your second question," Alicia said, "When I was in grad school we took some courses in the Geology department so that we could understand how a crime scene might change over time. I'm no expert, but my guess is that gully is pretty much of a permanent fixture. Let's go over where we can see it, and I'll explain why I say that."

A couple of minutes later, Alicia continued, "See how the gully runs up to the base of the ridge? Now, look up the ridge. Do you see that narrow gap in the vegetation there? That's this same gully. It's an intermittent stream bed. Iwo Jima doesn't get much rain, but I'm betting that whatever rain does fall on top of that ridge funnels into that stream and then down to the gully. I think there's just enough flow in that stream to keep that gully scoured out but not so much as to deeply erode it. I would guess that that gully is periodically filled in and then scoured out as the storms come and go."

"So, if that's the case, what does that tell us?" Sam asked. "I'll bet you can answer that Sergeant Haney. Think like a squad leader."

Steve squinted his eyes and looked up the gully and then around at the open ground around him.

"If me and my squad were pinned down here and I found that gully I'd try to get us into it. And then, if I had really big balls, I'd move us up that gully to try to knock out some of the Japanese positions."

"Colonel Sanders, sir, would you agree?" Sam asked, smiling.

"Yes, it makes sense. And that's why we found those bones there in the gully."

"Hold on, wait a minute," Alicia said, "We found bones, but we don't know if they're American. If they're Japanese, this whole theory falls apart."

"How soon can we know?" Tom asked.

"It all depends on what other bones or artifacts we find. If we find a long bone, a humerus or a femur would be ideal, or a good portion of the skull, I can give you an answer pretty quickly. If we can't find more bone or something definitive like a dog tag, then it's going to take a while."

"How do you want to proceed?" Tom asked.

"I want to get back down there as soon as I can to start digging that bone out and checking the other anomalies around it. I'd like Sam and Gunny to expand their search around where we will be working."

"Sam, how does that sound to you?"

"Yes, we can do that, and then I'd like to recommend that we focus our search in and around the gully rather than out here in the open."

"Anyone see a problem with this?" Tom asked.

When no one spoke, Tom said, "All right. Make it so. We have a new search plan."

♦ ♦ ♦

Iwo Jima: Amphitheater Search Area
Saturday 24 June
Search Day 2
0745 Hours

Sam started working Gunny at the southern end of the gully where it merged with the flat plain south of the Amphitheater. The brush that was sparse out in the open was thicker here, and the going was slow. Sam wanted to make sure that Gunny got his nose into and under the brush, so he constantly had him, "Check close, check close." This was Gunny's least favorite type of search. He much preferred to be on his own, letting his nose determine where he went. However, he was a good dog and did what he was told with only an occasional look back at Sam.

Gunny's expression when he looked at Sam was the same you would expect from a bored teenager being made to clean his room.

Sam could see that Alicia was working intently on her hands and knees. Jim Stewart had volunteered to help her, and he was sifting dirt through a screen and looking for anything that might be a bone or a human artifact. Alicia was very interested in something, but she wasn't asking for his help, so he just ignored what they were doing.

After about an hour of searching and just after Sam had given Gunny a water break, Gunny ignored Sam's command to "Check close" and drifted toward the bottom of the gully with his nose working rapidly. Sam muttered, "Trust Your Dog," and let him go.

Gunny tracked back and forth across the gully and then focused on a small area of soft sand in the creek bed. He sniffed at the ground and pawed a few times and then looked up at Sam.

Sam interpreted Gunny's look to mean, "There's something here, but I don't know what it is." Dogs, in general, and dogs like Gunny in particular, are drawn to any odor that is different or anomalous, so he went down to check.

Gunny sat back, and Sam got down to look where Gunny had pawed. There was something there, but what was it? He brushed more of the sand away. It was something metallic and round. He brushed some more sand and worked his fingers around the object. It was something familiar but he couldn't quite ...

Sam had never carried an M-1 rifle, the standard Marine weapon of WWII after Guadalcanal, but he had seen plenty of them. He had no doubt that what he was seeing and feeling was the muzzle and front sight of an M-1.

Sam had just grabbed his radio to call Tom Sanders and let him know what he had found when Alicia's voice stopped him.

"Tom, this is Alicia. I need you over here at our scene as soon as possible."

Sam was surprised that he could hear Alicia without his radio. He looked up to see that the dig site was only about twenty yards away. He and Gunny had covered more ground in the last hour than he thought, over a hundred yards anyway.

By the time he and Gunny got to Alicia's location, she was holding something out and showing it to Tom like a first-grader at show-and-tell. Even though the object was discolored and encrusted with dirt, it was easily identifiable—it was one-half of a human skull.

"This was about two feet down where we had a GPR hit" Alicia was saying. Turning to Sam, she said, "And yes, it was right under one of Gunny's green flags."

"Can you tell anything from that given the condition it is in?" Tom asked.

"Oh, for sure. I should be able to determine race once I get a good look at it in the lab, but I can tell you right now that I'm 90% confident that it is Caucasoid."

"You think it's one of our missing Marines?"

"Well, the good news is that there are several intact teeth in the upper jaw. Since we have the dental records of our missing Marines, we should be able to determine if this skull belongs to one of them."

"I may have another piece of the puzzle" Sam interjected. "Gunny found what I am pretty sure is the barrel of an M-1 rifle about twenty yards downstream."

"That's great," Alicia said, "Jim, would you be willing to take the GPR and your tools down there and check that out? If you don't see any other artifacts with the GPR, you should be able to dig that rifle out pretty quickly. Meanwhile, I'll take all the bones back to the lab and get a better look at them."

"Whoa, hold on," Tom said, "Jim, have you ever handled an M-1?"

"I've never handled any type of rifle, why?"

"Sam, would you go back with Jim and make sure that weapon is safe before he tries to move it?"

"Do you really think that rifle could be loaded and dangerous after all these years?" Alicia asked.

"If you want to stay alive and keep all your body parts you always, always treat any weapon you come across as loaded and dangerous. In fact, let's make it a rule that anytime you or Jim need to work on or around anything that is, or might be, a weapon that I,

Sam, or Steve will be there to make sure it's safe. Any problem with that?"

"Not for me," Alicia said with a smile. "I have an emotional attachment to my body parts."

Before Tom could reply, his radio crackled.

"Tom, this is Steve, over."

"Go ahead, Steve."

"I'm afraid I've got something here you're not going to like."

"Oh? What might that be?"

"I think Luke's found an artillery round."

◆ ◆ ◆

Iwo Jima: Amphitheater Search Ares
Saturday 24 June
Search Day 2
1115 Hours

A few minutes later, Tom and Sam reached Steve and Luke where they were taking a break at the base of the slope that rose up from the gully.

"What have you got, Steve?"

"Well Tom, Luke gave me a very positive indication in the brush a couple of yards up the slope there. See where I put that orange flag?"

"Yeah, I see it. What do you think it is?"

"Right next to where Luke was sitting I could see an inch or so of corroded metal sticking out of the sand. I'm pretty sure that was the base of an unexploded artillery round. If I had to guess, I'd say 155mm."

"OK, I've already alerted Japanese EOD, and they're on their way. How far away do we have to be to stay safe when they blow it?"

"I'm pretty sure they're going to want us completely out of the area."

"Shit! Just when we're starting to make some progress."

"OK," Tom continued, "I'm going to tell Alicia and Jim that they have to finish at their dig site and get everything back to the lab. Sam, will you help Jim check out that M-1 and, if it's safe, get it out of the ground?"

"Sure, no problem."

"You found an M-1?" Steve asked. "Cool! That'll look great over your mantelpiece."

"Hey, I hadn't thought about that. Do you think Team Liberty would let me keep it, Tom?"

"I don't think Team Liberty will be a problem, but I'm not sure what the Japanese will think about it. I'll check it out."

"OK, tell Matsuyama I'll buy him a bottle of good sake if he says yes. He looks like a sake drinker."

"OK, will do. Let's get back and get everyone to work."

◆ ◆ ◆

Iwo Jima: Amphitheater Search Ares
Saturday 24 June
Search Day 2
1310 Hours

Almost two hours had elapsed by the time the EOD team had arrived, confirmed Luke's find, and were prepared to destroy the unexploded round. This gave the team time to complete the excavation of the original bone site and the M-1 rifle. Sam and Gunny had also worked the last twenty yards up to the bone site and a little past with no other finds.

When EOD informed Tom that they were ready, Tom gathered the team together.

"OK, EOD is ready to go, so we need the clear the area. However, I got us permission to observe the blast if we do it from at least five hundred yards away. The best place would be up on the top of the western side of the Amphitheater. The ground there is high enough that we can be a safe distance back and still see. Would that be of interest to anyone?"

Alicia and Jim nodded enthusiastically. Sam and Steve just shrugged.

"What will we being seeing, Steve?" Alicia asked.

"They've put a one-pound block of C-4 explosive over the exposed base of the round and attached electrical blasting caps and covered the whole thing with a layer of sandbags to direct the force of the explosion downward. They've run the wire up to a detonator above the rim of the ridge, and that's where they'll set it off."

"If you see a bright, orange flame without much smoke and hear a sound like a sharp crack that means that the TNT in the artillery round was inert and all that went off was the C-4. If you see a larger, darker explosion with a lot of smoke and dirt and hear more of a deep, booming sound, then you'll know it's a good thing Luke found that round before somebody stumbled over it."

"OK," Tom said, "Let's get moving."

Fifteen minutes later, they were in place atop the Amphitheater. Looking across, they could see the Japanese EOD jeeps and, as they watched, red flags appeared at the top of the radio antennas on each vehicle. Then they faintly heard a Japanese accented voice:

"Fire in the hole. Fire in the hole. Fire in the hole."

A moment later, there was a flash of orange and black fire, and a column of dirt and smoke flew a hundred feet in the air. Half a second after that there came the whump of a sudden change in air pressure and a deep booming sound like a nearby lightning strike.

Alicia and Jim stood open-mouthed.

"My God," Alicia said, "That was just one artillery round. What must it have been like during the battle?"

"As close as I can determine," Jim said, "the Marine 155mm battery fired sixty rounds during Baker Company's battle that day, and the 105mm battery fired another sixty or so. That would mean at least 120 explosions like the one we just saw and, of course, those Baker Company Marines were a lot closer to them than we are."

"OK, folks," Tom said, "Let's take a break for lunch, and we'll get back to work as soon as we get clearance from EOD."

"Tom, I'd like to get these bones back to the lab and start examining them in detail."

"OK. Your call. Let's eat and get back to work."

Across the Amphitheater in a cave twenty yards above where the smoke and dirt from the explosion were settling something stirred. Something that had once been human, but had sacrificed its humanity and been lost in deep, deep darkness for over seventy years. Its mind and senses were dull, but it was becoming aware.

"I am Watanabe, the descendant of great samurai!"

He became aware of another, a presence he hated and feared. He stayed quiet and tried to remember. He must remember his duty, then he must act.

SEARCH DAY TWO: RESULTS

"When the Man waked up he said, 'What is Wild Dog doing here?' And the Woman said, 'His name is not Wild Dog anymore, but First Friend because he will be our friend for always and always and always. Take him with you when you hunt.'"

Rudyard Kipling: Just So Stories

Team Liberty Iwo Jima Base Camp
Saturday, 24 June
Search Day 2
1815 Hours

"OK," TOM SAID, "LET'S GATHER AROUND and get comfortable. We'll try to keep this meeting short. Alicia, would you start?"

"Sure. We got a lot done despite the interruption from the artillery round. I'd like to thank Steve and Luke for doing such a good job of taking care of us."

Steve nodded his head as the other four members of the team gave him a Luke a round of applause.

"I spent the time after lunch cleaning and examining the bones from our first find. Everything is preliminary and will have to be confirmed with full lab tests that I can't do here, but I'm pretty confident that the three pieces of bone we have are from the same individual and that that individual is a Caucasian male. I think the rifle that Gunny found supports that idea, but I'll let Sam talk about that."

"The rifle is definitely an M-1, and it was in amazingly good shape," Sam said. "A lot of the wooden stock was gone, and the metal was rusted, but it was intact. It was also fully loaded with eight rounds, one in the chamber, and the safety was off. I don't know if it would have fired, but it was certainly potentially dangerous. I had to spray a bunch of WD-40 on it to be able to get the bolt back and extract the rounds, but it's safe now. It's in the lab if anyone wants to look at it."

"The important thing about the rifle," interjected Jim, "is that we were able to get the serial number off it. I've sent that back to my students at BYU, and they are going to see if they can determine to whom it was issued. That could tell us a lot, especially if we can match it to one of our missing Marines."

"As for the rest of the afternoon, Gunny and I continued to search the gully, but we didn't get a lot done. It's hard work for him in that gully, and I had to rest him a lot in the heat of the afternoon."

"How much farther do you have to go to complete the search of the gully?" Tom asked.

"About another 125 to 150 yards."

"Can you finish that tomorrow?"

"I think so if we start early and don't have any problems."

"OK, let's try to do that. Alicia, what's your plan for tomorrow?"

"I think I'll stay in the lab unless Gunny finds something for us."

"I'll stay back too," Jim said, "And try to get more detailed physical descriptions to help Alicia with identification."

"OK, we've got a plan. Take a break and try to get plenty of rest. We've got a lot of work to do tomorrow."

The team drifted apart to different tables to drink a beer or to use their laptops to catch up on e-mail. After a couple of minutes, Jim sat down next to Sam.

"I've enjoyed watching Gunny work. Is it any different when he's looking for a live person?"

"Oh, yes, quite a bit different, especially compared to what we're doing here. With a live search, there is typically a lot more scent for Gunny to work with than when we're looking for small pieces of old bone. That means that he can range a lot farther out from me and work the wind to try to find scent."

"Have you made any live finds?"

"Yes, just one, but that one made it all worthwhile."

"I'd be interested in hearing about that and about how you and Gunny got started in search and rescue. Would you tell me about it?"

"Sure, but it'll cost you a beer."

♦ ♦ ♦

Team Liberty Iwo Jima Base Camp
24 June

Search Day 2
1845 Hours

Sam took a long pull from his new bottle of Kirin. As Jim went to get Sam's beer, he had spoken to the other members of the team who were now gathered around the table.

"OK kiddies, storytime. Two stories actually, how Gunny and I got started in SAR and how we helped find a missing person."

"If anyone gets bored, feel free to hit the rack. As our esteemed leader has reminded us, we've got a long day tomorrow."

"OK, where to begin ...

"My wife, Rebecca, and I retired to a small house in the mountains of northern Utah about eleven years ago. We're both skiers, so we went to work at Snow Peak as ski instructors. We worked the minimum number of days per week to get our season passes and spent the rest of the time skiing."

"Are we allowed to ask questions?"

"Only if you raise your hand first, Alicia."

Alicia dutifully raised her hand.

"So, you're married, and you're a good skier?"

"Yes, and yes, and why do you act so surprised?"

"I don't know. I guess I just never pictured you with a wife. What does she think about you being over here?"

"I think I've just been accused of being a male chauvinist," Sam said with a chuckle, "To answer your question, Rebecca was a Marine Wife for almost eighteen years. This ain't her first rodeo.

"So, to continue. One of our plans, when we retired, was to get a dog. We'd had Goldens before, and that seemed like the logical choice. We did our research and contacted a breeder in eastern Wyoming with a good reputation. We didn't realize that there are Golden Retrievers and then there are dogs like Gunny. These breeders did a fantastic job of breeding and raising healthy, well-socialized dogs, but these dogs were bred for hunting. They're about as much like your average Golden as a racehorse is like a child's pony.

"It didn't take long for us to realize that we were in over our heads and we needed some help."

"What sort of problems were you having?" Jim asked.

"He was just a very active little puppy who needed to be doing something all the time. If he got bored, which happened very quickly, then he found a way to get in trouble. Our previous experience with pets simply hadn't prepared us for this."

"So, what did you do?"

"Well, one day I talked to a friend of mine on the ski patrol who had a young dog with him, a beautiful GSD named Kaiser."

"What's a GSD?" Alicia asked.

"A German Shepherd Dog. This dog was about the same age as Gunny, about nine months, and even stronger and more active, but so much better behaved and in control. He knew all the basic commands, and he was already training to be an avalanche dog.

"I told his owner, Kurt, about Gunny and our problem and asked for his advice. He said it sounded like my dog needed a job, and that the ski patrol would be testing new dogs the next weekend, and I should bring Gunny up to see what he could do.

"The next weekend was cold and windy, about ten below with a fifteen mile per hour wind up on the mountain. I wasn't sure how Gunny would do in that weather. When I let him out of the car, he took about one second to look around and then headed for the nearest pile of snow and dove right in. When they tested him, he passed every test with flying colors.

"Kurt said that Gunny was born to be an avalanche dog.

"And, as they say, the rest is history. It took about a year to get him certified for avalanche search, and then we joined our K9

Search and Rescue team, and within another year he was certified in wilderness search, cadaver search, and water search.

"Did you ever do any avalanche rescues?" Tom asked.

"No. We did several searches of unobserved avalanches to make sure that there was no one in the debris, but no actual rescues."

"How do dogs do water searches, and what are they looking for?"

"Well, Alicia, I'm sure you've worked some drownings in your time, right?"

"Sure, but we've never used dogs, and I don't understand how they could help."

"Think about what happens to a body when it been in the water for a while. The skin softens and begins to slough off, right?"

"Yes, of course."

"Those skin cells and other products of decomposition then tend to work their way to the surface where a trained dog can detect them and indicate the approximate location of the body underwater. Dogs typically don't find a body, but they can significantly reduce the size of the search area for the divers."

"But as the bodies begin to decompose the gases generated will cause them to float and that's how we find them."

"That may work fine in Tennessee, unless, of course, the body gets snagged on something, but in a deep mountain lake the water is often so cold that decomposition never advances far enough for the body to float.

"Gunny and Kaiser once located a body in 110 feet of water in a high mountain reservoir at seven thousand feet above sea level."

"That's very interesting for you forensic anthropologists and cadaver dog handlers to talk about," Jim said, "but we historians have more delicate stomachs. Perhaps we could move on to the next story?"

Sam smiled and pointed his finger at Alicia, "It's her fault, she's the one asking the questions."

"Yes," Alicia responded, "and I have many more, but I'll save them for when we can have a more detailed discussion. Go on and tell us your next story."

"OK. It was late September a couple of years ago. That time of year can be tricky in the mountains. It can be warm and sunny one minute and snowing the next. That particular day was like that. It had been in the fifties with a warm sun until about three o'clock, then the clouds came in, and a cool breeze started up. The forecast was for light rain and sleet with snow possible above sixty-five hundred feet. We got a call that a young girl had gone missing earlier that afternoon in the next county over and the Sheriff was requesting K9 help.

"Gunny and I were the only team immediately available. Kurt and Kaiser would respond, but they were farther away, and our other live-find teams were unavailable for different reasons. It took about an hour for us to get to the scene, a remote cluster of vacation cabins at the end of a dirt road on the side of a mountain at about seventy-five hundred feet.

"These were cabins only in the broadest sense of the term. They were more like rustic McMansions. There were four of them with each one set on its own one-acre lot. Two of them were occupied, both with large families.

"I checked in at Incident Command and met the Sheriff who filled me in on what had happened.

"One of the families had a thirteen-year-old daughter with Down Syndrome. Kids from both families had been playing together, and some of the boys from the other family thought it would be fun to scare the 'retard.' They told her some scary story, and then one of the kids dressed up in a costume and jumped out at her from behind a bush.

"The poor little girl, her name was Julie, panicked and ran off into the woods. That had been at right around two o'clock. The two families searched for over an hour before they called 911. The Sheriff and his SAR team had arrived and searched the area behind the houses with no luck.

"By the time I had been briefed, it was close to five, and the east side of the mountain where we were was already in shadow. The temperature had dropped to the low forties, and a light, cold drizzle had started. Julie was only wearing a long-sleeved T-shirt, shorts, and sneakers. The Sheriff didn't think she would survive a night out in the woods if the weather continued to go to shit. The Sheriff wanted to send Gunny and me higher up the mountain on an ATV to expand the search area.

"I asked the Sheriff if I could talk with the parents to learn more about the girl. I spoke to the Dad who told me that Julie had the mental capacity of a six-year-old, but that her only real physical problem was poor coordination. When I asked him how far he thought she could run in those woods, he said that he was surprised that she had been able to run at all. He couldn't believe she had gone farther than the quarter-mile or so that they had searched up the mountainside.

"I told the Sheriff that I thought that Gunny and I should focus on the area immediately behind the houses since that was the most likely place Julie would be. He said his SAR team had already searched that area.

"I replied in my usual tactful manner that if the area hadn't been searched by a dog, then it hadn't been searched. I also told him that Kurt and Kaiser would be along in the next thirty minutes or so and, if necessary, he could send them out farther to expand the search area. Finally, I told him that there was a good chance that Julie had been so scared she had gone into hiding and had not responded to the searchers because she thought they were the "monsters" the boys had told her about.

"He reluctantly agreed, and I went to get Gunny and myself ready. The Sheriff assigned a member of his SAR team to act as my flanker and to maintain radio communications. As soon as we got saddled up, we headed out."

"The mountainside sloped gradually up behind the houses and the breeze was blowing upslope. I planned to head uphill about a quarter-mile and then work a grid pattern coming down into the wind covering an area about a quarter-mile wide. This meant we would be searching a forty-acre area and it should take about an hour to check it with the wind we had.

"I took Gunny to the edge of the woods and explained to him that this was for real and we had to find this little girl soon. Then I gave him his live search command...

"Gunny! Go Find!"

"Do you think he could understand what you were saying?"

"Steve, I bet you can answer Alicia's question for me, can't you?"

"Sure," Steve said, "Dogs don't understand anything we say beyond the commands they are trained on, but they are great at picking up on clues from our emotions and body language. I'm sure that Gunny understood that this was something different, something special and that he had to do his best job."

"I couldn't have said it better myself. Thanks, Steve.

"So, long story short, we worked up the hill through fairly thick trees and moderate brush and then started a grid back down. We had made two passes across the width of our search area when I noticed a change in Gunny's behavior. His nose and tail were up, and he was starting to move more downhill, working back and forth across the wind. I quickly lost sight of him and realized how dark it was getting. Luckily, I could follow him on my GPS.

"I was pretty sure Gunny was in scent, and I hoped it was Julie he was tracking. I started to follow him down the hill, checking his location periodically on the GPS. He was over a hundred yards away when he stopped moving for a moment and then started heading back uphill. When he was about fifty yards away, I called his name to let him know where I was.

"I heard the bell on his harness just before he appeared out of the gloom. He ran up to me, jumped up, and put his front paws in the middle of my chest. It was the best alert indication I had ever seen him do. I told him, 'Good boy! Show me!' and he took off back down the hill.

"I followed him as quickly as I could, but he was way ahead, and I lost sight of him. Usually, if I'm too slow in following him, he'll come back and give me another indication, but he didn't do it this time. I looked at my GPS, and he was stopped in about the same location where he had turned around before. I wasn't sure what he was doing, and I was getting a little worried.

"When we got to where the GPS showed Gunny should be, there was no sign of him. I was about to call out to him when I heard something. I held my breath for a second until I was sure. It was a child's voice speaking very low, and it was coming from under a downed tree about ten yards away. The tree had fallen against the branches of another tree, and it was propped up at an angle close to the ground. It was a pine tree, and its thick branches reached to the ground and formed a small, green cave.

"I told my flanker to call IC and get the paramedics out there and then got on my hands and knees and crawled under the tree. The first thing I saw was Gunny sitting very still, and then I understood why. A little girl, too small for a normal thirteen-year-old, was sitting next to Gunny with her arms wrapped around his neck and her face buried in the fur of his chest. The sound I had heard was her voice. She kept repeating, 'Doggy, doggy, doggy.'"

"So, she was OK?" Alicia asked.

"Yeah, she was fine. She'd stayed a lot drier up under those tree branches than I was. The paramedics checked her out and transported her to the hospital for observation, but she went home the next day."

"That's a great story," Jim said, "I assume the parents were grateful?"

"Yes, in fact, they made a nice donation to our SAR team, but there's an even better end to the story."

"What could be better than saving a little girl's life?" Jim asked.

"Well, the parents had no idea that Julie knew anything about dogs. They had never had a dog because they assumed a dog would frighten her. They think that one of her teachers or therapists must have read her stories about dogs, and when Julie saw Gunny, she felt safe with him.

"Anyway, I introduced them to a friend who works with *Canine Companions for Independence*. They got Julie into the CCI program, and now she has her own companion dog, a Golden Retriever-Lab mix named Roscoe who goes with her everywhere. The parents told me just before I came over here that Julie's language skills, cognition, and IQ have all made big jumps and that she has started making friends with other kids, and they're sure that the credit goes to Roscoe and CCI."

"And Gunny!" Jim said.

"Yeah, well, Gunny too, I guess," Sam said with a broad smile.

"OK, team," Tom said, "This has all been very enjoyable and heartwarming, and it gives us an even better understanding of what dogs like Gunny and Luke can do for us. However, I may have mentioned that we need to get a lot of work done tomorrow, so let's finish our beers and hit the rack. Reveille at 0600."

♦ ♦ ♦

Team Liberty Iwo Jima Base Camp
Saturday, 24 June
Search Day 2
2130 Hours

Gunny was dreaming again about the man dressed in green. He could see and hear the man more clearly now. He was younger than The Man, and he smiled a lot, and he looked friendly, but, without being able to smell him, Gunny couldn't be sure.

"Good boy, good boy. That was Corporal Hanks you found. He was a good guy, and now he can go home. But you gotta keep looking boy, there's more, there's more."

"There's more," that's the sound The Man made when he wanted Gunny to keep searching after he'd found something. He hoped The Man would take him out to search for more tomorrow.

Gunny's dream was starting to fade when he heard something new. It was a voice, but it was not like any voice he had heard before. It sounded like an angry voice. Gunny didn't hear angry voices very often because he was a Good Dog, and this voice was worse than anything he had ever heard. There were no sounds that he recognized, and he was starting to be scared.

"Don't listen to him, boy. That's a real mean son of a bitch, and he just wants to hurt you. Don't listen to him, boy."

But Gunny had to listen, he had no choice, and the more he heard, the more scared he became. He whined softly, then a little louder, then...

"Gunny! What's the matter? Are you OK?"

Gunny's eyes popped open, and for a second, he didn't know where he was. Then he felt The Man's hands on either side of his head, gently rubbing, and he was OK.

"OK, buddy, settle down. I think you just had a bad dream. This place will do that to you. You're OK now, go back to sleep, buddy.

"Sam, is Gunny OK?"

"Yeah, I think so. He was acting like he had a bad dream. That's unusual for him."

Sam looked over at Steve and Luke. Luke was sitting up and sniffing the air as if searching for an elusive odor.

"What about Luke?"

"I'm not sure. He's acting a little strange too. This is how he would normally react when someone approached us in the dark when we were in Afghanistan."

Luke had heard the angry voice too, and he didn't like it, but it didn't scare him. Unlike Gunny, Luke had heard plenty of angry voices, and he knew about dealing with angry men. He also saw the man from his dreams before, and the man had talked to him again.

"You gotta help your buddy, you gotta protect him. That's a real nasty bastard that's talking, and he's gonna try to hurt your friend. Keep an eye on him, help him."

Luke didn't understand the sounds the man was making, but he was supposed to do something, and it had something to do with Gunny. He decided he would just try to watch Gunny and make sure nobody tried to hurt him.

It was strange that he couldn't smell the man with the angry voice, and that worried him a little. But this wasn't the strangest thing he'd ever encountered. Luke would be ready if the man with the angry voice showed up.

SEARCH DAY THREE, STORM DAY ONE

*The best laid schemes o' mice an' men gang
aft agley*

Robert Burns, "To a Mouse', 1785

Team Liberty Iwo Jima Base Camp
Sunday 25 June
Search Day 3
0645 Hours

SEARCH DAY 3 HAD DAWNED WITH OVERCAST SKIES, a brisk wind out of the East and spitting rain. The team had just finished breakfast and was preparing to return to their huts to get ready for the day when the door to the dining facility opened, and Commander Matsuyama walked in followed by his interpreter, a young lieutenant.

Matsuyama's interpreter spoke.

"Please be seated, I have some information for you from Commander Matsuyama.

"The Commander asks me to say that all unnecessary outdoor work is canceled for today and tomorrow due to bad weather. This includes your search activities."

"What?" Sam exclaimed, "What bad weather? We can work through a little wind and rain. What's going on?"

"You should be aware that there is a typhoon approaching from the East," said the lieutenant.

"I'm aware of the typhoon, but it's not supposed to come any closer than a hundred miles of this island," Tom said.

After conversing with Matsuyama, the lieutenant said, "It is standard procedure to cease all activities at the airfield if a major storm is expected within 150 miles."

"That may make sense for airfield operations," Tom said, "but we will be only a short distance away and can easily return to shelter if the weather starts to become dangerous."

There was another exchange of Japanese and this time Matsuyama spoke sharply to his lieutenant.

"The Commander says that this is the rule, and it applies to everyone. There will be no exceptions!"

The Team was stunned into silence, and then Sam spoke in a quiet, polite voice.

"May I ask a question?"

The lieutenant nodded.

"I'm just wondering why the Commander is speaking to us through an interpreter. I notice that he's wearing pilot's wings, which means that at some time he learned to speak English since that is the international language of air traffic control. It would be pretty difficult to make an instrument approach to Iwakuni without speaking English. Has the Commander forgotten how to speak English, or is he just being an asshole?"

Commander Matsuyama stiffened and glared at Sam.

You understood every word I said didn't you, you son of a bitch, but you can't admit it now without losing face.

Matsuyama spoke in a torrent of angry Japanese to his interpreter and turned and stalked out of the hut, slamming the door behind him.

The lieutenant, copying the Commander's glare spoke directly to Sam.

"The Commander says that he will not tolerate any deviation from his orders. If you attempt to disobey, he will see to it that your authority to search further is rescinded!" Then, turning on his heel, he followed Matsuyama out of the hut.

"That son of a bitch! Are we going to let him get away with this shit?"

"Settle down, Sam. Let's see if we can think this through."

"Yeah, yeah, Tom, I'll settle down. Just give me a minute. Can he really shut us down?"

"I don't know. I'll try to get in touch with our State Department liaison, but she's in D.C., and it's Saturday afternoon there. I may not be able to reach her until sometime Monday."

"What about those State Department people who briefed us in Okinawa?"

"Yeah, I'll try them too, but it's Sunday, and I doubt I'll have much luck."

"I'll bet Matsuyama planned this out to the minute. I mean, look out there; it's nothing more than a drizzle. We can get in a full day of work before this gets bad enough to make us stop."

"Wait a minute, Sam. He certainly didn't plan this storm."

"No, Alicia, but he saw an opportunity, and he took advantage of it."

"Why would he do that?"

"I don't know, but the bottom line is that he's shut us down for at least two days and we didn't have that much time to start with."

"Tom, I may have an idea."

"What's that, Jim?"

"I'd rather not say until I've made some phone calls. Let me get my sat phone and check this out, and I'll let you know what I find."

"OK, but sooner would be better than later."

"I'll get right to work."

"In the meantime, what can we do?"

"I've got the bones and artifacts we've found to work on so I can stay busy. With any luck, we could get a positive ID on our first Marine."

"OK, Alicia. Let us know if there is anything we can do to help. It looks like Steve, Sam, and I will be twiddling our thumbs for a while."

♦ ♦ ♦

Team Liberty Iwo Jima Base Camp
Sunday 25 June
Search Day 3
0930 Hours

It had taken Jim Stewart over an hour on his computer and with his sat phone to find the phone number he needed. When the call went through, it was answered by a man speaking Japanese.

"Odenwa arigatou gozaimasu."

"Hello. Is this Professor Okada? This is Dr. Jim Stewart calling from Iwo Jima."

"Dr. Stewart, what a pleasure to hear your voice! How are things going on Iwo Jima?"

"Up until this morning we were doing well, but we've run into a problem, and that is why I'm calling. You said that you might be able to help us if we had difficulties with the government."

"Yes, I may have some influence. What is the problem?"

"It's Commander Matsuyama, the commanding officer here. He has been somewhat less than helpful since we arrived. This morning he shut down our search for two days on the pretense of a storm that does not appear to be much of a threat. As you know, we only have ten search days allotted to us, and losing two will have a serious effect."

"I see. This may be difficult. The government will be reluctant to interfere with the commander on the scene, especially if, in his judgment, there is an issue of safety. However, let me make some phone calls and see what I can find out. I will call you back as soon as I can."

"Thank you, Professor. I'm sorry to impose on you like this, but I didn't know what else to do."

"Nonsense, Jim. You know how interested I am in your work there, and I will help in any way I can."

"Thank you, Professor. I'll look forward to your call."

Two hours later, Jim's phone rang.

"Professor Okada?"

"Yes, Jim. I've done some checking, and I have some information and an idea for how we might proceed."

"That's great news. What have you learned?"

"Your Commander Matsuyama is a member of the Issuikai Movement, which is one of Japan's right-wing political parties. Although most of our right-wing parties are pro-US, the Issuikai see the Japanese government as an American puppet state and demand 'complete independence'. Furthermore, they seek to justify

Japan's imperialism before the Second World War, and they deny that Japan committed atrocities or war crimes during the war. It is possible that Commander Matsuyama is deliberately trying to sabotage your efforts."

"What can be done?"

"Very little at the moment. Matsuyama has done nothing wrong. The Issuikai is a legal, political party, and he is well within his purview as a commander to take whatever safety precautions he decides are necessary."

"Then we're stuck? He can just keep throwing up obstacles until we run out of time?"

"Perhaps not. I have spoken to a young colleague of mine, Dr. Edward Akiyama, who has offered to help."

"What can he do?"

"If you agree, he will travel to Iwo Jima where he will act as my 'eyes and ears' there. If Matsuyama does something that exceeds his authority, he will tell me, and I will try to intervene if possible."

"But he won't be able to help with our immediate problem?"

"No, I'm afraid not, but he may be able to help you avoid additional problems in the future. Also, he may be able to help your Dr. Phillips."

"How is that?"

"He is also a forensic anthropologist. In fact, when I explained the situation to him, he asked me to ask you to say to Dr. Phillips, 'Go, Vols.' Do you know what that means?"

"Vols could be short for Volunteers, which is the name of the sports teams at the University of Tennessee."

"Exactly. Ed Akiyama spent some time studying there, they may know each other."

"That will be great. I'm sure Alicia can use some help, especially if we begin to find more remains."

"Good, then I will tell him to get there as soon as possible. Hopefully by tomorrow evening."

"Professor Okada, you've been a big help. Thank you."

"My pleasure, Jim. Good luck to you and your team. I have a personal reason for my interest in your search that I hope to tell you about in due course."

"I will look forward to that. Thank you. Goodbye."

◆ ◆ ◆

Team Liberty Iwo Jima Base Camp
Sunday 25 June
Search Day 3
1200 Hours

Over lunch, Jim Stewart recounted his conversation with Professor Okada for the rest of the team.

"So, just who is this Professor Okada?" Sam asked.

"Professor Okada is a distinguished professor of history at Tokyo University, and he is the leading expert on the modern history of Japan. I corresponded regularly with him while we were preparing for this search because he has insights on the war in general and the battle for Iwo Jima in particular from the Japanese perspective that were very helpful to me."

"More importantly, for our current situation, he indicated that he has some influence with the government in Tokyo and that he might be able to help us if we encountered problems."

"Why would he do that?" Tom asked.

"I'm not sure, but he has mentioned several times that he has a 'personal interest' in our search. He's a bit mysterious about it, but he says he will tell me everything when the time is right."

"Do you think we can trust this guy?"

"Yes, Sam, I do. Very few Japanese share Commander Matsuyama's political beliefs, and Professor Okada is a highly respected academic who did his undergraduate work at UCLA and is known to be a friend of the US."

"Alicia, do you know this Dr. Akiyama?"

"I met him a couple of times at Tennessee. I think he was doing some post-doctoral work there when I was getting started in forensic anthropology. From what I know of him, he has an excellent reputation. When do we expect him to arrive?"

"I just got an e-mail from Professor Okada who said that Akiyama will fly here tomorrow on a military aircraft and should be here by late afternoon or early evening."

"Assuming that Matsuyama opens the airfield."

"Professor Okada's e-mail ensured me that would not be a problem, Sam."

"Huh. Maybe this guy has some clout after all."

◆ ◆ ◆

Team Liberty Iwo Jima Base Camp
25 June
Search Day 3
2200 Hours

That night the outer edge of the typhoon started moving across Iwo Jima. The rain that fell began changing the search area. Some changes were beneficial. Others were potentially dangerous.

As Alicia had predicted, most of the water that fell at the top of the Amphitheater was funneled to the gully where it ran down to the base of the ridge and into the old creek bed. Because the porous soil absorbed so much water, the flow in the creek was far from a raging flood, but it was enough to remove a few inches of dirt.

Farther up on the eastern slope of the ridge above the gully something that looked like a black rock with metal prongs protruding from it was dislodged and rolled a few feet down the hill into a shallow hole where it stopped with the prongs facing up. Fine mud made from the black volcanic sand flowed around it and anchored it in its new home.

Close examination of this object would show that it was not a rock at all. It was a Japanese landmine that had been emplaced in front of a fighting position many years before.

This particular mine had been assembled during the war in one of the small shops in the heart of Tokyo that were being used more and more for munitions production as the B-29 bombing raids took their toll on Japan's industrial base. The young woman who was responsible for the final, delicate mating of the Model 23 grenade to the firing mechanism and detonator had a fiancé in the Army from whom she had not had a letter in over a year. She believed that if she did her work very, very well it would help to ensure Japan's final victory and her reunion with her loved one.

As a result, she took extra care to make sure that the entire device was well waterproofed with the grease and wax she was provided even though she had been reprimanded several times for working too slowly and using too much precious material.

Because of this woman's love for her fiancé the mine that now sat with only the prongs of its firing mechanism exposed was just as dangerous as it had been on the day it had been put it into its original position.

The young woman's fiancé never returned from the war, and she never learned what had happened to him.

SEARCH DAY THREE, NIGHT DREAMS

Monsters are real, and ghosts are real too.
They live inside us, and sometimes, they win.

Stephen King

Team Liberty Iwo Jima Base Camp
Sunday 25 June
Search Day 3
2200 Hours

STEVE TOOK A SPOONFUL OF YELLOWISH MUSH out of the green can and put it in his mouth.

God! This tastes like shit! What the hell is this stuff?

Wait a minute, I know what this is. It's C-ration ham and lima beans. How in the hell do I know that?

As he swallowed, he tried to take stock of his situation.

Oh shit, not again. I'm back on Iwo Jima. I'm in a hole, there's a battle going on all around me, but nothing is landing too close, I'm filthy, I've got a BAR across my lap, and I'm so hungry that even ham and motherfuckers (how do I know that) is starting to taste good.

He was so intent on his thoughts that he didn't hear the noise outside his hole, and he almost had heart failure when a large Doberman Pincher landed in his lap and started licking his face.

That's right, the Marines used a lot of Dobermans in the war.

The dog's handler said something to Steve. "What? Oh no, he's OK. He's just being friendly."

When the dog and his handler had left, Steve sat there trying to figure out what was happening to him.

I know this is a dream, but it's not like any dream I've ever had before. It's too real, and there's this sensation that I've done all this before, and there's this other sensation like I have some vague idea what's going to happen.

Steve's thoughts were interrupted when another Marine slid into his hole.

That's Corporal Jeff Hanks.

"Billotti's dead."

"Shit"

I knew that. I knew it when I saw him on the beach, but how. I remember...Stewart, Jim Stewart told us at the briefing. Oh God, I know what's going to happen to all these guys. This dream really sucks! I knew Billotti was going to get killed and Hanks - Hanks is one of the missing.

But, who the hell am I?

♦ ♦ ♦

Team Liberty Iwo Jima Base Camp
Sunday 25 June

Search Day 3
2300 Hours

The night before Sam had gotten a full nine hours of much-needed sleep. He had been worried about a repeat of his dream, but he had slept straight through except for a couple of trips to the bathroom, something that was becoming more common for him as he got older.

This night would be different. He had been asleep for a couple of hours when he found himself back in combat on Iwo Jima. Once again he was pinned down in the open, but he wasn't on the beach anymore, he was on flat, featureless ground with high rocky ridges in front and on both side of him. The noise and the volume of fire were, if anything, even worse than it had been on the beach.

Oh shit! I'm in the Amphitheater!

A loud *Crack* followed by a booming explosion made him raise his head just enough to see the turret of an M-4 tank, with the tank commander still hanging out of his hatch, lifted in the air and turn over to land with the unlucky Marine crushed under it.

Oh God, this has to be a dream, but it's so real.

Somehow, above the noise, he heard someone yelling, a voice that, for some reason, was familiar.

"First Squad, over here! Move toward me! There's cover!"

First squad, that's me, that's us.

Sam started crawling toward the voice. After a minute, he could see another Marine who was half standing gesturing him and three others forward.

That's Hanks, Jeff Hanks. That crazy bastard is going to get himself killed.

Sam got up to Hanks, who pointed and said, "Down there! That little gully. You'll have cover. Get down there, and I'll send the rest of the squad."

Sam crawled as fast as he could and tumbled into the shallow creek bed. A few moments later, three other Marines rolled in on top of him. Sam looked up just as Jeff Hanks raised up to make sure everyone was safely under cover.

This is the gully where we've been searching, this is where Gunny found the ilium and the rifle. Oh God, I know what's going to happen! I don't want to watch!

But he had no choice, and he saw the instant that the sniper's bullet found Jeff Hank's chest. Hanks fell almost on top of him and rolled over limply on his back. Sam watched as the blood welled up in his mouth, and his eyes began to lose focus, and Jeff Hanks spoke his last words.

"You... you've got the squad."

Sam bolted upright in his bed, his mouth dry and his heart pounding.

I just watched Jeff Hanks die. I know who we found in the gully.

Yeah, great, but who am I gonna tell? They'll think I'm psycho.

♦ ♦ ♦

Team Liberty Iwo Jima Base Camp
Sunday 25 June
Search Day 3
2200 Hours

Tom looked down at Jeff Hank's body. All around him was the noise of a vicious battle, but all he could think about was what Hanks had just said to him.

I've got the squad. Goddamn it, I'm not a squad leader. What the hell do I know about leading a squad?

But that wasn't right. He'd spent twenty-two years in the Army, he was a Ranger, he knew a lot about leading a squad.

But I'm not me, I'm someone else. I'm a scared young Marine on Iwo Jima, but which one? Who am I?

Tom should be able to figure this out, but he was having trouble thinking clearly. Above all the other battle sounds he could hear the boom-boom-boom of the big machine gun up on the ridge, the gun that was tearing his company apart.

We've got to get that gun. Somehow, we've got to get that gun.

Tom's mind kept repeating,"..get that gun, get that gun" as he slowly drifted back to sleep.

◆ ◆ ◆

Team Liberty Iwo Jima Base Camp
Sunday 25 June
Search Day 3
2330 Hours

Since Gunny had found those bones on the first day of the search, Alicia had been doing a lot of thinking, augmented by some online research, and had concluded that she had been wrong. She didn't like to admit something like that, but she was a good scientist, and she knew she had to evaluate new data objectively and change her hypothesis if warranted. Once she admitted to herself that she had been wrong about Gunny, she understood that the other team members had not been disrespectful of her, they had simply known more than she did. That hurt her pride, but it also calmed her down a lot. The night before she had slept well, and she had fallen quickly to sleep tonight.

After a couple of hours, she began to dream that she was skiing. She had enjoyed skiing when she was young, but there hadn't been much opportunity once she moved to Tennessee. It was a pleasant dream at first; she was floating down through soft powder snow, and the feeling was exhilarating, but soon she began to feel cold. That's when she realized that she was only wearing the shorts and short-sleeved shirt she had gone to bed in, and she started to shiver. It was icy cold like a cold bath and...

Alicia jerked upright, her eyes flew open, and there he was at the foot of the bed, the same man she had seen two nights before. He stood there not moving, just calmly looking at her.

She opened her mouth to scream, but all her breath was gone, and all that came out was a thin, low whine.

He was dressed exactly as he had been before, nothing had changed except that now she could smell him, and it was a smell she recognized. It was the smell of one of the old bodies at the Body Farm, a body that had been there for a year or two and was completely skeletonized. It was the smell of old bone.

She fought for breath so she could scream for help, but then she looked into his eyes. There was no threat there, no menace, only sadness. As she slowly calmed and they looked at each other, the coldness ebbed away, and she was warm again.

I don't know who, or what, this is, but he's not here to hurt me.

"Who are you? What do you want? Do you need help?"

A sad smile slowly worked its way onto his face, a smile that had been a long time coming, and he started to talk.

"What? I can't hear you. What do you want?"

The man continued to talk, but it wasn't working, and he paused. When he started again, he was slowly repeating one word over and over. She leaned in closer.

He was saying, "Hanks, Hanks, Hanks."

"Hanks? Do you mean Jeff Hanks? Corporal Jeff Hanks?"

As Alicia spoke, she reached out to touch him, but, suddenly, there was nothing there, he was gone.

Just before he disappeared, he nodded his head.

◆ ◆ ◆

On the Eastern Ridge of the Amphitheater
Iwo Jima
Sunday, 25 June
Search Day 3
2330 Hours

Watanabe was seething with anger. Why were there Americans here? How could they be allowed back after General Kuribayashi had defeated them and thrown them back into the sea? Oh! How Watanabe wished he could have been there when Kuribayashi had come to his senses and unleashed the great Banzai attack, but no, Watanabe had been deprived of that glory by the traitor Okada.

The Americans were coming to desecrate his bones. He must stop them to give his countrymen time to find him. Then Watanabe would be taken out into the light again and be reunited with all the other heroes at Yasukuni, and live there in glory forever.

SEARCH DAY FOUR, STORM DAY TWO

*Our flag's unfurled to every breeze
From dawn to setting sun
We have fought in every clime and place
Where we could take a gun
In the snow of far off northern lands
And in sunny tropic scenes
You will find us always on the job
The United States Marines*

Third verse of The Marines' Hymn

Team Liberty Iwo Jima Base Camp
Monday 26 June
Search Day 4
1500 Hours

ALICIA LEANED IN TO GET A CLOSER LOOK at the X-ray image on her laptop. She then looked at the piece of bone she had spent most of the day before cleaning, photographing and X-raying. What she saw was the left half of a human skull with the upper jaw intact and a fragment of the lower jaw still barely attached. There were four teeth in the upper jaw and one in the lower jaw fragment.

After carefully measuring the spaces between the teeth, she said, "I've got numbers eleven, twelve, fourteen and sixteen on the maxilla, and seventeen on the mandible. Is that what you're seeing?"

"Uh, the maxilla is the upper jaw, right?"

Trying hard not to roll her eyes, she said, "Yes, Jim. The upper jaw."

It had been very nice of Jim Stewart to volunteer to help her with the tedious process of trying to identify this skull, but she thought she could almost certainly do it faster on her own. A few months ago, she would have simply told Jim to get out of her lab and let her work. Was her personality changing, or was she losing her edge?

Jim turned to look at his own laptop that showed the images of the dental charts for the five missing Marines.

"Laskey was missing twelve and Lawrence was missing seventeen. The other three had all five of those teeth on their charts. That means we can eliminate Laskey and Lawrence."

"Concur. Now I'm showing what looks like a filling on the lingual surface of number fourteen. It's about one millimeter across and two millimeters deep."

"And the only one of our remaining three who had a filling there is Corporal Jeff Hanks," Jim said, "So, I'm guessing it has to be him."

Hanks? Is that what that man...oh, bullshit, Alicia, that was no man, and you know it, it was something else. Something you're afraid to admit. Whatever he was, he said, "Hanks." Was that Hanks? Am I going crazy?

"Alicia, Alicia, are you OK?"

"What? Huh? Oh, sorry Jim, I guess I just spaced out for a second. What were you saying?"

Get your shit together, Alicia, don't look like a fool.

"I was saying that this must be Corporal Jeff Hanks."

"Not necessarily."

"Why do you say that?"

"Those dental records are dated from before the Fourth Division left the States. One of the other Marines could have had a filling put in en route to Iwo."

"But how likely is it that one of those two Marines would get a filling in the same place on the same tooth as Hanks?"

"Not very likely at all," Alicia said, "But a good defense attorney would cut you to pieces if you presented evidence like that in court."

"But we don't need legal proof."

"Don't we? Are you willing to go to Corporal Hank's next of kin and say that you have positive identification of their missing loved one if there is any doubt in your mind?"

"No. You're right, we need to be sure."

"OK, so review for me what we know."

"Corporal Jeff Hanks was a twenty-year-old white male who was five feet nine inches tall and weighed approximately one hundred forty-five pounds. Nothing we've seen in any of the three bones is contraindicative of an individual of this race, age, and size. Also, the remaining teeth in the upper and lower jaw match Corporal Hanks' dental records exactly."

"However," Alicia replied, "None of this evidence is conclusive. I agree that it is highly likely that this individual is Corporal Hanks, but it's not something we could take to court or say to his family with one hundred percent certainty."

"Don't forget what we just heard from my students about the rifle," Jim said.

"Yes," Alicia replied. "The fact that the rifle Gunny found had been issued to Corporal Hanks is additional corroborating evidence, but still not conclusive."

"What do we do next?"

"I'm going to work on extracting some pulp from one of those teeth. They're in pretty good shape, and I'll bet we can get enough pulp for DNA analysis. That's what we need to be certain."

Alicia continued, "Then I'm going to tell the rest of the team that, with your help, I have tentatively identified our first missing Marine as Corporal Jeff Hanks pending final confirmation by DNA. Sound OK?"

"Yes, and thank you for letting me help. This gives me a whole new perspective on history."

♦ ♦ ♦

Team Liberty Iwo Jima Base Camp
Monday 26 June
Search Day 4
1700 Hours

The team was just getting organized for dinner when Commander Matsuyama's interpreter came in with another man who was almost a head taller than the lieutenant and solidly built.

"Your attention, please! This is Dr. Akiyama. He has been sent here by Tokyo to oversee your operations to ensure that you do not violate the terms of your agreement with the government or disobey any orders of Commander Matsuyama. In effect, he will be in charge of your search from this point on."

Having delivered this speech, he left the hut before the team could ask any questions.

Dr. Akiyama watched him leave and listened to make sure he had gotten into his vehicle. He then spoke to the team in flawless, unaccented English—British English.

"He's an obnoxious little bugger, isn't he?"

After a second of stunned silence, the team broke out in laughter.

"Dr. Akiyama, welcome to Team Liberty," Tom said, "Can I assume that all that stuff about you being in charge is just your cover story?"

"Precisely, Colonel Sanders. Your dear friend Commander Matsuyama was very interested in finding out how I had commandeered a military aircraft and flown here on such short notice. The 'cover story' was Professor Okada's idea, and he even provided me with an official letter from the foreign ministry detailing the story the young lieutenant just told you.

"Please allow me to introduce myself properly. I am Ed Akiyama, and I'm a forensic anthropologist at Tokyo University. As I'm sure you have observed, I am a mixed-race Japanese. My father worked in the Japanese foreign office, and my mother was in the British embassy in Tokyo. They met and fell in love, hence me and my somewhat unusual name.

"I am here at the request of Professor Okada to help in any way I can. As a forensic anthropologist, I am excited to be here, and I am anxious to get my hands dirty in this fascinating search of yours."

When he had finished speaking, Alicia said, "Dr. Akiyama, I'm Dr. Alicia Phillips, the team's forensic anthropologist. I believe we met when you were at Tennessee."

"Yes, Doctor, I remember. I also remember that when we met, you had already established an excellent reputation. I look forward to working with you."

"I'm sure that it will be my privilege, and I look forward to learning from you."

Alicia then introduced Akiyama to the rest of the team.

After everyone had added their welcome Alicia said, "Dr. Akiyama, would you like me to brief you on what we've been doing?"

"Yes, Dr. Phillips, very much, but on one condition, that you, and the rest of the team, call me Ed."

"OK, Ed. I'm Alicia."

"Where shall we do this?"

"Why don't I give you the outline over dinner and afterward I can show you what we've found so far."

"That sounds perfect. I'm starving."

During the meal, Alicia and the rest of the team brought Ed Akiyama up to speed on what they had done since arriving on Iwo Jima.

When they had finished, he said, "One thing that jumps out at me is that the two dogs have played a major role in this search."

"Yes!" Alicia said, "Our dogs, Gunny and Luke, have been absolutely essential. Without them, we'd still be back at square one."

"Our dogs?" Steve thought. *That's interesting.*

"Well, I'll look forward to watching them work."

As everyone was about to get up from the table, Jim Stewart said, "Alicia, don't we have some information for the team?"

Alicia shook her head and grimaced, "Of course, I'm not thinking. Thanks, Jim. If everyone will sit back down Jim and I will bring you up to speed on our investigation of the remains we've been working on."

Jim smiled at being included as part of the investigation and Alicia continued, "With Jim's help I've examined the remains that

Gunny located for us, and we've reached a tentative identification pending confirmation by DNA analysis."

Sam, who had been unnaturally quiet all day suddenly blurted, "Hanks! It was Corporal Jeff Hanks!"

After a brief silence, Alicia said, "Why, yes. Yes, we think it's Corporal Jeff Hanks, but how did you know?"

"Because I saw... Nothing, I don't know. It just popped into my head."

There were looks of disbelief on everyone's faces except Jim's and Ed Akiyama's who merely looked quizzical.

"Look, I'm sorry, I've had a lot on my mind today. Forget what I said. I'm going to go take Gunny for a walk." With that, Sam got up and left the hut.

Sam and I have got to talk Alicia thought.

♦ ♦ ♦

Team Liberty Iwo Jima Base Camp
Monday 26 June
Search Day 4
1930 Hours

Other than a couple of walks and some training with The Man, Gunny hadn't done much. That didn't mean that he wasn't ready for a nap after dinner. The Man and the others were over at the other hut talking, so Gunny and Luke did what most dogs do best, curled up and went immediately to sleep.

Gunny had only been asleep for a short time when he began to hear noises like the ones the other night. At first, there was an angry buzzing like a small insect flying around his head, but as it got louder, he could tell that it was a man's voice—the same, angry voice.

Gunny did not like these sounds, and he whined, and his legs twitched. These were not sounds like The Man or anyone else he knew made, and they were so angry they scared him.

He could also hear, barely in the background, the other man, the one he now thought of as the Good Man.

"Don't listen.....hurt you.......bad"

Gunny tried to hear what the Good Man was saying, but the constant angry voice of the other man was too loud.

On the other side of the hut, Luke was whining and thrashing in his sleep like Gunny.

The sounds got louder, and Gunny became more scared. The voices wanted him to do something, but he had no idea what that could be. He was whining louder and becoming more and more upset.

He began to see an image. It was faint, but it was a man, not like any other man. The man was short and round. His round face was angry, and he was yelling. This was the man that was making the noise.

"Don't listen......bad man."

Yes, this is a bad man, and he wants me to do something.

When the door opened, and Sam and Steve walked in both dogs jerked awake and started barking frantically.

"Hey, hey, guys, what's the matter? What's going on?" Sam said.

Both men went to their dogs and tried to calm them.

As Luke settled down, Steve said, "What do you think that was all about?"

"I don't know it was like we woke them both up from a bad dream or something. What do you think they were barking at?"

"No idea. I mean Luke didn't seem to be focused on anything, he was just barking up in the air."

"Yeah, Gunny too. And now they're just sitting there with kind of a glazed look in their eyes."

After a couple of minutes, the dogs settled down, and their eyes returned to normal, but they were panting as if they had just run a long way. Both suddenly stopped panting and looked toward the front of the hut, and then they stood and walked to stand by the door.

Sam was about to grab Gunny when he saw that both dog's tails were wagging. A second later, there was a knock.

"Sam, Steve, it's Tom and Alicia. Is it too late to come in?"

Steve walked over and opened the door, "No, no, come on in. Sam and I were just...uh, playing with the dogs."

Alicia came in first, and her sharp eyes focused on Steve and Sam's faces. "OK, Tom, I'm glad we came over here. Somethings going on. Right, Sam?"

"I don't know what you mean," Sam said.

"Bullshit! None of us believed that crap about Jeff Hank's name just 'popping into your head.' You know something, or you've seen something, and now you and Steve are upset about something. Right?"

"No. The dogs were just having some bad dreams or something."

"Oh, them too, huh?" Tom said.

"What do you mean, them too?" Steve asked.

"OK," Alicia said, "I'm sorry if I came on too strongly, but it's been a strange night. Let's sit down and talk for a minute."

When they all had a spot on one of the bunks Alicia continued, "After the meeting tonight, Tom told me something that explained a few things for me, and I hope that the two of you can explain some more. Tom, would you tell them what you told me?"

"I've been having some bad dreams ever since we got here. Not every night, more like every other night. I dream that I'm one of the Marines we're looking for, I don't know which one, and I'm here fighting on Iwo Jima. The dreams are very realistic and very, very scary. Last night I dreamt I saw Jeff Hank's body shortly after he was killed lying in the gully where we've been searching."

"Sam, when you blurted out Jeff Hank's name at the meeting, I felt like someone had thrown a bucket of cold water on me. I knew you were right before Alicia said anything."

Sam and Steve hung their heads like a couple of schoolboys caught in a prank.

"Yeah, OK," Sam said, "I've been having dreams too. Last night I was in the Amphitheater, and Jeff Hanks saved our asses. He's the one who found the gully and got us in there. I saw him get shot and killed before he could get down there with us."

"Sam, you're talking like you were actually there like you were watching what actually happened," Alicia said.

"I wasn't just watching. Like Tom said, I was one of those Marines, one of the guys we're looking for, and, yeah, I have no doubt that I saw what actually happened."

"What about you, Steve?" Alicia asked.

"Yeah, me too, same kind of dreams. And I even have a way of telling how real they are. Do you guys know what ham and lima beans are?"

"Sure," Sam said, "They were the most hated meal in a box of C-rations, although I kind of liked them."

"Did they have a nickname?"

"Yeah, we called them ham and motherfuckers, excuse me, Alicia."

"I've never eaten C-rations, they were phased out long before I joined the Corps, so I'd never heard any of that before, but last night I dreamed that I was eating ham and lima beans and I even knew what they were called."

"God, what a horrible dream," Tom said with a slight smile.

"So, what about you, Alicia?" Sam asked. "Have you had dreams?"

"Not dreams, at least I don't think so, but before I tell you, I'd like to try a little experiment. Are you guys up for a short walk?"

"I'd rather not leave Gunny here right now."

"That's OK, bring the dogs, just put them on a leash. I'd be interested to see what they do."

"OK, why not," Sam said, "Tonight can't get much weirder."

Alicia shook her head. "Oh, yes, it can."

♦ ♦ ♦

Team Liberty Iwo Jima Base Camp
Monday 26 June
Search Day 4
2015 Hours

Alicia led them over behind her hut to where she had seen the ghost the first time.

Might as well call a spade a spade. After what I just heard, if that guy's not a ghost, I don't know what he could be.

"OK, this is about the right spot. It's a bit early, but, for some reason, I don't think that matters."

"Are you going to tell us what this is all about?" Tom asked.

"Give it a few minutes. If nothing happens, I'll try to explain, but it's better if you can see it for yourself."

"See what?"

"Shhhh, just wait."

They stood around self-consciously for several minutes and nothing happened. The dogs were lying at their feet and going back to sleep. Suddenly, both dogs stood and looked out into the darkness, and a low growl started in their throats.

Sam whispered, "What is it, Gunny?"

"I don't like this," Steve said, "Luke's telling me something."

Alicia pointed off to their left and said, "There he is!"

The three men looked where she had pointed and saw a man carrying a rifle walking slowly toward them.

"That guy's armed!" Steve said.

"It's OK, he's not here to hurt us."

As the man came closer, the dogs growled louder, and then— they went silent. Both dogs had relaxed, and their tails were wagging.

Gunny recognized the Old Bone scent of the Good Man and tried to go to him, but The Man held him back.

The ghost walked toward them without any sign of recognition until he came abreast of the two dogs. He paused, looked at them, and smiled briefly, and then continued. Soon, he was through the fence and down the ridge into the Amphitheater.

Alicia stepped in front of the three men who were staring fixedly at the point where the ghost had disappeared. "Do you gentlemen have any questions?"

◆ ◆ ◆

Team Liberty Iwo Jima Base Camp
Monday 26 June
Search Day 4
2100 Hours

Sam reached under his bunk and pulled out a well-worn seabag with the names of all the places he had served stenciled down one side. He reached inside and pulled out a bottle of twelve-year-old

Jameson's Irish Whiskey. He held the bottle up to the light. It was almost full.

"Anyone want to join me?"

He took a healthy pull and passed it to Steve, who did the same and gave it to Tom, who had his share and handed it to Alicia. She hesitated for a moment and then took a healthy swallow.

"Do the dogs get any?" she asked.

Steve and Sam chuckled, "No!"

"You asked for questions, here's my first," Sam said, "Why isn't Jim here?"

"Tom and I sounded him out earlier, and we're pretty certain he hasn't experienced what we have so we thought we'd wait until we knew more before bringing him in."

"OK, good idea, but what do we think we know? I mean is there really such a thing as ghosts?" Steve said.

"Don't ask me, I'm an anthropologist, not a parapsychologist, but until someone gives me a better explanation, I'm gonna say yeah," Alicia said with a slightly slurred voice.

"I agree." Steve said, "And I'll tell you what convinced me was the way the dogs reacted. As soon as they got his scent, they not only calmed down but acted like he was their new best friend. They knew that guy, and they trusted him."

"His scent, yes, of course, his scent. Did you smell him?" Alicia asked.

"No, did you?"

"Not tonight, but I did last night when he was in my room."

"In your room???" the three men said together.

"Yeah, yeah, I'll tell you about that later. But I was right up next to him, and I could smell him, and he smelled like old bone."

"Old bone?" Tom asked. "What the hell is that?"

"You know," Alicia said, "like a skeletonized body when all the flesh has decomposed."

"I'm pretty sure we wouldn't know that Alicia," Tom said.

"Actually, I know that smell," Sam said, "Gunny and I did some training at the body farm at Western Carolina University a few years ago, and I know just what you're talking about."

The room was quiet for a moment, and then Tom asked, "So who is this ghost? Is it one of our Marines, or just your generic Marine ghost, model 1945?"

Sam replied, "Based on absolutely no evidence whatsoever, just a feeling, I think it's not only one of our Marines, but it's the same Marine we've been inside of in our dreams."

"Yeah," Steve said, "That sounds right, that feels right."

"So, what do we do now?" Sam asked.

Tom reached for the bottle and took another drink, "First, let's share all our stories, so we know what each of us has seen or experienced. Then we'll need to bring Jim up to speed."

"What about Ed?" Alicia asked.

"Let's see how things go while we're working tomorrow." We don't know him very well yet. By the time for the team meeting tomorrow evening we should have a better idea of what to do."

The four of them spent the next couple of hours talking about their dreams and experiences with the ghost. By the time they were done, the whiskey bottle was empty, and they all stumbled into bed.

♦ ♦ ♦

On the Eastern Ridge of the Amphitheater
Iwo Jima
Monday 26 June
Search Day 4
2100 Hours

Watanabe was satisfied. The dogs had heard him and had been scared. It had taken a lot of energy to overcome the interference from the other, and now he was dangerously weak. He remembered more every hour, and his plan was forming.

There were many things that he did not understand, but the dog was key. The dog was the one that might find the cave and must be stopped, but how? He longed to hold his sword in his hand once more. He would make short work of that dog then, but now he had no way to do anything physically to the dog. He might be able to manipulate it, though. Perhaps he could lure it into something dangerous, something deadly, something like… yes! The minefield! That is how he would kill the dog, but, first, he must become stronger.

SEARCH DAY FIVE

There are more things in heaven and earth,
Horatio, Than are dreamt of in your
philosophy.

William Shakespeare: Hamlet Act 1, scene 5

Iwo Jima, Amphitheater Search Area
Tuesday, 27 June
Search Day 5
0700 Hours

AFTER AN EARLY BREAKFAST, the teams started on their various assignments. Alicia and Ed were in the lab working on extracting a sample from the remains for DNA analysis and preparing it for shipping. Sam and Steve took the dogs out to the search area where the storm runoff had removed some of the soil in the gully.

Sam asked, "Steve, do these dogs seem right to you?"

"No, Luke is acting kind of spacey and Gunny doesn't look like his normal self either. Do you think they're OK?"

"I don't know. After last night I wouldn't be surprised if they were a little off. Tell you the truth, I'm a little off myself."

"A little off because of the ghost or the whiskey?"

"Some of both I guess, but the dogs weren't drinking whiskey, so I'm guessing their problem is the ghost."

"Do you think they can work in the state they're in?"

"Only one way to find out. Why don't you send Luke to that area where you said he was showing interest the other day and I'll have Gunny follow up on whatever he does?"

"OK"

"Luke...Search!"

Luke looked at Steve like he didn't understand, but then he shook his head and gathered himself and set off zig-zagging back and forth across the gully.

"He looks OK now," Steve said.

"Yeah, hope that works for Gunny."

Luke worked back and forth with his nose to the ground for about twenty yards until he got near the area where he had shown interest three days earlier, and then he slowed down, and his nose started working faster. It was clear to Steve that he was in scent, but there was nothing strong enough to make him go to his final alert.

After about twenty minutes, Luke had wandered around an area about ten yards wide and twenty yards long centered on the gully. Steve had placed orange flags in six places to mark the outline of Luke's interest.

When Steve had taken Luke out of the area, Sam turned to Gunny.

"Gunny! Look Close! Adios!"

The Man's commands sounded muffled and distant, and they barely registered. For the last hour, Gunny had heard the same voices from his dream, the angry, buzzing one he couldn't understand and the calmer, gentler one that kept saying, "Good boy, good dog."

Without that calm, soothing voice, Gunny would have been unable to do anything. The other voice was mesmerizing and confusing him. No man had ever spoken like that to him before.

Finally, Gunny understood what The Man was saying. It was Time to Go to Work. Training and instinct took over, and Gunny started searching for the Old Bone.

Gunny had watched Luke doing his search, so he had an idea of where he was supposed to be looking. As he got close to the area with the green flags, he began to get the scent of Old Bone, but it was very confusing. Not only did the scent seem to be coming from all around him, but he could tell that there were different Old Bone smells.

The image that was forming in Gunny's mind was very complex, but he had worked difficult scent pictures before, so he did what he always did. He first walked with the wind at his back until he lost all of the Old Bone scent then he turned and moved slowly into the wind. He ignored the fact that the scents were different and focused on finding where the scent was the strongest. Each time he came to a point of stronger odor he would paw at the ground or, if it was particularly strong, he would sit and bark so The Man could come and mark it and give him a treat and tell him he was a Good Dog.

This was not something The Man had taught him to do. This was something that dogs and their wolf ancestors had been doing for millions of years. Gunny was just using his natural, instinctive ability to get what he wanted, a treat and a pat on the head. For an animal that had evolved to find the burrow where the rabbit was hiding in a field covered in buffalo dung, this wasn't that hard a search.

It took over an hour, and Gunny had to take several breaks, but when he had finished, the search area inside of Luke's orange flags was covered with ten green flags marked with Gunny's "G." These ten flags appeared to be grouped into three distinct clusters.

"OK, Sam, what do we have?" Tom asked.

"There's definitely something there, and it looks like it's concentrated in those three, separate spots, so I'm guessing it's more than one set of remains. I think we'd better get Alicia and Ed down here with the ground-penetrating radar and all their gear. I think we may have to move a fair bit of dirt, but I'm confident we're going to find some remains."

"What about you, Steve? Anything dangerous down there?"

"There was nothing that put Luke on alert. There's probably some explosive reside, maybe from rifle cartridges or grenades, but nothing near the surface that's going to go bang. I should run Luke on the area every time we move some dirt to make sure there's nothing deeper down there."

"OK, I'll call Alicia and get them moving."

Suddenly, Luke and Gunny both spun around facing the ridge above and began a chorus of barks that sounded like something between anger and fear.

For the first time, the angry voice was making words. Gunny had never heard these words before, but he understood the tone. Someone was giving him a command in a loud and angry voice. At the same time, Gunny began to smell a new Old Bone scent.

"Don't listen to him, boy. Don't listen to that son-of-a-bitch he's just tryin' to hurt you."

The Good Man's voice was not loud enough to block out the Bad Man's voice, and Gunny kept hearing the same thing over and over.

"***Inu wa koko ni kimasu!***"

Gunny started to go toward the steep slope rising above the search area.

"Sam, grab Gunny! We haven't cleared that area yet!"

Sam grabbed Gunny's collar and snapped on his leash.

As quickly as it had started, the dog's barking stopped, and both dogs plopped down on the ground panting like they had just been on a long run.

"What the hell is going on?" Sam asked.

"I don't know, but I don't like it. Luke is just not acting right, and I don't want to put him on search in the condition he's in."

"I agree," Tom said, "We've got plenty of other stuff to do. Let's give the dogs a break and get Alicia down here. Jim and I can help her and Ed. You guys focus on your dogs."

"Thanks, Tom. The last thing I want is a distracted bomb dog working in front of me."

"Yeah and I don't need Gunny running into any place he shouldn't be. Maybe they just need a little time off."

♦ ♦ ♦

Iwo Jima, Amphitheater Search Area
Tuesday, 27 June
Search Day 5
1000 Hours

Alicia and Ed had just finished re-packaging Corporal Hanks' remains when the call came in telling them about what Luke and Gunny had found. They closed up the lab and, together with Jim Stewart, headed out to the search area.

Once on-site, Tom showed Alicia what the dogs had done. This was going to be a much more extensive search than the one for Corporal Hanks.

After she and Ed had walked the area and looked at all the flags, they made a quick decision about a plan of action.

"Tom, if you and Jim can get the GPR over here we'll take a look at the areas immediately under and just around where Gunny's flags are. If he's found anything, it should be right around those flags, and the GPR should give us a good idea of what we're dealing with."

The two men started rolling the GPR toward the first group of flags struggling to move it in the loose soil around the gully.

"This is going to be tough," Tom said, "Moving this thing around this large an area is going to take a while."

The GPR system they were using was mounted on a low-slung cart that looked a little like a lawnmower with over-sized wheels. The combination transmitter and receiver sat at the bottom of the cart so that its antenna was less than an inch above the ground. On top of this was the analyzer and display system, essentially a high-powered computer that interpreted the signals reflected from the ground below and displayed an image of the subsurface on a screen.

GPR is an incredibly powerful tool for finding buried objects without having to dig for them. Like most tools, however, it has its limitations. The system weighed about fifty pounds, which was why they were having so much trouble moving it through Iwo Jima's volcanic soil. When it was in place, it could take only a single image of a piece of ground about twenty-five inches on a side. Once that image had been viewed and recorded the system had to be moved about two feet forward to take the next picture with a slight overlap.

Alicia wanted to get a quick look at the most promising spots to see if there was anything there to justify spending a whole day on. Although she was learning to trust Gunny, her instinct was to believe what she could see or touch.

Alicia and Ed set to work to measure and mark the locations where the GPR would be positioned for each image. Tom and Jim did the heavy lifting to move the GPR into each position.

It took about four minutes to position the GPR, activate it to capture the image, and then quickly review and save the image file. After six images, Alicia told everyone to take a break while she and Ed discussed what they had already seen.

"What do we have, Alicia?" Tom asked

"A lot! In just these six images, I see numerous pieces of what are probably bone and several metallic objects, and they're all jumbled together. All of the objects are between eighteen and thirty inches below the surface. I'm guessing we have some remains mixed up with some items of equipment. Do you agree, Ed?"

"Yes, and I think one of the metallic objects could be part of a rifle."

"What do you want to do?" Alicia asked.

"Let's focus on this first cluster of Gunny's flags. It will take us another couple of hours to finish imaging the area around these first flags. Then we can download the images to the laptop and look at them while we break for lunch. Then we can make a dig plan to recover the most promising, and easiest to get to, artifacts so we can see what we're dealing with. After that, well, we'll just have to see what happens."

"What would we do without Gunny's flags?" Tom asked.

"Yes, I'm very impressed by what the dogs have been able to do," Ed said.

"Yeah," Alicia said, "Without Gunny, we'd still be wandering around out in the middle of the Amphitheater with no idea where our missing Marines might be. I've learned some valuable lessons on this trip."

"We all have," Tom said, "OK, good plan, let's get back to work."

♦ ♦ ♦

Team Liberty Iwo Jima Base Camp
Tuesday, 27 June
Search Day 5
2000 Hours

Alicia had underestimated the difficulty of moving the GPR around in the broken ground of the gully, and it had taken almost three hours to finish imaging the area around the first cluster of flags. After that, she and Ed had spent the rest of the afternoon carefully digging in three places where their analysis of the imagery had shown they had the best chance to find bones or artifacts that could be used for identification.

They had arrived back at base camp at about five with several boxes full of carefully packaged items. They then had gone directly to work unpacking, preserving, documenting, photographing, and doing an initial analysis of what they had found. They worked through dinner, occasionally pausing for a bite of a sandwich or a sip of coffee. Alicia called it quits only when they were getting tired enough that they were going to start making mistakes.

The two scientists walked slowly into the dining facility, went straight to the beer cooler, signed for a beer, and then slumped to a seat at a table with the rest of the team.

"Looks like you guys have been having fun," Sam said.

"This is incredible," Alicia replied. "This isn't like investigating a crime scene, this is like digging through the ruins of Pompeii. There are so many artifacts, and they're all jumbled together without any order that I can find."

"What sorts of things have you been finding?" Tom asked.

"Lots of bone," Ed replied. "No 'smoking guns' so far that might lead to a definite identification of an individual but enough that we can see that we have at least three sets of remains. My guess is that they must have died farther up the gully and their remains migrated to this location over time as the gully periodically filled up and then was scoured out. That's the only thing that would explain why everything is so jumbled up."

"And you think you have three different sets of remains?"

"We won't know for sure until we get a chance to do some microscopic and X-ray analysis, but that's what it looks like."

"Do you think these are three of our Marines?"

"Unfortunately, it looks like one set of remains is non-Caucasoid."

"You mean you think it's a Japanese soldier?"

"That's the most likely explanation."

"Alicia, why do you say 'unfortunately," Sam asked.

"I meant that it is unfortunate because now we'll have to get Commander Matsuyama involved again. Isn't that right, Tom?"

"Yeah, our agreement with the Japanese government is that we're required to inform Commander Matsuyama immediately if we discover any remains that might be Japanese. I'll do that as soon as we're finished talking."

"I was afraid of that. Is that asshole going to cause us another problem?" Sam asked.

"I hope not, but it's hard to tell with that guy. Is there anything else we need to discuss right now before I go call his duty officer?"

"Yes," Alicia said, "we need to talk about a few things."

"The first and most critical is that we only have five search days left. If the rest of this area is like what we've seen so far there is no way we could do all of the imaging, digging, recovering, preservation and analysis of what's down there in thirty days let alone five. And, even if we could do all that, we still only have evidence for three of our five Marines. There are two more out there."

"Could they be in that same area?"

"Certainly. They could also be somewhere totally different."

"Is the situation really that serious?" Tom asked.

Alicia and Ed both said, "Yes!" at practically the same time.

"OK, what's the second thing?"

"We need a plan for tomorrow. Even if I've grossly overestimated the time we will need to finish the work at this site, we can't afford to waste any of the time we have left."

"OK. Sam, Steve, how are your dogs doing?"

"As soon as Gunny got away from the search area he seemed to return to normal, except that he's acting like he's exhausted."

"Yeah, Luke's the same."

"So they should be able to work tomorrow?"

"I don't see why not."

"Sure, no problem."

"Alicia, will you need Gunny tomorrow?"

"I'd like him to take another sweep through that area now that we've disturbed some of the soil to see if he hits on anything else, but that shouldn't take long. After he finishes, we'll go back to doing more of what we did today."

"OK, so let's get Luke started on clearing that slope above the gully and Gunny can start by working with Alicia's team. Jim and I will continue to help Alicia and Ed."

"Sound like a plan?"

After everyone had agreed, Tom turned to Alicia, "I guess I know what the last subject is."

"Yes, we just need to decide about Ed."

"Ed," Tom said "We need to talk about something that is rather, well, strange I guess is the best word. You're a member of the team, and we'd like to include you in this, but you may think we've all gone crazy."

"Oh, I see, you're finally going to tell me about the ghost."

♦ ♦ ♦

Team Liberty Iwo Jima Base Camp
Tuesday, 27 June
Search Day 5
2100 Hours

Jim Stewart was the first to break the stunned silence, "Ghost? What ghost? What are you talking about?"

Tom replied, "It's a long story, and we'll tell you all about it, but first I'd like to know what Ed meant by his comment."

"I'm sorry if I was too dramatic, but I couldn't resist. I was walking back to the lab last night because I had left my phone there, and I saw all of you standing around over by Alicia's hut. I was about to ask you what you were doing when I heard the dogs growling. I was afraid they were growling at me, so I stopped. Then I saw what you were looking at—the ghost."

"What made you think it was a ghost?" Alicia asked.

"Who, or what, else would be walking around at night dressed like a World War II Marine, and have the ability to pass through a metal fence and float down the ridge into the Amphitheater?"

"You don't act very surprised," Alicia said.

"It's a cultural thing. I'll explain, but first I'd like to hear the whole story. I was dying to walk in on your discussion last night, especially since I'm a big fan of Irish whiskey, but I thought it would be better to let you take the initiative to tell me."

"You were eavesdropping on us!" Sam said.

"Just for a moment, there's still a lot that I'm anxious to hear."

"You're anxious? I have no idea what you people are talking about!"

"I understand, Jim, and we're going to explain right now."

Alicia went first and described her encounters with the ghost. Then each of the men recounted being in the body of one of the missing Baker Company Marines and what they saw.

"That's absolutely incredible. If I didn't know all of you, I'd say you were the victims of some sort of group fantasy. You're not making this up, are you? This isn't some sort of joke?"

"No, Jim. As far as we know, this is real." Sam said, "It gets even stranger. We're pretty sure that the dogs have been seeing this guy too. They recognized him last night."

"That's incredible!"

"You know I just thought of something."

"What's that, Sam?" Alicia asked.

"I haven't been able to figure out how Gunny got the scent of that ilium back on Search Day One. He should have been a lot closer than he was to get that scent."

"Are you saying you think he had some sort of supernatural help?"

"I don't know, Alicia, I just thought of it, but it's the only explanation I've been able to come up with so far."

"OK, let's assume that you all haven't gone crazy. I have two questions. The first is why am I the only one who hasn't seen this ghost or had these dreams?

"I don't know," Alicia said, "but I have a theory about the dreams. The only ones who have had the dreams are our three combat veterans. Right?"

"Yeah, good point," Sam said. "But what does that mean?"

"I don't know; maybe you're the only ones that could have understood what was happening."

"Yeah, maybe, but why hasn't Jim seen the ghost?" Steve asked.

Tom said, "Maybe he just wasn't in the right place at the right time."

"Or maybe I just wasn't meant to for some reason, which brings up my second question. What's the purpose of all this? Why is it happening?"

"Excellent Jim!" Alicia said, "Depend on the historian to ask the right question."

"Well, I'm no historian, just an old, broke-dick, retired Marine, but I've been wondering the same thing."

"OK, Sam," Alicia said with a smile, "spare us the good ol' boy, 'Aw shucks' routine and tell us what you're thinking."

"I agree with what Tom said last night. I think that the ghost and the Marine we've been dreaming about are one and the same and that he's trying to help us."

Tom said, "Sam, I think you're right, although I wish he'd find a better way than making me re-fight the battle of Iwo Jima in my dreams."

"Yeah," Steve said. "He led us to the gully, he showed us where Hanks was killed."

"So, is everyone convinced that we are being... I don't know, is 'haunted' the right word?" Tom asked.

"May I make a comment?"

"Of course, Ed."

"Although I wouldn't characterize myself as someone who believes in ghosts, I'm not surprised by what's happening here for two reasons. First, I've been conditioned by my culture to be less skeptical about these things than, perhaps, someone from the West. We Japanese have legends and stories about literally hundreds of ghosts and demons that have been part of our society for over a thousand years. I know many people, people who would not be out of place in this group, who firmly believe in the existence of spirits."

"Secondly, and perhaps more to the point, if there is any place on earth where there could be ghosts, then surely it is here. This blood-soaked rock was the site of months of indescribable suffering and violent death and is home to the remains of many thousands of young men who never had the chance to live their allotted span of years."

"I understand what Ed is saying about cultural conditioning, and I agree with him," Jim said. "As a Mormon, I believe in the eternal life of the spirit, and our First Prophets, Joseph Smith and Brigham Young, believed that the spirit world was very close to our physical world and that, under the right circumstances, it is possible for a spirit to cross over. Although this isn't Church Doctrine, I and many others share this belief. If it weren't for that, I'd think you had all gone crazy."

"I went to Catholic school," Sam said. "Catholics, like all Christian religions, believe in the afterlife, but no doctrine requires a belief in earthly spirits. There are, however, many warnings in canon law against doing anything that might conjure a spirit. Don't forget 'The Exorcist.' Part of that movie was based on fact. The Catholic Church has a well-defined liturgy for the exorcism of demons."

"All right," Tom said. "We know that many cultures and religions have beliefs about ghosts and demons, but what about scientific proof? Alicia?"

"This is not something that is amenable to study by science. Science focuses on observable, measurable phenomenon, and it requires controlled, repeatable experimentation to determine the truth of any hypothesis. When we talk about spirits, demons, ghosts, whatever, none of these things apply."

"So, you're saying that there is no scientific proof for spirits?"

"Yes, but lack of proof is not proof of lack. I'm just saying that this is not an area where science is going to be much help."

The room filled with the buzz of excited conversation as the team tried to make sense of what they were hearing.

"OK, OK," Tom said. "let's wrap this up. We still have work to do, and we need to move on. We need to figure out what, if anything, we should do about this."

Sam was the first to speak.

"I don't see that there's much we can do. I think that the important thing is that we now know that this isn't just something we've been imagining. That we're all experiencing pretty much the same thing. I would suggest we just be aware of what's happening, and if any of us see or feel something new, we let everyone else know right away."

With agreement all around the meeting broke up, and everyone headed toward their beds.

♦ ♦ ♦

On the Eastern Ridge of the Amphitheater
Iwo Jima
Tuesday, 25 June
Search Day 5
2100 Hours

Watanabe was furious that he had failed to destroy the dog that afternoon, and he did not know why he had so little effect on the Americans. Could it be because of the other presence, the American coward that Okada had stopped him from killing? How could such a coward be stronger than Watanabe?

Watanabe had been so weak after he had tried to command the dog that he was afraid he would slip back into the darkness where he had been for so long—the darkness that was so empty and so much blacker than where he was now. He was getting stronger, but he must be careful. He must save his strength for one great effort that would be Watanabe's own Banzai attack that would defeat the Americans yet again.

He must rest and wait for the right moment to strike and then strike with all his power. Once the dog was destroyed, then there would be time to take his vengeance on all the Americans.

As he thought about what he would do to the dog, his fury slowly turned to almost joyful anticipation.

SEARCH DAY SIX

*I am tired and sick of war. Its glory is all
moonshine. It is only those who have never
fired a shot nor heard the shrieks and groans
of the wounded who cry aloud for blood, for
vengeance, for desolation. War is hell.*

William Tecumseh Sherman

Iwo Jima, Amphitheater Search Area
Wednesday, 28 June
Search Day 6
0710 Hours

WHEN THE TEAM ARRIVED AT THE SEARCH AREA, they were
surprised to see a dozen Japanese soldiers arrayed in a circle around
the flags from yesterday's search.

Tom asked the others to wait by the vehicles and walked toward
the soldiers. Commander Matsuyama's interpreter walked quickly
toward him with his hand raised in an order to stop.

"This area is off-limits. Please get back in your vehicles and return to your camp immediately!"

"What do you mean this is off-limits? We have an agreement with your government to search this area for five more days."

"Commander Matsuyama has determined that your agreement is no longer valid now that you have disturbed the remains of Japanese soldiers!"

"Commander Matsuyama is wrong. Our agreement specifically includes the recovery and identification of Japanese remains. I demand to speak to him immediately!"

"You have no right to demand anything! You are not welcome here! Get back in your vehicle now, or will be removed, by force if necessary!"

Having exhausted his limited supply of diplomatic tact, Tom reverted to a role in which he was more comfortable - a Lieutenant Colonel of the U.S. Army Rangers. Drawing himself up to his full height, he stepped forward and glared down at the lieutenant who was a good head shorter.

"You listen to me you worthless little cockroach. You wouldn't make a good pimple on the ass of one of the Japanese soldiers who fought and died on this island. We will go back to our camp, but if Commander Matsuyama does not call me or come see me personally within the hour, I will see to it that you spend the rest of your time in the army shoveling shit in the Senkaku Islands."

"I resent..."

"GODDAMNIT LIEUTENANT! THE ONLY WORDS I WANT TO HEAR OUT OF YOUR SLIMY LITTLE MOUTH ARE 'YES SIR.' DO YOU UNDERSTAND ME?"

The young man could not have been more shocked if he had been slapped in the face. Stepping back without a word, he spun around and marched back toward his soldiers.

Tom watched him and then turned and walked back to the team.

"Hey, Colonel, that looked like fun! Can I go yell at him for a while?"

"No, Sam. I think I did enough damage for this morning. That worthless little prick ..."

"Don't get pissed at him. Matsuyama's the one we need to deal with."

"Yeah, but right now our options are limited. Let's head back to camp and see if we can figure anything out."

Standing behind and a little apart from the team, Ed Akiyama had watched the encounter with interest. After a moment of thought, his mouth widened into a slight smile, which he quickly erased before joining the others in one of the vehicles where he sat next to Jim Stewart and whispered something into his ear.

◆ ◆ ◆

Team Liberty Iwo Jima Base Camp
Wednesday, 28 June
Search Day 6
0945 Hours

An hour later, the team sat dejectedly around one of the tables in the dining facility. Since it was almost midnight on the East Coast, they had not been able to contact anyone at the State Department or with the Team Liberty headquarters who could help. Alicia had even called Dr. Jefferson, the head of the forensic anthropology department at Tennessee, and gotten him out of bed. He had promised to try to help, but there was nothing he could do until morning. They had left messages and sent e-mails, but there was no hope for any action today.

And, of course, Commander Matsuyama had not been heard from.

"I guess I shouldn't have pissed that lieutenant off."

"Aw, bullshit, Tom, you know better than that. That little turd is just Matsuyama's designated ass-kisser. He has nothing to do with this."

"Yeah, Sam, I know. I'm just frustrated. I really thought we had a chance to pull this off and now it looks like we're going home empty-handed."

Alicia said, "That's not true. We have Corporal Hanks' remains, and we have discovered the probable locations for at least two other Marines. I would say that's pretty significant and that this team has done a great job."

"Thanks, you're right, I need to stop feeling sorry for myself. Let's huddle up and see what we can get accomplished while we're waiting for help. It's now ten o'clock. What do we do with the rest of the day?"

"I guess I'll do some training with Gunny, what about you, Steve?"

"Yeah, that's about all we can do."

Alicia said, "Ed and I are going to do a little more work in the lab to finish up on what we were doing yesterday. I would suggest we all plan on getting some rest this afternoon. It'll be a busy night once folks start getting to work back in the States. Remember, ghosts or no ghosts, Matsuyama is still our biggest problem."

"OK, Alicia, sounds good. Let's set the time between lunch and dinner as team rest time. Dinner at 1800 and we start making phone calls at 1900."

"Agreed?"

The other four each mumbled some form of assent and went their separate ways.

◆ ◆ ◆

Team Liberty Iwo Jima Base Camp
Wednesday, 28 June
Search Day 6
1845 Hours

Everyone on the team had finished dinner, and most were having a second cup of coffee instead of a beer since this promised to be a long night.

It was then that Commander Matsuyama entered the dining hall without his interpreter and, in excellent English, politely asked to speak with Tom.

Bowing low, Matsuyama spoke quietly, "I apologize if my actions have been misunderstood. My intention was only to ensure the safety of all of the remains, both Japanese and American, until your team was ready to recover them. My men have been withdrawn from the site, and I would be pleased if you would return there and continue your work as soon as possible."

"Thank you for clarifying the situation, Commander," Tom said. "We will continue our work tomorrow morning."

As soon as Matsuyama was out the door, the entire team was laughing, cheering, and fist-pumping.

"I'll be damned," Tom said. "I guess I owe those State Department guys an apology."

"Never, ever apologize to the State Department," Sam said. "It just makes them even more insufferable than they already are."

Jim Stewart spoke up, "If you want to know who is responsible for Commander Matsuyama's sudden change of heart, I don't think you have to look further than Dr. Akiyama here. On the way back from the search area yesterday, he asked to borrow my satellite phone, and I saw him making some calls yesterday afternoon."

As the whole team's eyes focused on him, Ed Akiyama bowed his head and smiled.

"I called Professor Okada, and it appears that he is not without some influence with the government."

After he had been congratulated by each member of the team, Ed continued.

"I also brought Professor Okada up to speed on what we have accomplished since I arrived. He was very interested in hearing about the remains we found and uncovered yesterday, and he asked me several questions about the location of our find. He was very knowledgeable about our search area, even to knowing about the gully where we have focused our search. He asked if we had searched the face of the ridge above the place where we found the latest remains and I said that we would do that as soon as Luke checked it for explosives."

"When I had finished briefing him he said, 'I must come there. You are getting very close. I have some information you will need.'"

"'You are getting very close,' what does that mean?" Alicia asked.

"I have no idea, but we'll find out soon. He will be here in two days, Friday evening."

♦ ♦ ♦

Team Liberty Iwo Jima Base Camp
Wednesday, 28 June
Search Day 6
2200 Hours

Sam was crawling along in the bottom of the gully, struggling to keep his BAR out of the sand. Somehow through the deafening roar of battle all around him, he could distinguish the sound of the big machine gun up the ridge a hundred or so yards ahead.

He paused to catch his breath and looked behind him where the remaining Marines in his squad were following.

I'll be damned, all three of 'em are following me. I expected Laskey and Hobbs, but I wasn't too sure about that shitbird Lawrence. I guess he's a better Marine than I thought.

Wait a minute! That's Lawrence, Laskey, and Hobbs behind me. That means I must be Durance, PFC Robert L. Durance! They call me Robby.

Sam's brain raced trying to assimilate all the new information. He was flipping back and forth between two minds, two sets of memories.

Got to get that gun....got to get that gun.....I won't be a coward

This is crazy! How do I wake myself up before I get killed?

"Durance, hey Robby, what the hell's going on? What are we doing?"

That's Hobbs. Hobbs is one of my Marines. He's my responsibility. I've got to get my head out of my ass and start acting like a Marine.

With that thought, Robby's mind took over completely.

Gotta find that big gun. Maybe the arty took out some of the Japs around it, and we can get close enough to throw in a couple of grenades. If we can take out that gun maybe the Company can fight their way outta here.

He was focused entirely on what he was doing, but there was a small voice in the back of his mind that kept saying, "If you do this you will die, If you do this you will die." He knew that the voice was right, but he ignored it. His entire life, everything he had ever done, and all he had ever been, had come down to this moment. He believed that this was where he was supposed to be and that he was doing what he was supposed to do. Once that became clear, everything fell into place. There was no fear, no rage, and no indecision. He was either going to get that gun, or he was going to die. The only thought he had time for was, "I hope Daddy understands."

He crawled for a long time, and the sounds of the battle around him never diminished. The other three were moving slower and had fallen ten yards or more behind. Laskey was the farthest back, about five yards behind Hobbs and Lawrence.

He was almost under the big machine gun when he felt the blast from two grenades exploding close behind him and the stabbing of several pieces of hot metal slicing into his back and upper legs. A second later he heard four rifle shots.

When he turned around, two Japs raised their rifles with long, wicked bayonets high and then plunged them down into something below them. There was a terrible scream. Was that Hobbs? Then the Japs were turning toward him and bringing their rifles to their shoulders.

They never had a chance. He clamped the BAR to his hip and fired two short bursts. The big .30-06 rounds tore through the Japs' torsos, and they were dead before they hit the ground.

After ten days of fighting, these were the first Japs he had killed face-to-face. The first that he knew he was responsible for killing. He spared them not one second of thought or pity as he crawled down to where the rest of his squad lay.

It didn't take long to realize that he was all alone. Hobbs and Lawrence had been hit by grenade shrapnel, shot, and stabbed and were obviously dead. Laskey was still gasping for breath, but he was horribly mangled by a grenade that had gone off right beside him. As he watched, the breaths came farther and farther apart and then, mercifully, stopped.

He wanted to cry, he wanted to feel sorrow, he wanted to feel something, but there was no time. The big machine gun was still hammering, and Marines were still being killed in the Amphitheater. He turned and started moving slowly and painfully toward what looked like the best approach to his objective. Behind him, he left a broad trail of blood.

Sam jerked awake and sat up just in time to hear a gasp of breath from across the room and see Steve bolt upright. Both dogs also came awake and started barking.

"Jesus, Steve! I just had an incredible, awful dream."

"Yeah, me too. And I know who I am, I mean who we're dreaming about; I'm Durance, Robby Durance."

Sam took a second to get his breathing under control. "I know, but I wasn't dreaming, I **was** Robby Durance, and I saw three guys, Lawrence, Laskey, and Hobbs get killed and I killed two Japs."

"Yeah, me too, I saw all the same stuff, and I wasn't just watching it or dreaming it, I was **doing** it."

Sam called Gunny over to calm him down, and Steve did the same for Luke, and this gave Sam a minute to collect his thoughts. "This time we both had the same dream only it was more than a dream, is that what we're saying?"

Before Steve could answer, there was a brief knock at the door, and Tom, Ed, and Jim walked in.

"I heard the dogs barking, and you two talking. Did you guys have dreams tonight?"

"Not dreams, Tom," Sam said. "A dream. We both dreamed the same thing only it was more than a dream we were actually in Robby's mind."

"Robby? You mean Robert Durance? That's who I was dreaming about too, but then it was like he took over the dream."

The men talked in a rush for several minutes and quickly concluded that they had all had the same dream and experienced being in the mind of PFC Robby Durance during the battle in the Amphitheater.

"What about you, Jim, Ed? Did either you have a dream tonight?" Steve asked.

"I'm not sure," Jim said. "I know that I was dreaming that I was cold, and then I woke up and there was a Marine, a World War II Marine, standing at the foot of our bunks and looking at Ed and me. I think he was trying to say something to us, but I couldn't hear him. Then Tom sat up with a big gasp—I thought he was having a heart attack—and the ghost disappeared."

"I think I woke up from my dream - I dreamt I was swimming in icy water - a few seconds before Jim, and I saw the same thing he did except I'm pretty sure I could hear him, and he was saying 'Robby.'"

"What about the dogs?" Tom asked. "Do you think they were dreaming about Robby Durance?"

"No." Steve and Sam said almost together, and Sam continued, "I think they were just barking tonight because we both startled them when we woke up so quickly. I don't get the sense that they're disturbed about anything."

"Yeah, I agree," Steve said.

There was a knock at the door, and Alicia said, "Is this an all-guys party, or can I come in?"

"Come on in and tell us your ghost story," Tom said.

Alicia walked in and said, "How do you know I have a ghost story."

It took several minutes for each of the men to tell about the dream and seeing the ghost. When they were done, Alicia said, "You guys had a lot more excitement than I did. I just saw Robby Durance standing at the foot of my bed for a couple of minutes."

"How do you know it was Robby?" Sam asked.

"He told me. He said several times, 'I'm Robby Durance, please find me,' and then he just faded away."

"All right," Tom said, "We need to talk about this and decide what it means. Let's go over to the mess and brew some coffee and have a team meeting."

"Don't make any coffee for me," Sam said. "I doubt I'll be sleeping anytime soon."

◆ ◆ ◆

Team Liberty Iwo Jima Base Camp
Wednesday, 28 June
Search Day 6
2330 Hours

No one else opted for coffee, so the team settled quickly around a table, and Tom spoke first, "Does anyone think they understand what has been happening?"

"I only see two possibilities," Sam said. "Either someone is spiking our food with LSD, or the ghost of Robby Durance is trying to help us find our missing Marines."

"Anyone disagree with Sam's second option?" Tom asked.

When no one responded, he continued, "If we agree that we're getting help, how does that affect our search plan?"

"Well, now we know, or believe, that there are the remains of three Marines and two Japanese soldiers buried in the gully," Alicia said. "That agrees with what we have uncovered so far. If the dreams that you, Sam and Steve had are true, and I don't doubt that they are, then Robby Durance is somewhere up on that ridge above the gully."

"You think we should focus our search up there?"

"I think we should get Gunny working up that way as soon as possible."

Steve broke in, "Don't forget we haven't cleared that area yet. Luke and I will have to go first."

"That's fine, we can use Gunny down in the gully until you tell us it's safe to send him and Sam up the hill."

"OK," Tom said. "I think we have a plan. Any other ideas?"

When no one responded, the team sat around for the next hour or so talking listlessly about anything they could think of that had nothing to do with ghosts or Iwo Jima before heading back to bed.

◆ ◆ ◆

Team Liberty Iwo Jima Base Camp
Wednesday, 28 June
Search Day 6
Earlier that evening

Sam had been partly wrong about the dogs not having dreamed about Robby. Gunny hadn't, but Luke had had a pleasant but puzzling dream. The Good Man was stroking his fur and speaking softly but firmly to him.

"Take care of Gunny. Watch your friend. He'll need your help tomorrow."

Luke didn't understand the words, but they were like the words the Good Man had said to him after he had the dream about the Bad Man, so he knew what he had to do.

Luke had to protect Gunny. He would, or he'd die trying.

SEARCH DAY SEVEN

If there are no dogs in Heaven, then when I
die I want to go where they went.

Will Rogers

Iwo Jima, Amphitheater Search Area
Thursday, 29 June
Search Day 7
0710 Hours

EVEN THOUGH NO ONE HAD GOTTEN MORE THAN A FEW HOURS
OF SLEEP, Tom had had no problem getting everyone up and ready
to go early. This was the earliest they had been on-site with all the
gear unloaded and in place since the search had started. The whole
team was ready to get to work and make up for lost time.

Steve had already put Luke on search on the face of the ridge
above the gully. Sam was ready to send Gunny inside the green
flags to see if he alerted on any new spots. Once Steve declared that
the area above them was safe, then Sam and Gunny would move up
onto the ridge.

"Gunny! Look close! Adios!"

Gunny started his search by quickly crisscrossing the area. At the places where the earth had been freshly dug, he smelled the same Old Bone smell that he had the last time, but there was less of it now. This meant that the Old Bone that had been there had been moved and Gunny just pawed at the dirt but did not sit and bark. Once he had checked all the holes, he did as he had done the last time and moved downwind until he lost the Old Bone scent and then turned and started working his way down.

As he turned, he looked up and saw that Luke was up on the hill working with his Man. Gunny didn't know what Luke was searching for, but it wasn't Old Bone, and so it was none of his business.

Gunny was just getting a hint of Old Bone scent when.....

"***Inu wa koko ni kimasu!***"

The angry voice of the Bad Man was louder than anything Gunny had ever heard. It filled his body and his brain and drove out every other thought. He could no longer smell the Old Bone. He could not hear what The Man was saying. He did not understand the voice, but, somehow, he knew what he must do.

"Sam!" Ed Akiyama yelled, "Someone is calling Gunny! Someone bad! Grab him quickly!"

Sam had also heard the voice and sensed its evil intent even if he could not understand what it was saying. He didn't realize that the voice was speaking to Gunny. It took a second for Ed's words to register.

That was a second too long.

Sam took two steps and reached for Gunny's harness but grasped only air. Gunny was gone, sprinting as fast as he could toward the face of the ridge where Luke and Steve were working.

"Steve! Grab Gunny!"

Gunny easily dodged Steve and continued up the hill faster than a dog his age should have been able to run.

Gunny's mind was filled with only two things, an almost overpowering scent of Old Bone and an image of a dark place that he must find.

Watanabe was exultant. He wanted to yell another command at the dog, but he was too weak and must be careful not to fall back into the darkness. He had used almost all his strength, but it had worked! The dog was coming right where he wanted him. Soon the dog would be dead, and the Americans would leave, and Watanabe would be free!

Gunny was close to the dark place, and the Old Bone scent filled his nostrils. He thought he could see a slight dip in the face of the hill, and that was where he must go.

What Gunny did not see were the three small prongs of the mine that were sticking less than an inch out of the ground just a few feet in front of him.

Gunny would be at the dark place in just a few more strides. He was almost exhausted and running more and more slowly but he would not, could not, stop.

As his front paws touched the ground on his next stride, he felt a violent shock. Something slammed into his side, and everything went black for an instant. Then he was off his feet and flying through the air. He hit the ground hard and began tumbling down the hill and stopped only when he crashed into a large rock. He tried to rise, but it was as if a heavy weight was holding him down. He started to struggle, and then he felt something hot and moist on his face.

Gunny opened his eyes. Luke's angry, snarling face was staring down at him just a few inches away. Luke's paws were planted firmly on Gunny's chest, holding him down, and his message was clear, "DON'T MOVE!"

Gunny was confused, and he could not remember what had just happened. He didn't know why Luke was angry with him or why he had knocked him down, but he knew what he had to do.

He bowed his head submissively, closed his eyes, and let his body relax.

What had happened? The dog had stopped coming. Where did it go? He must bring the dog back up to be destroyed. Did he have enough strength for one last command? He must try.

An instant later, everyone in Team Liberty was shaken by a voice that boomed across the entire search area.

"GO TO HELL YOU SON OF A BITCH!!!"

The shock of that voice slammed into Watanabe, and it was many times stronger than the bullets that had torn into his chest so long ago. He was blasted backward, and then he was falling, falling into that horrible darkness and Watanabe would never see the light again.

"Holy shit! Did you hear that???"

Steve had tackled Sam when he tried to run after Gunny. They had both watched in amazement as Luke caught Gunny and knocked him down the hill. As the echoes of the last voice faded in their minds, Luke got up and walk a few feet up the hill and then went to alert at a spot very near where he had rammed Gunny. Meanwhile, Gunny lay unmoving where Luke had left him.

"Sam, don't even think about going up there to get Gunny" Tom yelled from the bottom of the hill. "I've got my binos on him, and he doesn't look like he's hurt and I can see that he's panting. He just looks like he's really tired. Just hold on a minute, and we'll do this right."

"Yeah, Tom. OK, but let's not take too much time. I'm worried about Gunny."

"Tom, I can call Luke down here and get him out in front of us, and we'll go up and get Gunny. Will that work?"

"Yeah, Steve that'll work, but I'm coming up to help."

"OK"

"Luke! Come!"

Luke came down to Steve, casting a worried glance at Gunny as he passed him.

A few minutes later, the three men cautiously followed Luke back up the hill.

When Sam approached him, Gunny struggled to his feet and stood with his head bent low and his tail tucked between his legs. Sam had never seen him looking so remorseful or so fearful.

"It's OK, Gunny. It's OK. I don't know what just happened, but it wasn't your fault. Come here, buddy."

Sam knelt down, and Gunny took a couple of steps forward until Sam could put his hands on either side of his head and slowly begin to rub his fur. Then Gunny just collapsed and buried his head in Sam's lap.

"It's OK, you're a good dog. It's over now, and nothing is going to hurt you. Good boy, good dog."

Soon Gunny's tail began to wag slowly.

Sam stayed with Gunny while Steve sent Luke back on search. When Luke went on alert, Steve slowly walked up to him and carefully examined the ground.

"You guys aren't going to believe this, but I can see what looks like the prongs on the top of the firing mechanism of a mine here. And here's a dog paw print less than a foot away."

"There are a lot of things about this morning that I'm going to have a hard time believing," Sam said. "But I have no doubt that Luke just saved Gunny's life."

"OK," Tom said, "I'll call EOD and get them up here."

"Hold on a minute, Tom. I've got a suggestion. Why don't you let me mark this mine and keep searching up here? That way we won't have to stop everything while we wait for EOD and they can destroy this and anything else we find at the end of the day."

"You think it will be all right for us to continue to work down in the gully?

"Trust me. If I see something that I think could cause any danger, I'll let you know ASAP."

"OK, make it so. Sam, do you need any help with Gunny."

"No. I think he can walk. I'll just get him down the hill."

"OK, but keep him on a leash. We don't need any more excitement right now."

"Yeah, will do, but, you know, for some reason it feels like whatever or whoever that first thing was that was yelling is gone."

"I think you're right, but we need to try to figure out what happened before we turn Gunny loose again."

"Roger that, Colonel."

♦ ♦ ♦

Iwo Jima
The Eastern Slope of the Amphitheater
Thursday, 29 June
0735 Hours

Robby was tired, but it was the good kind of tired like after a hard basketball game that your team won in the last second.

Watanabe was gone, and Robby didn't think he'd ever be back. It had been a gamble staying quiet so long, but he didn't want Watanabe to find out just how strong he was. He almost had to yell at Gunny, and that would have given him away to Watanabe, but Luke had done just what he'd told him to do the night before. It was close, though, and Robby was glad that both dogs were OK.

It had felt good yelling like that, almost like he was alive again. He didn't know if he had sent Watanabe to hell, but he had gone someplace else, and that was all that mattered.

Robby didn't worry about slipping into darkness, his place was in the Light. He was only here in this dark place for a little while to be a guide. When he and the rest of his squad were found he could go back into the Light where he belonged.

Gunny knows where I am, and he's going to find me soon. Then we can go home.

◆ ◆ ◆

Iwo Jima, Amphitheater Search Area
Thursday, 29 June
Search Day 7
0745 Hours

The team gathered back around the vehicles near the gully. Steve was giving Luke a short break in the shade of one of the trucks before going back up onto the ridge. Gunny was lying next to Luke soundly and peacefully asleep.

When they could delay it no longer, they began to talk to understand what they had just experienced.

"So, what did that first voice say, Ed? It was speaking Japanese, wasn't it?"

"Yes, Sam, it was saying, 'Dog, come here!' It was such a commanding voice that I almost started to go up the hill, myself."

"You know what, Ed?" Alicia said, "I think I took a couple of steps that way, too, and I don't even speak Japanese!"

"So, what do we think that was all about?"

"May I say what I think?"

"Of course, Ed," Tom said.

"Based on what we have seen and heard in the last half hour and our experiences last night, I believe that there is a fairly simple explanation of what has happened."

"Huh!" Sam exclaimed. "You really think you understand this shit?"

"It is very simple. We have had an encounter with a particularly nasty Japanese demon!"

The team stared at Ed in shocked silence until a slight smile appeared on his face, and then everyone broke out in laughter.

"I was only partially facetious. I think that an encounter with a demon is the most likely explanation for what is happening."

"And how do you arrive at that conclusion?" Alicia asked.

"You recall last night I said that many Japanese believe in the existence of spirits that can interact with mortal humans? Well, that is especially true for evil spirits or demons. So, the idea of a demon as the explanation for this came naturally to me."

"Once I had a basic hypothesis, I did what I always do when I am faced with a problem like this. I refer to the words of the first, and I believe greatest, forensic criminologist, Mr. Sherlock Holmes, who often said to Dr. Watson, 'when you have eliminated the impossible, whatever remains, *however improbable*, must be the truth.' I suppose that's the British in me coming out."

Again, Ed's remarks elicited smiles and laughter from the team.

"But seriously, my suggestion is that, until another explanation arises, we operate under the assumption that we have been dealing with an evil spirit and try to decide what means to our mission."

"OK," Alicia said, "If the first voice was an evil Japanese spirit, what about the second voice?"

"It was obviously an American voice, a southern American voice I think," Tom said, "and it was trying to...what, exorcise the demon?"

Steve said, "My question is how we know if that demon is still around or did that second voice scare it away?"

Before anyone could answer, barks and growls erupted from behind the vehicles and everyone ran to see what new crisis they were facing.

Gunny and Luke were running around barking and nipping at each other, play growling and rolling in the dirt like a couple of puppies. It was the first time anyone had seen the two ordinarily serious dogs actually playing together.

"Steve, I think that's the first piece of evidence that our demon has hit the road."

"Yeah, Sam, I agree. I haven't seen Luke that playful in a long time."

"But why would a Japanese demon want to try to hurt Gunny in the first place?" Alicia asked.

Ed replied, "The only thing I can imagine is that we are in the middle of a feud between an American ghost, who appears to be benign and perhaps helpful toward us, and a Japanese demon who may be trying to stop our search by killing our search dog."

"I thought I'd seen some strange shit in Afghanistan," Steve said, "But this is in a whole 'nother league."

"OK, everyone," Tom said, "Let's try to figure this out later. We've lost a bunch of time this morning, and we need to get back to work. But I want anyone who sees, hears, or feels anything the slightest bit out of the ordinary to let the rest of us know right away. I agree with Ed that, until we have a better explanation, we assume that we have an evil spirit looking over our shoulders and that he does not wish us well."

Within fifteen minutes, everyone on the team was back at work. Gunny was taking the rest of the day off, so Sam put him up in the back of one of the vehicles and went to help at the recovery site. Steve and Luke headed back up the hill to continue their search.

Sam watched Steve and Luke for a while to see how they were doing. Steve had taken an old ski pole up with him, and Sam was curious why. It soon became apparent that walking across the side of the hill was difficult for Steve, especially when his prosthesis was on the downhill side. He was using the ski pole like a cane to help with his balance, and occasionally he would poke it into a bush or use it to check someplace where Luke had pawed.

He's an amazing kid. We never notice that he's only got one leg, even when he's wearing shorts. He just acts so naturally that it never registers for us. It's only when he's doing something out of the ordinary, like walking across a hill covered in rocks and volcanic sand, that we notice and, even then, you have to really be paying attention.

I've got to do something nice for him. After all, Luke saved Gunny's life today. How can I pay him back for that? I'll have to give this some thought.

After watching for a few more minutes, it was time to move the damn GPR again, so Sam went back to work.

♦ ♦ ♦

Team Liberty Iwo Jima Base Camp
Thursday, 29 June
Search Day 7
1745 Hours

That day the team made a lot of progress with Sam, Tom and Jim doing the heavy lifting and Alicia and Ed supervising and analyzing results while Steve and Luke worked up above them.

Back at camp after everyone had gotten a shower and cleaned up, Tom called the team together for a quick recap and to make a plan for the next day.

"Alicia, you go first. What did you accomplish today?"

"Thanks to all the help from Ed and you other strong, manly types we got a lot done. We've finished a GPR map of the areas where Gunny's flags were and dug a few test holes to confirm what we were seeing."

"And what was that?" Tom asked.

"A lot of stuff! Even more than I had thought before. There are numerous bones, at least two rifles and a couple of things that might be helmets. This is all based on my preliminary visual examination of the GPR images. Once we get them downloaded and do some computer enhancement I'm sure we'll see a lot more."

"More than we can recover in the next three search days?"

"More than we can recover in the next three search weeks, but that's OK, we have a plan for that. You want to tell him, Ed?"

"Alicia and I have agreed, and we are sure that Dr. Jefferson and Professor Okada will support us, that this site will be an excellent training ground for our Ph.D. students. She will select two students from Tennessee, and I will select two from the University of Tokyo, and I'll supervise them on the recovery project."

"And I'll try to get back here for at least part of the time."

"That sounds great, but we'll have to get approval from the Japanese government."

Ed smiled and said, "Professor Okada has assured me that will not be a problem."

"That sounds good to me. At least now we won't have so much time pressure on us."

"Steve, how did your day go?"

Steve had been the last one back to the camp because he had stayed to show the EOD team what he and Luke had found. When he had come into the dining facility, he had walked with a slight limp, the first time the team had seen any effect of his missing leg.

"Based on our dream of Robby I figured that the most likely place to find him would be on the ridge above where Lawrence Laskey and Hobbs are and to the north to the point where the gully goes up toward the top of the ridge."

"Right," Alicia said, "Because we think that they were killed at some point upstream from where they are now, and their remains migrated downstream over time. That makes sense."

"Yep, but we also worked twenty-five or so yards downstream just to be on the safe side."

"What did you learn?" Tom asked.

"First of all, it's going to be tough to search because it's so steep and rocky. Just moving around up there is hard work. Secondly, you can't see it from down below, but that hillside has a bunch of small, shallow depressions in it. After Luke had pawed at a couple of them, I decided to check one out. I had Luke double-check it to make sure there wasn't anything nasty waiting for me, and I poked my ski pole into the middle of the depression."

"At first it was just like sticking a pole into the ground, but after it had gone in eight or ten inches, it suddenly broke through and went all the way to the handle. I almost fell on my ass!"

"When I pulled the pole out, Luke went over to sniff in the hole and immediately went into a full alert. After I rewarded him, I carefully dug around and enlarged the hole and confirmed what I had been thinking."

"That shallow depression was the entrance to a cave or fighting position that had been covered up over the years by sand and rocks sliding down the face of the hill. I saw at least ten more of those depressions and, I'm guessing some other cave entrances have been more completely filled in."

"How sure are you of this, Steve?"

"Near the top of the ridge at the point where it curves around to the west, Luke went to full alert on another depression. This one already had a natural hole through to the cave beyond. When I showed it to the EOD guys a little while ago, they dug it out enough to be able to shine a light in. When they did, I thought the guy looking in the hole was going to faint."

"What was it?"

"When I looked in, I was looking right into the muzzle of a 47mm Japanese Type 1 anti-tank gun. Probably the one that knocked those two tanks out on the first day of fighting in the Amphitheater."

"That had to be scary. Why do you think it was still there? Why hadn't it been destroyed?"

"All I can figure, Sam, is that it was either damaged or they ran out of ammo and abandoned it. The hole was just large enough for the gun tube to stick out and, with a little camouflage, and if nothing were shooting out of it, it would have been very hard to see. It could have just been bypassed."

"Yeah, OK. That makes sense."

"Anyway, that's two depressions, two fighting positions. I'm afraid we may have to check out a lot of holes."

"What do you think, Sam?"

"I think we'll have to check those holes out pretty well. If Robby had been killed somewhere out in the open, he'd have been found a long time ago."

"What do you want to do?"

"How about if Steve and Luke follow us. If we find one of those depressions, we can have Luke check it, then poke a hole into it and let Gunny see if he gets any human remains scent from it."

"Steve, are you going to be OK going back up on that hill tomorrow?

"What, me? I'm fine, Tom. No problem."

Tom looked at Steve for a long moment.

"OK, Marine. Your call."

"Did you and Luke find anything else up there?"

"Yeah. We worked that hillside really well, and we found two more dud artillery rounds."

"Wow. Is EOD going to blow them?"

"They already did."

"I didn't hear anything."

"They only needed a small charge to blow the landmine, but that thing was definitely live. They got a good secondary off it, but it was only a hand grenade sized charge so you wouldn't have heard it back here."

"The two artillery rounds turned out to be inert, so, once again, there was no big boom like we had the other day."

"So, are you pretty confident you've gotten everything?"

"Everything on or near the surface that could be a danger, yes. We'll still want to be careful and not have folks running all over that hill, but it's safe."

"By the way, I learned something interesting from the EOD guys."

"What's that?"

"They said that the hillside had been swept by the Japanese army with metal detectors at least three times in the last ten years."

"Really? What did you say to that?"

"Well, I followed Sam's example and told them if it hadn't been swept by a dog, then it hadn't been swept. That kind of pissed them off until I showed them the mine and the two artillery duds and then they didn't say much."

"Ah yes," Sam said, "The United States Marine Corps—making friends through tact and diplomacy since 1775."

When the laughter had died down, Tom said, "OK, looks like dinner is here. Let's eat."

With a mixed chorus of "Yes, Sir!" and "Yeah, yeah, whatever" the team started getting the tables set for dinner.

♦ ♦ ♦

Team Liberty Iwo Jima Base Camp
Thursday, 29 June
Search Day 7
2230 Hours

Usually, Gunny could go to sleep within a couple of minutes of lying down, but it had taken a long time tonight. Although dogs live in the moment, they have good memories, and Gunny was disturbed that he couldn't remember much of what had happened that day.

He certainly remembered that first voice, it had scared him so badly. He remembered running and wanting to stop but not being able to. The next thing he remembered was Luke standing over him and snarling at him.

Gunny remembered the second voice too. It was the loudest man sound he had ever heard. That voice didn't scare him, though. It was the Good Man, and Gunny thought that he was yelling at the Bad Man. It was right after this second voice that Gunny's mind began to clear. He could remember everything that had happened after that.

In particular, he remembered that Luke had nudged him awake a little later and made a play bow. It had been fun playing with Luke, and Gunny was relieved that Luke wasn't angry at him anymore.

With his mind swirling with these strange thoughts, Gunny slowly became aware that someone was speaking to him. He settled down and soon the Good Man was speaking very softly.

"Gunny, good dog! Good boy! I'm glad you're OK. You don't have to worry about that mean bastard anymore. He's gone, and he won't be back. He can't hurt you anymore."

"You remember that dark place he was trying to bring you to? That's where I am, Gunny. Come get me, boy. I want to go home."

Gunny didn't understand most of what the Good Man was saying, but it made him feel better, especially now that the Good Man knew his name.

He remembered something about a dark place. There had been a dark place before, and there had been Old Bone scent there. Gunny brought up his memory of that scent and... yes! It was the same as the Old Bone scent he smelled when he saw the Good Man.

There was a dark place on that hill very near where Gunny had gone, and the Good Man was in the dark place. Gunny could find the Good Man!

With that thought, Gunny slipped into a peaceful, sleep.

SEARCH DAY EIGHT

When you go home
Tell them for us and say
For your tomorrow
We gave our today

Inscription at the entrance to the 5th Marine
Division Cemetery on Iwo Jima –

Iwo Jima, Amphitheater Search Area
Friday, 30 June
Search Day 8
0710 Hours

ONCE AGAIN THE TEAM WAS ON SITE early and eager to work. With only three search days left, everyone wanted to get as much done as possible before they had to pack up and leave. The anthropologists were excited about having both a treasure trove of artifacts and a new recovery problem to solve.

But no matter how much everyone wanted to get started in the gully, it was clear that the primary focus of interest was on Sam and Gunny. Would they be able to find the remains of Robby Durance?

Though they all tried to maintain a professional detachment, Robby Durance had become the sentimental center of attention of the search. Everything they had learned told them that he was a decent, brave young man who gave his life trying to help his fellow Marines and had died fighting. Without any discussion or formal decision, Team Liberty Iwo Jima had made Robby Durance their number one priority.

So, it was not surprising that all work in the gully slowly came to a halt when Sam, Steve, and Tom, along with Gunny and Luke, walked to the base of the ridge.

"OK, Sam. What's your plan?"

"Tom, Steve, correct me if I'm wrong, but this is about where Gunny ran up the hill yesterday, right?

When they both replied in the affirmative Sam went on.

"Gunny was moving with a purpose yesterday, and he ignored everything we tried to do to stop him. Gunny will sometimes disobey me if he thinks I'm being an idiot and trying to do something stupid—and he's usually right—but he will at least acknowledge me. Yesterday, it was like he didn't even hear me."

"Yeah," Steve said, "When I tried to grab him, he dodged right around me, but he never even looked at me."

"What do you think all this means?" Tom asked.

"This is the part that's going to sound crazy, but I think he was under the control of that demon or whatever it was that was yelling in Japanese. Like Ed said yesterday, I think that it was making him go up that hill to lure him to that landmine so he would be killed."

"But how could this demon or ghost know there was a landmine there?"

"I have no idea, but I can't think of another explanation."

"What do you think that means?"

"It means that, if I'm not completely crazy, there's something important up there where Gunny was heading, and where Luke found that mine. What's more, I'm pretty sure that's what Gunny thinks too."

As Sam said this, all three men looked down at Gunny. He was almost quivering with excitement. His gaze was fixed straight up the hill, and a low whine came from his throat.

"What do you think, Tom? Should I put him on search here?"

"Yes, but I want Steve and Luke right behind him. If he finds something, I want Luke to check it out before we do anything else."

"Roger that!"

"OK, Gunny let's see just how crazy I am. Let's see what you can find."

"Gunny! Look close! Adios!"

Gunny had been thinking about his dream from last night. Now that he was back here on the ridge, he remembered what had happened yesterday. He was pretty sure that the Good Man was just up the hill past where Luke had knocked him down. He didn't know exactly where but all he had to do was get close enough to smell the Old Bone.

The Good Man was in a dark place, so that meant he was under the ground. So, this would be like an avalanche search except that he was looking for Old Bone scent instead of live man scent. Gunny could do this.

Gunny was a little worried about Luke. He still didn't know why Luke had gotten angry with him, and he didn't want that to happen again. He decided to move slowly and keep one eye on Luke and stop if it looked like Luke was mad.

Gunny started slowly up the hill moving from side to side with his nose near the ground and sniffing rapidly. To Sam and Steve, it looked like he was following his own scent trail from the day before.

As soon as Gunny had started up the hill, he began to hear the Good Man's voice. It was very soft and faint, but it was clear, and Gunny knew what it meant.

"Good boy, good dog. Keep coming, Gunny."

The face of the ridge where Gunny was searching pointed almost due west, so it was still in shadow while the top of the hill was exposed to the early morning sun. As the air above heated up, it began to rise, pulling the air along the ridge up with it creating a flow going uphill. With no breeze to bring scent down to him, Gunny focused on following his track.

When he got to the point where Luke had knocked him down, his track stopped. In front of him was a small crater a couple of feet across and a foot or so deep that had not been there before. Gunny's nose filled with the sharp tang of fresh explosive residue, but he blocked that out and continued to search for the Old Bone scent.

Without a track to follow Gunny started moving a few yards to the left then back and then a few yards to the right then up a little and back across. There was a slight depression in the ground ahead of him, and he remembered seeing that yesterday. As he got close to this depression, he swung around to the right and went above it to sample the flow of air across its face and.... there it was! Old Bone, and not just any Old Bone but the Old Bone he smelled when he saw the Good Man.

There was another Old Bone smell, and he thought that might be the Bad Man, but the Bad Man was gone, so he ignored it and focused on the Good Man smell.

Sam watched Gunny's change of behavior and noticed that he was standing just above one of the depressions in the ground that Steve had talked about. Gunny pawed at the ground and then begin to dig furiously into the face of the hill.

"Gunny! Sit! Sit!"

"Steve, get Luke up there I think Gunny's found a cave!"

When Sam had yelled at him, Gunny had paused for a moment, but then he went back to digging. Sam ran up and grabbed Gunny's harness and pulled him away with Gunny barking and clawing to get back to the hole he had started.

"Easy, Gunny, easy. Let's let Luke check it out then you can go back up there."

Gunny relaxed slightly but continued to strain at his harness while Luke went forward and began to check where Gunny had been digging.

Steve watched Luke paw at the ground in a couple of places but not go to his alert, so he turned to Sam and Tom.

"He's got a little interest here but not much. I'm going to see if I can poke my pole in here and let him check that."

"Luke, sit!"

Steve moved forward and started pushing his ski pole into the hole where Gunny had been digging. After about six inches it broke through into a void. Steve worked the pole around to create a larger hole and then called to Luke, "Luke! Check, check."

Luke moved up next to Steve and stuck his nose in the hole. He sniffed for a few seconds then slowly sat back and looked at Steve with his head cocked to one side.

"I've never seen him do an alert like that before. I think he's telling me that there's something in there, but not anything he thinks is too dangerous."

"Tom, can you bring that entrenching tool up here so we can see if we can enlarge this hole enough to shine a lantern in there?"

"Sure. Sam, are you and Gunny OK?"

As soon as Steve had poked his ski pole into the opening Gunny had begun barking urgently and Sam was having trouble holding him back.

"Yeah, Tom, but don't take too long, I'm getting tired of holding this damn dog."

Tom moved up next to Steve and started thrusting the small shovel into the hole Steve had made. The dirt in the depression was not well consolidated, and he soon had a hole large enough to reach in with a flashlight and look at what lay beyond.

"OK, this is definitely a cave, and I see something that looks like a couple of bundles of rags lying on the floor. You want to bring Gunny up here and see what he thinks?"

"Sure, on the way."

As Sam started up the hill, Gunny suddenly broke free of his grip, ran up next to Tom, rammed his head and shoulders into the hole, and, before Tom could grab him, gave a push with his hind legs and disappeared into the cave.

As soon as Gunny had vanished the rest of the dirt and debris around the cave entrance collapsed and, to Steve's amazement, Luke broke his "Sit" and followed Gunny into the cave.

Gunny had never smelled so much Old Bone before and in the dim light now flooding the cave he could see where the Good Man's Old Bone scent was coming from.

He was about to go to the Good Man when Luke's growl from just behind stopped him cold. He turned and saw Luke's angry face and slowly sat and stayed still while Luke moved past him and began to search around where the Good Man was lying.

"Steve! What's going on?"

"I'm not sure, but it looks like Gunny is just sitting there and Luke is searching. Yep, there. He just put his nose on something and went to full alert. I'm going to go in and check."

"Careful, Steve."

"No worries, Tom. Luke wouldn't let me go in there if there was a problem."

Sam and Tom watched anxiously from the entrance as Steve moved past Gunny and next to Luke.

"You guys won't believe this! There's a full skeleton, well, except for one leg, dressed in Marine utilities and Luke is indicating on a grenade attached to the Marine's cartridge belt."

As Steve was talking Gunny slowly came out of his "Sit" and moved toward the head of the skeleton which Tom and Sam could now see clearly in Steve's light.

Gunny moved to the skull and sniffed it twice and then gently licked it, and then sat back and gave a single bark.

Sam turned to Tom and said, "I have no idea what's going on. But I think we just found Robby Durance."

◆ ◆ ◆

Iwo Jima, Amphitheater Search Area
Friday, 30 June
Search Day 8
0730 Hours

Down in the gully Alicia, Ed, and Jim had watched as Gunny, then Luke and then the three men had disappeared into a hole that was barely large enough for Tom's shoulders to fit through. They had been out of sight for several minutes, and Alicia and others were starting to worry.

Just then, Tom crawled out of the hole and stood up and yelled down to the team.

"Everything is OK up here. You can all come up, just don't wander too far away from our tracks."

As Alicia, Jim and Ed made their way up the hill, the other two men and the dogs emerged from the hole.

When they got up closer, Alicia asked, "What's going on, Tom? Have you found something?"

"Yes, we have, but I don't want to say anymore. I want you to see it for yourself with no preconceptions. I don't think we disturbed things in there very much so you should have a pretty clean scene to investigate. The scene is safe except for one hand grenade which Steve has marked with an orange flag. I would like you and Ed to look at the scene together."

Alicia did not understand why Tom was so formal, but she noticed that all of them, men and dogs, were unusually quiet.

She got a flashlight from Tom and Ed got a flashlight from Sam, and they entered the cave. Once inside, they moved to the center of the space and knelt down side by side.

As their eyes adjusted to the dim light, they looked around. Ed drew in a deep breath, "Oh...my...god."

"OK, Ed, let's do this by the book. Tell me what you see."

Ed shone his light around into the darker corners of the cave, then said, "I see a cave approximately two meters high and roughly circular in shape about five or six meters across. The floor is flat, compressed dirt and fine stone. I see what look like two sets of skeletonized remains. One set looks to be complete the other set appears to be missing its left leg from just below the knee. The remains with the missing leg are covered in what I recognize to be U.S. Marine Corps combat utilities from the World War Two era. The other remains are wearing what looks like the field uniform of a Japanese Army officer from the World War Two era. Lying next to these remains is what looks like a Japanese samurai sword."

"Did I get everything?"

"What's that in the back there under that small ledge?"

"Damn! I missed that. It's a weapon of some type, and it looks like it might be a Browning Automatic Rifle."

"Yes, those are the main features. There's one thing I want to check."

"Be careful of that grenade, Alicia."

Alicia looked over her shoulder. Steve was watching her intently from the cave entrance.

"Don't worry, I'm not going close to it."

Alicia moved closer to the remains in the Marine uniform. She leaned over the body and shone her light down into the neck and upper chest of the skeleton.

"What are you looking for?"

"Dog tags, and there they are. I can't read them, but once we recover them and get them cleaned up, they should give us a pretty positive initial identification."

"Do you think this could be Robby Durance?"

"I would be very surprised if it isn't, but we want to do this right. Let's get out of here so we can come up with a plan for doing our investigation."

◆ ◆ ◆

Iwo Jima, Amphitheater Search Area
Friday, 30 June
Search Day 8
0750 Hours

After Ed and Alicia had emerged from the cave, Tom called them over to join the others.

"What did you see and what do you think, Alicia."

"Ed and I saw a scene with two sets of remains, one probably American and one probably Japanese. The artifacts with these remains are all from the approximate time of the battle of Iwo Jima. The American remains are missing the left leg from just below the knee, and there is a set of dog tags resting in the chest cavity."

"OK, where do we go from here? Steve, you go first."

269

"From my perspective, that's easy. We need to get that grenade out of there."

"They're not going to blow it up, are they?"

"No, they'll bring a containment box and carefully move the grenade into that, and take it out to be destroyed elsewhere. I've already notified EOD, and they are on their way. I don't think it will take them more than an hour or so to get our scene cleared."

"Ed, what do you think?"

"I know this won't be a popular suggestion, but I think I should notify Commander Matsuyama that we have found what we believe to be the remains of a Japanese officer and invite him up here to view them."

"Thank you, Ed," Tom said, "I should have thought of that. It's the right thing to do."

"Yeah," Sam said, "I agree, but just let me know before he gets here so I can be somewhere else."

"Alicia, what's your plan?"

"Once we've done all those things we just talked about, the next step is to get a complete survey with photographs of the scene. That will mean we will need lights and a generator. Maybe once we make nice to Commander Matsuyama, he could help with that?"

"I'll ask when I speak to him," Ed said.

"I can handle the survey, which will take several hours. Ed, I think you should use that time to finalize a plan for how you'll continue the work at the scene in the gully after we've gone because I don't think we're going to get much more done down there in the next three days. I think we will be lucky to finish the work up here before we run out of search time."

"I agree, Alicia. Does that sound right to you, Tom?"

"Yes. Any other ideas?"

"One more thing I just thought of Tom."

"What, Sam?"

"We're going to need a couple of flags, and I'd like to see if we can get an honor guard from the Third Marine Division here. When we move those remains, both the American and Japanese, out of that cave, it should be done properly."

"Are you thinking of flag-draped coffins, Sam?"

"Yes, Alicia. Can you do that?"

Alicia looked thoughtful for a moment.

"Sure. You get me the coffins and flags, and that's how we'll transfer the remains out of the cave."

"I'll head back to camp now and make some phone calls."

"OK, folks. We have a plan. Let's get to work!"

◆ ◆ ◆

Iwo Jima, Amphitheater Search Area
Friday, 30 June
Search Day 8
1100 Hours

Three hours later, the entire team, including Sam, was gathered below the cave entrance when Commander Matsuyama emerged with the tracks of tears evident in the dirt smeared on his face.

When he saw the team, he stopped and went to a rigid position of attention. Then, bowing deeply at the waist, he said, "Thank you for granting me the privilege of paying my respects to these two brave warriors. It would be a great honor if you would allow me and my men to assist you in recovering these sacred remains and returning them to an appropriate place of honor."

Tom addressed Matsuyama. "Thank you, Commander, for your kind offer of assistance. Since we have only two more days before we must leave, we plan to recover the American Marine first. We hope to have a brief ceremony on Saturday evening or Sunday morning when we bring his remains out. When we have left, Dr. Akiyama will supervise the recovery of the Japanese Officer. Will that be satisfactory?"

"Perhaps I can intervene with my government to extend your stay?"

"Thank you again, but we all have obligations back home and must leave on schedule," Tom said, In fact, the team had already discussed this with Ed, who, through Professor Okada, had much more influence with the government than Matsuyama, and decided that it would be impossible to change all of the plans for returning the team to the States.

Matsuyama looked thoughtful for a moment and then turned to study the cave entrance.

"I think it is entirely appropriate to have a ceremony to remove the remains. To do so properly you should enlarge the cave opening and build a ramp down to the flat ground and put a bridge over that gully. If you wish, I will have my engineering officer report to you within the hour to make the necessary arrangements."

"Dr. Phillips, what do you think?"

"I think that would be a great help. I was wondering how we were going to do all of that."

"Then we accept your generous offer, Commander."

Matsuyama bowed again to the team. As he returned slowly to attention, he locked eyes for a brief moment with Sam Webber. The two men nodded slightly in recognition that, perhaps, their relationship had changed. Matsuyama then walked down the hill. At the bottom, he began issuing orders to the small group of officers that had accompanied him to the Amphitheater.

SEARCH DAY EIGHT — EVENING

All officers of Chichi Jima, goodbye from Iwo

General Kuribayashi's last message –

Team Liberty Iwo Jima Base Camp
Friday 30 June
Search Day 8
1830 Hours

THE TEAM HAD WORKED UNTIL AFTER FIVE and staggered back to camp exhausted. After a short break, Alicia and Ed Akiyama had gone back to work in the lab cleaning and sorting bones and artifacts and working on GPR images until time for dinner.

As they were eating, Tom asked them to recount their day.

"Ed, why don't you talk about what you were doing down in the gully? I hardly got down there."

"Sure. My focus in the gully is on preparing the area for the work we will do after your team leaves. We're trying to identify all of the places where we will be digging and trying to get some idea of how much effort will be involved. It's going to be a big job, but I'm confident that we will be able to recover everything that's down there. Sorting it all out and identifying the remains is going to take a while."

"Everyone worked hard today. Thanks to all of you for your help. Jim really did a great job today. Where is he?"

"The last time I saw Jim," Sam said "he was sound asleep and snoring up a storm. I don't think he's used to a lot of outdoor labor, but he held his own today."

"Yeah," Tom said, "I'll bet he's lost ten pounds since he's been here and he acts like he's enjoying himself."

"What about the scene in the cave, Alicia?"

"I have to give Matsuyama credit, his men did a good job. It's a lot easier working in there with that entrance opened up. I got all the photos and started on the measurements. I had a chance to get a good look at both sets of remains, but I haven't touched them. I'll examine the American tomorrow starting with recovering his dog tags. Hopefully, they'll confirm what we're all thinking."

"Will you be able to get him ready to be placed in a coffin by tomorrow evening?" Sam asked.

"That shouldn't be a problem. I don't plan on doing a lot of analysis of the body here. That's a job for the JPAC folks back in Hawaii."

"By the way, Ed," Sam asked, "What was going on in the cave this afternoon and who was that guy in the robes with the long, pointy hat with Matsuyama and the two others?"

"Oh, yes, I should have mentioned that. That was a Shinto purification ceremony and that 'guy with the pointy hat' was a Shinto priest."

"What was that for?"

"It is a common practice in Japan to purify any place where violent death has occurred to get rid of any evil spirits who might still be around."

"Do you think Matsuyama knows what happened yesterday? Does he know about the demon?"

"No, I think it was just a common precaution."

"Wow, this place just keeps getting weirder and weirder."

"Yeah, you can say that again," Tom said, "Speaking of ceremonies, Sam, you want to brief us on the plan for the ceremony for Robby? Is it OK to call him Robby?"

"If that turns out to be anyone other than Robby Durance, then I'm going to need some serious psychological counseling. I don't know who that Jap...anese guy is, but I know that Marine is Robby Durance." Sam said.

"At the risk of sounding unprofessional, I have to say I agree with Sam," Alicia said.

"Anyway, the ceremony. The honor guard, the band, the flag detail, and the Assistant Division Commander will be flying in tomorrow evening with everything they will need, including the coffins and flags. The ceremony itself will be first thing Sunday morning."

"Band? Assistant Division Commander? What's that all about?"

"You won't believe what happened when I called our liaison officer at Third Marine Division. Once I explained what we had found and what we wanted he transferred me almost immediately to the Chief of Staff's office. The next thing I know I'm talking to a full Colonel, and he's making lists of all the things he's gotta do for us. This is going to be a real, full-dress ceremony."

"I'm glad to hear that," Tom said, "I think these guys deserve a ceremony after all these years."

The team had just finished eating when there was a polite knock on the door, and a moment later, Commander Matsuyama came in with another Japanese man. The other man was older with wispy, white hair. He was short with an erect posture and gleaming eyes that quickly scanned each member of Team Liberty as he walked in.

Following the two men was a Japanese soldier carrying a large, ornate wooden box with Japanese kanji symbols on it. At Commander Matsuyama's direction, he placed the box on an empty table and then left.

"Gentlemen and lady," said Matsuyama "This is Professor Okada from the University of Tokyo. He is to be the official representative of the Japanese government on your team. He has told me that he is here to assist you in your search."

"Thank you, Commander," Tom said, "We've been expecting him."

"Colonel Sanders, before you meet with Professor Okada, may I speak to your team for a moment?"

"Of course, Commander."

Matsuyama looked around the room at each member of Team Liberty and then, bowing his head, he spoke.

"Before you arrived at Iwo Jima I was told by people I trusted that your mission here was to disgrace and humiliate the Japanese soldiers who fought on this island and that you would be doing this for political reasons. Based on this, I am afraid that I behaved badly toward you. I have learned over the past few days that I was misinformed. Therefore, I offer you my humble apologies. As a token of this, I have brought a small gift for all of you. Professor Okada knows of this gift, and he has said that he will be kind enough to present it to you and explain its significance."

Having completed this speech, Matsuyama turned and left the hut.

After Commander Matsuyama had left, Jim Stewart stood and walked toward Professor Okada with his hand outstretched.

"Professor Okada, I am Doctor Jim Stewart from BYU. What a pleasure it is to finally meet you. Can you tell us what that was all about?"

"Doctor Stewart, the pleasure is entirely mine. The Commander has, in fact, provided a suitable gift and we will talk about that soon."

"Professor, I'm Tom Sanders, the team leader. Allow me to welcome you to Team Liberty Iwo Jima. May I introduce you to the rest of the team?"

"I don't believe introductions are necessary, Colonel Sanders. I have read so much about your team that I feel that I already know all of you. Dr. Phillips, Mr. Haney, and Mr. Webber. Correct?"

"One hundred percent, Professor."

"Professor," Jim said, "Ed Akiyama has told us that you have some information for us that you think is important. Can you share that with us now?"

"Yes, that is my reason for being here. Perhaps we can sit, and I will tell you what I know."

"Of course," Tom said, "We were just about to have our evening meeting. Can we offer you a beer or some sake?"

"A beer would be nice, but not the sake that you have here. I will explain why later, but it ties in with Commander Matsuyama's gift."

Okada saw the puzzled looks on everyone's face and said, "Don't worry. Everything will become clear soon."

After everyone had settled in with a drink, Professor Okada spoke.

"I understand that earlier today you found the remains of two men in a cave above the gully where you have been searching."

"Yes," Alicia said, "Two men, an American and a Japanese. We've been trying all day to figure out how they got there and how they both died there together."

"I had hoped to be here when they were found, but you worked much faster than I anticipated. I never expected that you would find them in only ten days and I assumed that a follow-up search would be required. I understand that you have some remarkable dogs working with you."

"Yes, Gunny and Luke have done an amazing job," Alicia said, "But I don't understand. You knew that the bodies were there? How is that possible?"

"Yes, I knew they were there, and I will explain how tonight. Ed told me that the American was missing the lower part of his left leg, is that correct?"

"Yes," Alicia said, "It's likely that he died from blood loss from that wound. We don't know yet how the Japanese officer died."

"I know how he died. My father shot him."

♦ ♦ ♦

Team Liberty Iwo Jima Base Camp
Friday 30 June
Search Day 8
1830 Hours

The team was stunned into silence. Professor Okada quickly continued.

"Please excuse me," he said, "I did not mean to be so melodramatic. Allow me to explain."

"I am named for my father, Superior Private Ichiro Okada, who served with the 4th Company of the 2nd Independent Mixed Brigade here on Iwo Jima. In fact, he fought in the area called the

Amphitheater, where you are now searching for the missing Marines."

"Wait," Jim said, "If I remember correctly, you were born after the war so that would mean ..."

"Yes, Dr. Stewart. That means that my father was one of the very few Japanese survivors of the battle of Iwo Jima."

"So," Tom said, "your father may have been a witness to the battle in which our five Marines went missing?"

"More than that, much more. I believe that my father watched all but one of your missing Marines die."

"Is your father still alive?" Tom asked.

"No, he died some time ago. When my father returned after the war, he felt dishonored. So few Japanese soldiers survived the war, and so many of our people thought that it was a disgrace not to die in battle or commit seppuku that he was treated as a pariah. The only job he could get was as an interpreter with the American Army and that only served to further alienate him.

"I am sure that his torment would have eventually driven him to suicide, but he, and by extension, I, had a stroke of good fortune. He met the young woman who would become my mother. She saved his life.

"My mother devoted her life to convincing my father that he was not a coward, but a brave and honorable man who had followed his conscience rather than blindly obeying orders. By the time I was a young man, my father had regained enough of his sense of self-worth to begin to tell us about what had happened to him on Iwo Jima. Once he started talking, he couldn't stop. It was helpful to him to tell his story, so my mother and I always listened attentively even though we had heard it many times.

"Finally, my mother convinced him to write down what he had experienced, and you will be the first, other than my mother and I, to read his story. But first, allow me to give you some background so that you will better understand what you will learn.

"In August, 1941, my father was preparing to leave Tokyo for his senior year at UCLA. He was studying English with the goal of being a teacher, but his real love was poetry. His favorite pastime was composing haiku, the seventeen syllable Japanese poem, in both English and Japanese. He was within a few days of leaving when a letter arrived from Army HQ. He was not allowed to leave Japan but was to report to the Tokyo induction center for immediate assignment to active duty in the Army.

"His father, my grandfather, was a kind man whose life revolved around poetry and the theater, and he could not understand this sudden change in his son's future. The sons of his friends had been deferred from service so far. Furthermore, the government had encouraged my father, and many others who were capable, to attend school in the US. The government had even provided Ichiro with a modest stipend. So, why this sudden change?

"My father knew all too well that the fault lay with his dear, sweet father. Too many times Okada-san had spoken indiscreetly about the government and its plans for the Greater East Asian Co-Prosperity Sphere. Too many times he had criticized General Tojo and the other military leaders saying the country would be better with a civilian government. Someone, the wrong someone, had heard and had spoken.

"My father's future had been changed by his father's words, but he could not be angry. He loved his father too much and, besides, he agreed with most of what his father said.

"Basic training in the Japanese Army was notoriously brutal. Even for young men accustomed to corporal punishment throughout their time in school, the beatings administered by their instructors were nothing less than sadistic. My father had expected this, and he found that his ability to lose himself in his poetry was a way to deal with the physical abuse. However, he had no defense from the psychological torment that was heaped upon him every day, especially when his instructors learned that he was not only a useless poet but that he had gone to school in the US and could speak the American's barbaric language almost as well as he spoke Japanese.

"When he completed his training he was assigned to the Kwantung Army in Manchuria or Manchukuo, as he and other Japanese had been taught to call it after Japan's invasion of China in 1931. He left for his assignment on the 6th of December, 1941. He learned of Japan's 'glorious victory' over the US fleet at Pearl Harbor when he arrived in China.

"Here he got his first piece of good luck since the letter from Army HQ. The Adjutant of the Second Independent Mixed Brigade was looking for educated men to serve as clerks, and my father fit the bill perfectly. While most of his basic training comrades were in infantry units fighting the Chinese guerrillas of Mao Tse Tung, or the pitiful army of Chiang Kai Shek, he was at Brigade HQ living in relative comfort and working a relatively normal routine.

"As Japan swept victoriously across the Pacific, my father had to pretend to feel the same sense of nationalistic pride and war fervor as his fellow soldiers. He was proud to be Japanese, but he knew more about the Americans than anyone in the Brigade. He had watched them at their games, they were fierce competitors, and most Japanese could not even conceive of America's material wealth. He did not believe that the war would be won as quickly and easily as he was being told.

"When the Brigade Commander read the latest battle news to the troops gathered at the morning formation, my father joined with a thousand others and yelled, "Banzai! Banzai! Banzai!" as loudly as he could. However, as time went on, he noticed that each speech had fewer and fewer details, and each victory sounded less and less plausible. He yearned for the day that the Country's leaders would swallow their pride and call for an end so that he could go home.

"When he was told, after almost three years, that he was leaving China, it was not in the way he had dreamed. The Second Independent Mixed Brigade was one of the units forming the 109th Division under General Kuribayashi and sailing immediately to a post in the Pacific. My father feared that his comfortable life on the fringe of the war was ending.

"After more than a month of travel, the old steamer that carried him and five hundred others in cramped, squalid holds came in sight of a small island marked by a towering volcanic cone. As the ship moved into its anchorage, he got his first whiff of the odor that he would be living with for the next months—an odor you are all familiar with—and he understood the reason for the island's name, Iwo Jima - Sulfur Island.

"When he arrived, the fortification of the volcanic cone, Suribachi, had been almost completed. The Fourth Company, along with the rest of the Brigade, was assigned to the center and north of the island. For the next three months, he lived the life of a mole, digging holes for bunkers, enlarging the existing caves and tunneling all around the curving ridge that would likely become his tomb. For the first month, his life was unrelieved tedium and exhaustion. Then the American bombers came.

"The first time the B-24's came over the few Zeros remaining at Airfield Number 2 flew up to meet them. Only a handful returned. After several days of bombing, the Zeros were gone, and the airfield was destroyed.

"My father was terrified the first time the bombs came shrieking down near him, but he and the other soldiers quickly learned that they had little to fear. As long as they were underground, they were in danger only from an unlucky direct hit. The positions on their ridge were particularly impervious to the bombs because of the steepness of the slopes into which they were dug. Many bombs exploded on the flat top of the ridge, but they were no danger to the moles who never stopped digging, even during an attack.

"Some of the soldiers believed the daily harangues from their officers that promised that mighty fleets of ships and airplanes were waiting just over the horizon and when the American fleet arrived they would surge forward and send it to the sea bottom. Most soldiers had only to look at the waves of modern, heavy bombers the Americans sent every day and then to the mangled remains of the pitifully small Zeros to know that they were being deceived. Their destiny was sealed, and they accepted this with various mixes of military fervor and stoic fatalism.

"My father and a few others were different. His exposure to American ideas of individual freedom and self-determination had weakened his belief that duty to his Emperor was more important than his life. However, his country was in a fight for its very survival, and if the Americans could not somehow be stopped, Japan would be destroyed in the final battle that would be fought in the Homeland. Like his fellow soldiers, he resolved to do his duty; to fight to the death and kill as many Americans as he could. He had no choice.

"My father spent almost all of his time on Iwo working with two others to enlarge and improve a small, natural cave on the eastern flank of the area you call the Amphitheater. The three young men were a machine gun team, and their mission was to provide protection for a larger machine gun emplaced farther up the hill. Their last task before the Americans arrived was to put in a small minefield on the slope below them to protect their position.

"Before the Americans landed, my father had been subjected to days of almost continuous bombing and naval gunfire. Even in their caves and bunkers more and more men of the Fourth Company were killed or wounded. Some were buried alive when their fighting position collapsed on them after a near miss from a large shell. However, my father did not see a live American until ten days after the landings, on March 1st, 1945, which is where his account begins."

♦ ♦ ♦

Team Liberty Iwo Jima Base Camp
Friday 30 June
Search Day 8
1900 Hours

"So, Professor, your father was a reluctant warrior, at best?" Alicia asked.

"No, that is not entirely correct. He certainly did not want to fight, and he had lost faith in Japan's leaders, but he did believe that he had a duty to protect his homeland and that duty overrode any other consideration. That, I believe, is why it was so difficult for him when he came home. It is a difficult concept for a non-Japanese to understand."

"Yeah," Sam said, "It'll take a while for me to wrap my head around that idea."

"I understand, Mr. Webber. Perhaps you will understand better when you have read the full story."

"I'm anxious to see what he wrote."

"Then let's begin. I have a copy for each of you. I suggest you read the full story and I will try to answer your questions when you are all finished."

Account by Superior Private Ichiro Okada, Fourth Company, 2nd Mixed Brigade, 190th Division, of the Battle on March 1st, 1945 on the Island of Iwo Jima

The American attack began with a heavy artillery bombardment. I sat cross-legged at the rear of the cave near the tunnel entrance. I could feel the shocks as the American shells slammed into the face of the ridge. The shells were landing near, but not too near. Only a few were hitting this side of the curving ridge where we were expected to fight—and die. There was nothing I could do until the shelling stopped, so I turned my mind to my favorite pastime to keep from thinking about what would happen next.

"The shells that were falling for hours

Seemed to have been falling for all time."

OK, I thought. *Not too bad a start. Seventeen syllables, but I don't like the way the first and second lines break. How can I change that?*

A better question would be, why am I sitting here thinking of an English haiku when I am sure to be dead in a few hours?

But then, what else would a poet do? Especially a poet misfortunate enough to write in both English and Japanese.

Suddenly there was a loud, harsh shout almost at my ear.

"Chui!!"

The two other members of my team and I sprang to our feet at the command of the platoon sergeant. We brought ourselves to a bow calculated to be the precise depth for the entrance of our esteemed platoon leader.

Lieutenant Watanabe strode into the cave like a royal prince into a room full of commoners. *And that is precisely the way he views himself.*

In my estimation, Watanabe, whom most of the platoon called Akuma, the Demon, behind his back, was the worst kind of Japanese of this generation. He was from a well-to-do merchant family that had prospered supplying the Kwantung Army during the invasion of China. He was not very smart, but he was very ardent in his patriotic devotion to the country's military ruling class and so always found preferment ahead of more able students in school.

During the war, many American newspapers caricatured the Japanese soldier as being short and squat like a toad with a wispy Fu Manchu mustache and thick, ugly glasses. The Japanese soldiers I knew were lean and fit, clean-shaven, intelligent and well educated, but Lieutenant Watanabe could have posed as the model for one of the worst of the American caricatures.

Watanabe was convinced that he was a direct descendant of 'Watanabe no Tsuna,' the founder of the original Watanabe clan of Samurai over fifteen hundred years ago. I thought this was a silly notion since Watanabe is one of the most common Japanese surnames, but Akuma believed it so fervently that he always carried a Samurai sword even when crawling through the tunnels, where it often got in his way.

Watanabe had joined the Second Independent Mixed Brigade shortly before its assignment to Iwo Jima and so had seen little or no combat. This did not keep him from assuming in his arrogance that he was the best fighter in the company. He refused to listen to advice from his more experienced NCOs, and he often berated them in front of the men. He was one of the firebrands who chaffed under General Kuribayshi's order against Banzai attacks. He seemed to believe that all he would have to do would be to lead a charge waving his sword, and the decadent Americans would flee in terror.

I thought he was a fool—a very dangerous fool.

On the other hand, Watanabe thought that I, the English speaking poet, was a useless dreamer and probably a degenerate who could not be trusted.

As soon as Watanabe saw me, he yelled, "Superior Private Okada!"

"Yes, Sir!"

"Why are you groveling here in the back of this cave? Why aren't you at your position to start killing Americans?"

"Sir, I am in obedience to the Company Order to stay away from the firing positions until the artillery stops and then to man our guns, but to hold our fire until the enemy is close!"

Watanabe swung without warning and hit me in the face, almost knocking me down.

"Do not speak to me of orders you coward! The only orders you have to obey are the ones that I give you. Get in position now! Perhaps the Americans will get lucky and kill you and save me the trouble later!"

My face burning with shame, I bent down and picked up the Nambu light machine gun that was my responsibility. As I passed Watanabe to emplace the weapon, he kicked me in the ass to add just one more humiliation that I must endure.

I emplaced my weapon by setting the bipod legs into two sockets that we had carefully dug into the rocky ground. By doing this, my Type 99 machine gun was pointed at the center of the twenty-degree sector that was my responsibility. My orders were simple, kill any American who came within my narrow field of view to protect the heavy machine gun that was sited higher up the slope. Three other Nambus were emplaced in such a way that there was no approach to the main position that was not covered by at least one gun.

Beyond this, I had no knowledge of the battle plan. I was expected to do exactly as I was told, no more, no less. My duty was to follow the "Courageous Battle Vow" issued by General Kuribayashi that was posted on the wall of the cave above my firing position. I will never forget what it said.

"Above all else, we shall dedicate ourselves and our entire strength to the defense of this island. We shall grasp bombs, charge the enemy tanks, and destroy them. We shall infiltrate into the midst of the enemy and annihilate them. With every salvo, we will, without fail, kill the enemy. Each man will make it his duty to kill ten of the enemy before dying. Until we are destroyed to the last man, we shall harass the enemy by guerrilla tactics."

The other two privates got into position on either side of me. One would act as a spotter to point out targets, the other would load fresh magazines into the top of the Nambu each time I emptied the previous thirty round magazine.

I could not see any explosions within my limited view, but I could still hear the shells shrieking down. Most of the rounds were heading toward the slope of the ridge to my right with only a few impacting on this side of the open bowl. Suddenly, there was the sound of a large shell that seemed to be heading directly toward me. I started to duck but stopped myself. I would not give Watanabe the satisfaction of seeing me act fearfully. As I looked out of the cave, I thought I saw for a brief instant a dark shape flash across in front of me and impact near the bottom of the slope to my right. I tensed involuntarily for the explosion, but it did not come. The round was a dud, and it was now buried in the hillside twenty meters away.

I chanced a quick glance back and was rewarded by seeing Watanabe getting up from where he had thrown himself to the floor of the cave.

Watanabe turned and moved toward the back of the cave but stopped at the tunnel entrance and said to me, "I am leaving to check my other positions, but I will be back. I do not trust you Okada, and if I see that you have shirked your duty, I will take pleasure in wetting the blade of my sword on your neck!"

As Watanabe and the sergeant exited the tunnel, the last of the shells exploded outside, and for a moment there was an eerie, fearful silence.

I did not see the Americans approach, but the sudden eruption of firing told me that they had entered the bowl of the Amphitheater. I kept my eyes on my small portion of the battlefield, ready for the first Americans to appear. I was so intent on this that I almost screamed when a hand clamped down on my shoulder from behind.

It, of course, was Watanabe. He ordered the other two privates to move to different fighting positions. He then squatted behind me, saying that he did not trust me and that he was going to keep a close eye on me.

I thought that was, as one of my UCLA classmates would say, bullshit. I was convinced, despite all of Watanabe's bluster and talk of being descended from Samurai, that the man was a coward. He had noticed that my position was more protected from the enemy's artillery than the other places manned by the platoon. I was convinced that the lieutenant was here for no other reason than to save his own ass.

The roar of the battle had gone on for many minutes before I saw the first American who was crawling slowly along the bottom of the gully below me. I had aimed my gun and was about to shoot when Watanabe stopped me.

"Wait," Watanabe said, "There may be others behind him."

I was surprised to realize that Watanabe was right, that was the correct decision. Even a blind squirrel finds a nut sometimes, as the Americans say.

A moment later, three others appeared. I was ready to fire again, but before I could two Japanese soldiers rose up behind the men and threw two hand grenades. When the grenades went off they each fired their rifles two or three times and then advanced on the badly wounded Americans with their rifles raised for a final bayonet strike.

Even above the noise of the battle, I could hear one of the men scream as the bayonet went through him. Then the two soldiers advanced on the last man.

But this man was not as severely wounded as the others. I watched him turn toward them with a large gun that I recognized as a BAR. I saw the muzzle flashes from the BAR, and the two Japanese soldiers were thrown backward and fell to the ground, obviously dead.

I watched the American crawl over to his comrades and sadly shake his head as he looked down at them. They must have been dead or very close to it. As I watched, the man turned away from his friends and looked up the hill where the big 12.7mm gun was still pounding away. The American then picked up his BAR and began to limp and crawl up the hill, leaving a broad trail of blood behind him.

Watanabe said, "Did you see what he did to those soldiers?"

"Yes," I said as my finger tightened on the trigger of the Nambu. "I will kill him now!"

"No! No! Don't fire. I have a better idea."

I could not imagine what Watanabe was thinking, but then everything that was happening had become more and more surreal. Why had he stopped me from shooting the American who was coming up the slope directly into my assigned sector of fire?

It wasn't that I wanted to kill this man, I didn't. I could see that he was very brave, and I admired him, but it was my duty to protect the machine gun position up the hill, and the only reason I was fighting at all was to do my duty and avoid dishonor.

As the American drew closer, I waited to see what Watanabe wanted me to do. Then he whispered into my ear, "We are going to capture this man and interrogate him. I will learn everything he knows, and it will be a great honor when I report all of the American secrets to the Captain! Wait until he gets to the landmines. If he gets past those, then shoot him in the leg and go and drag him in."

Even though I immediately understood that I would be the one to do the work and take the risks and Watanabe would claim all the credit, I still didn't understand. What secrets of any value would an ordinary soldier have and what good would it do to learn those secrets anyway? Everyone on the island knew that the Americans had overwhelming power, and the end of the battle was in no doubt. I was sure that the Captain would just laugh at Watanabe's tales of courage and stolen secrets.

Not that it mattered, l had to do what the bastard said.

I watched the man approach and again admired his courage. He was severely wounded and all alone, and yet he kept coming up the hill. He must know that he had no chance and that he must die soon.

If all of the Americans are this brave, the battle will be even shorter than I thought.

The American was almost at the point where we had emplaced the landmines. I thought that the best thing would be if he were killed outright by one of the mines, but that wasn't likely. The mines were adapted from old Model 23 grenades which weren't very powerful. They were intended to stop an attacker by blowing off a foot or lower leg and incapacitating rather than killing him.

A moment later, that is precisely what happened.

The man was lifted into the air by the explosion under his left foot and then slammed into the ground. I heard him scream once and then go silent.

I hope he's dead.

Watanabe's cry of glee told me that it didn't matter if the man was dead or not; I was going to have to go out and get him.

"Hurry, Okada. Get him up here before he bleeds to death! And bring his weapon with you. It will be a great souvenir."

Although most of the shooting was focused on the Americans in the flats below, there were still many bullets cracking into the slope beneath me, not to mention the occasional mortar or rifle grenade. I would be lucky to get back up to the cave alive with or without the American.

But I had no choice.

"What are you waiting for you coward? Go and get him!"

I slid out of the cave and scrambled down the slope toward the American. Besides the danger from the bullets and shells flying around, I had to be careful of the remaining landmines. I thought I knew where they all were, but I never imagined that I would be going back down there like this.

When I got to the American, he was alive, but barely. First, I took the man's BAR and slung it over my back. It was even heavier than my Nambu. I could see no easy or gentle way to get him back up to the cave, so I took a grip under his shoulders and, standing up as much as I dared, started dragging him up the hill. I could hear the man groan in pain each time the stump of his leg bounced against a rock, but there was nothing else I could do.

It wasn't long before I was so exhausted that I had lost all fear. All I could think of was getting this burden to the mouth of the cave where Watanabe lay and cursed me for my slowness.

Finally, I was close enough that Watanabe felt it was safe to reach out and help me pull the American inside. We dragged him to the middle of the cave and lay him on his back on the floor, and I collapsed next to him.

As I sat gasping for air, Watanabe said, "Give me your belt. Your belt, you fool. Hurry!"

I fumbled off my belt and handed it to Watanabe who wrapped it tightly around the man's leg just above the stump.

A tourniquet? Well, that may keep him alive for a while, but not long.

By the time I had gotten my breathing under control, the man was regaining consciousness, and Watanabe gave me my orders.

A moment later, I leaned over the man and said, "My lieutenant has told me to tell you that you are his prisoner. He says that if you cooperate, he will honor you with a quick death by sword. He says that he will now demonstrate what will happen to you if you do not cooperate."

I watched as Watanabe unsheathed his sword and stood over the man on the side of the injured leg. He then swung the sword like a golf club so that the flat of the blade smacked into the raw stump. The man screamed, and his whole body convulsed as if from a jolt of electricity. He then went utterly still.

"Is he dead?"

"No, lieutenant. I can see him breathing, but one more shock like that may kill him."

You bastard. What kind of animal are you?

"Very well. If he answers my questions, I will not harm him again."

I don't believe that for a second. How can I help this man?

Watanabe gave me my next instructions, and I leaned over the man again.

"My lieutenant says that you must tell him when the next attack is scheduled on this position."

The American tried to spit in my face, but he had no moisture in his mouth.

"Fuck you," he said.

I turned to Watanabe and said that the attack would be tomorrow morning. Watanabe gave me the next question, and I turned back to the wounded man.

"I told him that you said 'tomorrow morning.' Now he says you must tell him how many men will be in the attack. Say something different this time."

"Kiss my ass you fuckin' Jap."

I made up a number and told that to Watanabe.

"Now he wants to know how many tanks?"

"Go to hell."

The interrogation went on with more meaningless questions and equally useless answers. I could see that the man could not stay alive much longer and hoped that the end would come soon.

Watanabe sensed the same thing, and his next instructions made the hair stand up on the back of my neck. I tried to protest, and Watanabe punched me in the face even harder than before, this time knocking me to the floor. One eye swelled almost shut immediately.

"Tell him what I said, coward, or you'll be sorry!"

Picking myself up and kneeling over the American again, I said, "My lieutenant says that you have acted dishonorably by being too quick to tell your secrets and you do not deserve an honorable death. He says that you will die slowly and painfully. I think that's what the son of a bitch wanted all along. He says he will begin by cutting off your other leg. I'm sorry."

I watched as Watanabe positioned himself alongside the American. I instinctively backed away, I didn't want to see, but the cave was too small, there was no place to go. When I had moved just a foot or two, something jabbed me in the back.

The American's rifle, the BAR!

I had a split second to make a decision that would affect the rest of my life. Everything my father had ever taught me said that I must do something to prevent this atrocity, but if I did, I would be a marked man and a traitor. I thought for a brief instant of my father's dear face and made my choice.

As Watanabe raised the sword over his head, I stood and pointed the BAR at the lieutenant's chest. I had no idea if it was still loaded and I didn't know how to work the safety. I put my trust in fate and pulled the trigger.

I had never fired a weapon this powerful before. There were two almost simultaneous explosions, and I was driven back by the force of the recoil. I was stunned and nearly blinded by the muzzle flash, and I had no idea if I had hit or missed my target.

When my vision cleared, Watanabe lay on his back with two large holes in his chest. The ground beneath him was already turning red, and there was no light left in his eyes. I had murdered a Japanese Officer.

Maybe the best thing I've ever done, I thought.

When I knelt down alongside the American, he was almost gone.

"Hello, my name is Ichiro. I am very sorry for what has happened to you."

"Why....how...you speak English?"

"I went to school in America. UCLA, Class of 1942, although I missed my senior year for obvious reasons."

"You saved my life. Why?"

"I couldn't just sit here and watch that bastard cut you up. I'm glad I killed him."

"I'm going to die here, ain't I?"

"Yes, I'm afraid there is nothing I can do for you."

"Will you....will you stay here with me?"

"Yes, I will."

"Tell me your name again."

"I am Ichiro...Eee-chee-row."

"I'm Robby. Thank you, Eee-chee-row."

I watched Robby's face, and it began to go slack as the pain receded, and his brain slowly died from lack of blood.

"I think that you will soon be with your ancestors. They will be very proud of you. You fought bravely."

"I....don't feel brave. I'm.....scared."

Robby was looking at me as his eyes lost focus. Just before he stopped breathing a slight smile came to his lips, and he began to speak. I leaned in close to hear.

"Rusty" Robby whispered. "Is that you? Where've you been? Good ...good..."

After a minute, I reached down and closed Robby's eyes.

I don't know how long I sat looking at that dead young man, but I eventually became aware that the sounds of the battle were decreasing and that I must do something. If I were found with my platoon leader dead next to me and no way to explain how that had happened, I would be shot on sight. I wasn't thinking clearly, and I ran into the tunnel and turned toward my platoon's other fighting positions. I only went a short distance. The tunnel had been collapsed by a direct hit on one of the caves or bunkers. I turned the other way and went into the sector of our adjacent platoon, and that is what saved me.

After I had gone a short distance, I was stopped by an NCO I did not recognize.

"Who are you, and where are you going?"

"I am Superior Private Okada of Second Platoon, and I am carrying a message from Lieutenant Watanabe to the Captain."

The man looked at me suspiciously. "Where is your weapon?"

I had taken no weapon with me from the cave. I vowed to myself that I would kill no more.

"I can move faster without a weapon, and my lieutenant said that this is an urgent message. He has information about tomorrow's attack."

"Well, you're going the wrong way. The Captain is back that way."

GHOSTS OF IWO JIMA

"I know, but the tunnel is blocked. I must go through here and up to the top of the ridge and try to circle around."

"Hah! You'll never make it, but that's not my problem. Go on. Hurry!"

That was the start of my odyssey. Like Odysseus, I had many adventures and was almost killed many times, but the confusion of the battle, what is called the "fog of war," was on my side. Although we had repelled the Americans, we had taken many casualties, and units had to be reorganized. I found that if I kept moving and playing my role as a messenger, I could hide in open sight. I did this for ten days living on rations and water I took from the dead, both Japanese and American.

After ten days, the battle finally moved to the north, and I was left behind the American lines. Watching carefully, I selected a rear echelon unit that was less likely to shoot me immediately. I stripped off my uniform and, wearing only a loincloth, I walked toward them with my hands in the air. It worked, and I was taken prisoner.

◆ ◆ ◆

Team Liberty Iwo Jima Base Camp
Friday, 30 June
Search Day 8
1930 Hours

"My God, Professor, what a story," Tom said.

"Yes, and it explains so much," Alicia said.

"I have a question," Jim said, "I can understand how the two bodies in the cave could be overlooked but how was it that those three Marines in the gully were not found?"

297

"Ah! Good question. There is another element to this story that my father only mentioned one or two times because he did not think that it was important. I myself did not realize its importance until I started reading about your search."

"The night of March 1st a storm hit the island that was unexpected and intense. As you know, Iwo Jima normally gets only a few inches of rain in February and March, but on that night it got almost a full month's worth in a couple of hours."

"The rain was a blessing to many because the battle practically stopped while the fighters on both sides tried to find whatever meager shelter there was, but for the families of the men whose bodies lay in that gully it meant that they would wonder for over seventy years what had become of their loved ones."

"My father told us that he watched the next morning as the loose, volcanic soil, weakened by weeks of bombardment, formed a soupy mix that flowed down the steep part of the gully and into the creek at the base of the ridge. Although it seemed that it would stop at any moment, it continued to ooze inexorably until it had completely filled the creek bed almost to its top."

"The next day, when the Americans attacked again, there would be no gully offering cover from the Japanese fire and no sign that four of their own were buried just a few feet away."

"And then," Alicia said, "over the years other storms periodically scoured out and refilled that gully which is why all of those remains are so jumbled together today."

"I agree," Ed said, "We're just lucky to be here at a time when the gully is exposed."

"Professor, your father, was a real hero, and we should make sure that everyone knows this story," Sam said.

"My father gave no instructions to my mother or myself concerning his story, but he often said that the real hero was the young American named Robby. My feeling is that he would have preferred that he receive as little attention as possible, but I think that he would be happy to see his account used to help that young man receive recognition for his bravery. My father often told us that he thought of Robby every day, and his one regret was that he was not able to somehow save him."

"Professor, I think each of us feels that your father did everything possible under the circumstances. I can only hope that I would act as well if I had been in his place."

"Thank you, Colonel Sanders. My mother and I always felt the same, but it is good to hear someone else say it."

"Professor, I have a question."

"Of course, Dr. Stewart."

"Do you know who 'Rusty' was? I haven't come across that name in any of my research."

"No, I don't know, but my father said that he was clearly someone very close to this young man. A good friend, perhaps a brother or close relative?"

Tom said, "If it were a nickname, it wouldn't be in any of the official records."

"No," Jim said, "Our best hope is that this is either a friend or relative from back home or someone that he mentioned to his family, perhaps in a letter. As soon as we're done, I'll send an e-mail to my grad students. One of Robert Durance's younger brothers is still alive, and he has been very helpful to us. Maybe he'll know."

"I think we have a bigger problem than figuring out who this Rusty guy is."

"What's that, Sam?"

"What, if anything, do we tell Matsuyama about Watanabe?"

Tom said, "That is something that will have to be handled very delicately. Professor, do you have any recommendations?"

Professor Okada said, "I have given that a lot of thought. I assume that you would want to make my father's account a part of your final report and that a copy of that report would be given to the Japanese government?"

"Yes," Tom said' "That would be appropriate."

"Then I think that we can leave that problem to the government. They will have no desire to 'air any dirty laundry,' and they will decide how to handle Lieutenant Watanabe. I also see no need to say anything to Commander Matsuyama. The government will determine when, and if, he is to be told anything."

"I can tell you what I'd do with Lieutenant Watanabe if it were up to me," Sam said, "I'd have him ground up and used for fertilizer."

"Wow! That's pretty harsh."

"No, Alicia," Steve said, "That's 'Semper Fi.' That was a Marine he was cutting up, and we don't take kindly to shit like that. I'd do what Sam said."

"OK," Tom said, "I get it. But I want the two of you on your best behavior whenever we're around Matsuyama or Watanabe's body. Got it?"

Sam and Steve said together, "Aye, aye, Colonel."

"Professor, there is another issue that I have not had time to discuss with you, and your father's story reminded me of it."

"What is that, Ed?"

"Your father said that the men in his platoon called Watanabe 'Akuma,' the Demon. I think that there is a good chance that we encountered an evil Japanese demon during the search yesterday, and that demon tried to lure our dog Gunny to his death on a landmine."

Professor Okada leaned forward, looked intently at Akiyama's face, and spoke in a slow, measured voice. "Why do you say that, Ed?"

Ed, with help from the other team members, recounted what had happened when they had heard the disembodied voices the day before. He then went on to describe the strange dreams that everyone had had, and Sam and Steve described Gunny and Luke's odd behavior.

"So you already knew the identity of the American in the cave?" Okada asked.

"Yes," Ed replied

"And you all believe that these phenomena were caused by an evil demon?"

"I believe what we have been experiencing is a conflict between a demon and a benign or friendly spirit."

"Why do you believe that, Ed?"

"Because it is the simplest explanation I can think of and it requires the fewest assumptions."

"Ah, yes. Occam's Razor."

"OK, hold on a minute," Sam said, "Someone is going to have to explain that to this simple grunt."

"Mr. Webber," Okada said, "Occam's Razor simply refers to a heuristic technique or 'rule of thumb' which states that among competing explanations for an event you should choose the one that requires the fewest assumptions."

"OK, I understand that, but this explanation requires that we believe that there is such a thing as ghosts and demons and that's a pretty big assumption."

"Yes," Okada replied, "but that is an assumption that a majority of people in Japan have been making for almost two thousand years. I can see by the looks on your faces that you are either confused or skeptical. I will try to explain without being too long-winded. Ed, please feel free to add anything you think I miss.

"As you may know, the main religion in Japan for at least one thousand five hundred years has been Shinto. Approximately eighty percent of Japanese practice one of the many forms of Shinto. A belief in gods and spirits capable of interacting with the living is at the core of Shinto, so, you see, it is quite natural for a Japanese to believe in all types of spirits both benign and evil.

"Further, there are folk stories of literally hundreds of demons of all types. Some are gods or spirits that were never human; others are humans with an evil spirit who become demons when they die."

"Yes," Ed Akiyama said, "One way for a human with an evil character to become a demon is to be killed violently and without gratitude for his life or service. I would say that fits Lieutenant Watanabe perfectly."

"Yes, Ed, I would agree, and that has made me think of something else."

"What is that, Professor?"

"I think we should call Commander Matsuyama tonight and ask him to have a purification ceremony performed in that cave before anyone else goes in there. I am sure that there is a Shinto priest on this island somewhere."

"That's already been done, Professor. Commander Matsuyama took care of that this morning before we started work.""

"Of course. I'm not surprised, but I'm glad to hear that. I would be concerned about you spending too much time alone in there Dr. Phillips if it was not properly purified."

"Well, I've never worked a crime scene that has been purified by a Shinto priest before. I guess there's a first time for everything."

"All of this talk about demons and spirits brings up another issue having to do with writing our final report," Sam said.

"You mean, what do we say about the ghosts?" Tom asked.

"Exactly. Do we want to try to tell people who have never been to this place or seen and heard what we have that Gunny was led to the cave by the ghost of a Marine who has been dead for seventy years, or that a demon that used to be a Japanese officer tried to kill him?"

"I don't," Tom replied, "but what about the rest of the team? We need to make sure we're all on the same page. Alicia, what do you think?"

"I don't want to be known as the 'ghost whisperer' of forensic anthropology, so I would be happy with giving all of the credit for finding that cave and the other remains to Gunny and leaving the ghosts out of the report."

"Jim, what do you think?"

"If I were writing a novel, which I just might do, it would be a great sub-plot, but in an official report? No way."

"Steve?"

"I agree with Alicia, as long as Luke gets some credit for saving Gunny's life."

"Then we're in agreement; we'll keep the ghost stories to ourselves and give the dogs the credit that they deserve anyway. Right?"

When everyone nodded in agreement, he turned toward Professor Okada.

"This has been an amazing evening, Professor. Thank you very much." Tom said, "Let's have one more beer and relax for a few minutes then I'm going to hit the rack. We've got a lot to do tomorrow."

Everyone mumbled some form of agreement and headed for the beer fridge.

SEARCH DAY NINE

Here's health to you and to our Corps
Which we are proud to serve
In many a strife we've fought for life
And never lost our nerve
If the Army and the Navy
Ever look on Heaven's Scenes
They will find the Streets are Guarded
By United States Marines

Last Verse of The Marines Hymn

Iwo Jima, Amphitheater Search Area
Saturday, 1 July
Search Day 9
0700 Hours

ALICIA AND ED LEFT THE BASE CAMP as soon as they had gotten a bite to eat and went straight to the cave. There Alicia removed the dog tags from the American body while Ed videoed the entire procedure. Ed then did a detailed search of the Japanese body looking for anything that might confirm the man's identity while Alicia recorded.

The uniform cloth was brittle and falling apart, and Ed worked slowly and carefully. After fifteen minutes he sat back, shrugged his shoulders, and said, "Nothing here that I can find - no ID tag, no papers, nothing. His mouth is pretty unique; he's lost some teeth and had some interesting looking dental work, but I know that the personnel records for the soldiers on Iwo have never been found so there won't be any dental records for comparison."

"So," Alicia said, "He'll remain unknown?"

"Yes, it looks that way unless the Japanese government uses Private Okada's account to identify him and I think that is unlikely."

Alicia then left to go back to the lab while Ed went down to the gully for another day of work with the rest of the team.

As soon as the two dog teams had arrived Ed said, "Sam, Steve now that we know we're looking for three Marines and two Japanese soldiers I want to widen the search area to make sure we haven't missed anything. Can you do that while Jim, Tom and I work the GPR here?"

Sam and Steve both nodded, and Sam said, "How far do you want us to expand the search?"

Ed turned in a circle surveying the area. "I think we want to focus on the gully but work maybe ten yards on either side. I doubt that there's much upstream of us so go maybe twenty, thirty yards that way and maybe fifty yards downstream?"

Steve thought for a moment, "Yeah, we can do that. It'll probably take all day."

Ed said, "That's fine with me. I just want to make sure we don't miss anything by being too focused on this one area."

"OK, Ed. We'll let you know if we find anything."

Forty-five minutes later, Alicia's voice came over the team radios, "Hey everybody I've got some news. I cleaned the dog tags and checked the name and serial number. I also compared the photos we took of the face and jaw to the dental records, and there is a perfect match on everything. It's Robby Durance. One hundred percent sure."

♦ ♦ ♦

Team Liberty Iwo Jima Base Camp
Saturday, 1 July
Search Day 9
1930 Hours

Jim Stewart had been the last of the team to straggle back to the base camp at five-thirty. His shirt was clammy, and his skin was flushed and gritty from the covering of Iwo Jima sand.

I'm supposed to be a historian, not a ditch digger, but I admit that it feels good to get involved in literally uncovering history.

When he got to his room, there was a message on the satellite phone. He checked that and then headed for a quick shower. Fifteen minutes later, he plopped into his seat at the dining table and was gratified to see that everyone else looked at least as tired as he was.

Everyone was hungry, and dinner was a quick affair without a lot of talk. When they had all finished, Tom spoke.

"I know that everyone is tired, but let's have a quick team meeting and then we can all relax. Who wants to go first?"

"Tom, I have some information that will affect our schedule for the rest of the evening, so maybe I should go first."

"OK, Jim. You're up."

"I had a message from my grad students, and they have contacted Mr. Ed Durance, Robby's younger brother. He has agreed to talk with us this evening. We have a satellite hook-up scheduled for 9:45. Is anyone else interested in listening in on our discussion?"

Everyone said, "Yes!" almost in unison.

"OK, then. I'll hook the phone to a speaker so we can all listen in. That's all I have."

"Ed, what about you. You want to summarize what we did in the gully today?"

"Sure, Tom. First, I want to thank you and Jim for helping with that GPR. That damn thing is heavy! I couldn't have moved it around by myself."

"Anyway, I think you all know that Gunny and Luke did their usual good job and located two more small areas downstream that we have to include in the search. We only had time for a quick look with the GPR, but there's definitely something there. I'll need to spend some time tomorrow, adding those areas to our computer map."

"OK, Alicia. What about you."

"I spent most of the day getting the two bodies ready to go into their coffins and making sure that I had gotten all of the evidence that I could for identification. Along those lines, I removed three teeth from Robby to use for DNA analysis. They will be returned to the body before his final burial."

"Just a little while ago, six Marines and several Japanese soldiers showed up in a truck with the coffins. They got the coffins into the caves and moved the bodies, very reverently I might add, into the coffins. They also brought a coffin for Corporal Hank's body, or the few remains that we have, and he will be returned home with Robby in the ceremony tomorrow."

"What about Watanabe?" Sam asked.

"His remains will stay in the coffin in the cave until the Japanese conduct their own ceremony in a couple of days."

"Did you remove any of his teeth for DNA analysis?"

"No one suggested that I do that and so I didn't. I suppose the Japanese could do that, but it would be a huge effort to try to find a match, and I doubt that they will bother."

"So, he'll officially remain unknown?"

"Most likely."

Tom said, "Professor Okada, do you have anything to add?"

"Yes, just one thing. It has to do with Commander Matsuyama's gift. I know everyone is tired, but we don't have much time before we go our separate ways, and I think that you will find that this gift will help you relax somewhat."

"Sure," Tom said, "I don't think that any of us will be going to sleep tonight until after we talk to Robby's brother, so why don't you go ahead?"

"All right. If one of you could bring that box over here, I will explain."

After the box had been set in front of him, Professor Okada continued, "I understand that you have not drunk very much of the sake provided in the beverage refrigerator is that correct."

"Yes," Alicia said, "I'd never tried sake before, and I wanted to try it, but I didn't like the taste."

"I've had sake before," Sam said, "And I just didn't like what we had here."

"That's good, it shows you have good taste. I will explain what I mean, but first, I must give you a short lecture. I am, after all, a Professor.

"Do you know that in Japanese the word sake does not mean 'rice wine' but refers to any alcoholic beverage? If you want to order rice wine in a Japanese bar you should ask for *nihonshu,* the bartender or waiter will be very impressed.

"Next, you need to learn something about the different grades of *nihonshu.* The lowest grade is *futsushu,* and this is typically served only at poor bars or to unsuspecting gaijin. The *nihonshu* here is *futsushu,* and Commander Matsuyama chose it as an insult. If you had drunk a large amount of it, everyone on the island would soon know that you are unsophisticated gaijin. The fact that you did not drink it was, I am sure, disappointing to Commander Matsuyama."

Steve asked, "Excuse me, Professor, a gaijin is a foreigner, right?"

"Yes, very good. Many people believe that the term gaijin is a slur, but it simply means 'outside person'"

Professor Okada then removed a golden colored bottle shaped like a snowman without the head from the box.

"I won't bore you with the other classifications, but I will simply tell you that what we will drink tonight is *daiginjo nihonshu,* which is the highest grade of *nihonshu.* This particular bottle is *Suzuki Shuzoten Hideyoshi Flying Pegasus,* which, I believe, is the finest *nihonshu* made. There are five more bottles in the box, and this *nihonshu* is very expensive. This is a true act of apology by Commander Matsuyama."

Sam asked, "How will you warm it?"

"Not all *nihonshu* should be drunk warm. I put these bottles in the refrigerator a few minutes before dinner, and it should be at just the right temperature to bring out all the aroma and flavor."

Okada then removed from the box a small, elegantly carved, wooden case that he opened to reveal six sake cups beautifully hand-painted with views of Mt. Fuji.

"Those cups look very old and very fragile."

"Yes. We can't drink this *nihonshu* from a common cup. These are over three hundred years old."

"My god, Professor, I'm afraid to touch them, let alone drink from them," Alicia said.

"Nonsense, they are not as fragile as they appear. Please choose one and allow me to serve you."

"Also, for you, Jim, I have a bottle of non-alcoholic nihonshu if you would like to join us."

"That's very thoughtful of you, Professor, I would be happy to join you."

An hour later, the group had consumed two bottles of what was the best wine any of them had ever tasted. They were relaxed and warm, and, strangely, no longer tired. They talked together like old friends and in the hour left before the call to Ed Durance, they drank a third bottle of *Suzuki Shuzoten Hideyoshi Flying Pegasus.*

♦ ♦ ♦

Team Liberty Iwo Jima Base Camp
Saturday, 1 July
Search Day 9
2145 Hours

Everyone was feeling mellow when the time came to call Robby Durance's brother.

Before Jim made the call, Sam urged him not to say anything definite about finding Robby.

"The Marine Corps has a formal protocol for notifying the next of kin of Marines killed in combat, and they won't be happy if we mess that up. Just be vague."

"OK," Jim said.

"Also remember not to say anything about Professor Okada or his father," Tom said.

"Right, got it."

A few minutes later, the call went through.

"Mr. Durance, this is Dr. Jim Stewart calling from Iwo Jima. I hope we're not calling you too early in the morning."

"Doctor, I'm eighty-two years old, and I can count on the fingers of one hand the number of times I've slept past seven o'clock in the morning. I been up for two hours. Do you have any news about my brother, Robby?"

"Sir, we don't have anything definite yet, but we may have some leads. I need to ask you a question about your brother."

"I'll help any way I can. I was eight years old when Robby went off to the war. That was a long, long time ago, but I remember it clear, and I remember him. He was my big brother, and I pretty much thought that the sun come up in the mornin' 'cause Robby told it to. There ain't a day goes by I don't think of him."

"I understand, sir, and we will do everything we can to bring your brother home."

"Thank you. I appreciate that. Go on and ask your question."

"We're trying to identify someone whom your brother may have known, and we don't know if he was a Marine or someone from back home. Do you know if he ever had a friend named Rusty?"

"Rusty? Rusty? Hell yes, ever body in Roanoke County knew Rusty. Best damn dog that ever lived! The saddest day of my life was when we heard that Robby had gone missing and was prob'ly dead. Second saddest was the day Rusty died just before Robby left for the Marines. How'd you hear about Rusty?"

"We've found some papers written by someone who may have been with Robby when he died. Is it possible that your brother would have mentioned his dog as he lay dying?"

"Well, I wouldn't be surprised. He and that dog grew up together and you hardly ever saw one without the other. Hard to tell what folks might think about when they're dyin' but, no sir, if somebody said Robby was talkin' about Rusty when he died, well, he prob'ly was."

"Mr. Durance, thank you very much. This has been very helpful. I promise that as soon as we have some definite information about your brother, we will let you know."

"I appreciate all that you folks are doin' goin' way to hell over there to that godforsaken place to bring my brother home. It means a lot, but if you're gonna find somethin', sooner would be better than later. I ain't gettin' no younger."

"Yes, sir, we understand. I pray every night that we will find your brother and his friends."

"Thank you for that, Doctor. You keep a-prayin', but don't let it slow down your lookin' none, all right?"

"Yes, sir, we'll keep looking. Thank you. Goodbye."

"Well, I'll be damned!" Sam said.

"His dog? His last thoughts were about his dog? Does that make sense?" Alicia asked.

"Remember what we read," Tom replied, "He was a young man, far from home, dying in a strange place. He was probably thinking about something safe and familiar."

"I understand that, but why not his mother or girlfriend?" Alicia asked. "Sam, would your last thoughts be about Gunny?"

"I hope not, or Rebecca would kill me."

After a brief, shocked silence, everyone got the joke, and a quick burst of laughter relieved the tension that had been building.

"Hey, wait a minute," Jim said, "I think I may have a picture here."

Jim opened his laptop and typed quickly. After a minute he turned the computer so everyone could see the picture on the screen.

"The Durance family sent me copies of a bunch of old photos. Here's one of Robby Durance and his dog."

The picture showed a boy of about ten standing in front of a barn with a dog sitting at his side. The dog was medium size, a little smaller than Gunny. He was a mutt with maybe some collie in him. His fur was a patchwork of brown and white spots. His left ear stood up straight, but his right ear flopped over about halfway up. There was nothing special about him unless you looked at his eyes. Even in a grainy, eighty-year-old photograph, you could see his bright, intelligent eyes.

Steve said, "They look like good friends, don't they?"

Alicia peered more closely at the screen. "Yes, yes, they do."

The team looked at the screen for a long minute until Tom said, "OK, let's get back on topic. What have we learned here?"

"This backs up the Professor's account. We know for sure that his father met and spoke with Robby Durance," Sam said.

"OK," Tom said, "This has been a big day and a long one, and we've got the ceremony first thing in the morning tomorrow so let's get some sleep. We want to look sharp in the morning, and I'd like everyone to wear their team uniform shirt. We want to show respect for those two Marines we're sending home."

"Roger that, Colonel," Sam said, "See you in the morning."

ROBBY GOES HOME

UNDER the wide and starry sky,
Dig the grave and let me lie
Glad did I live and gladly die,
And I laid me down with a will.
This be the verse you grave for me:
Here he lies where he longed to be;
Home is the sailor, home from the sea,
And the hunter home from the hill.

"Requiem" by Robert Louis Stevenson

Iwo Jima, Amphitheater Search Area
Sunday, 2 July
Search Day 10
0700 Hours

THE FIRST RAYS OF THE RISING SUN were coming over the top of the Amphitheater as the body bearer detail, six Marines in their Dress Blue uniforms, emerged from the cave with the flag-draped casket containing the remains of Robby Durance.

As the detail moved slowly down the ramp cut into the side of the hill the Third Marine Division Band played *The Marines' Hymn* in slow-march tempo. On one side of the Band, a platoon of Japanese soldiers stood at rigid attention with their hands raised to the brim of their caps in salute. On the other side, a platoon of Marines in camouflage utilities stood with their M-4 rifles at the position of "Present Arms." In front of the Band, a Marine Brigadier General and Commander Matsuyama raised and then lowered their swords in salute.

The members of Team Liberty Iwo Jima, including Professor Okada and Ed Akiyama, stood with their heads bared. Tom, Sam, and Steve as retired military members had the privilege of rendering the hand salute, which they did. Jim and Alicia placed their hands over their hearts.

The detail carried the casket across the gully toward the Assistant Division Commander and placed it on a stand in front of him next to an identical casket that held a small bag containing the remains of Jeff Hanks.

Two hours later aboard a Marine C-130 Robby Durance and Jeff Hanks started their final journey home.

♦ ♦ ♦

Team Liberty Iwo Jima Base Camp
Sunday, 2 July
Search Day 10
2230 Hours

After the ceremony, it had been an easy day for Gunny and Luke. There was no sense in any more searching since Ed Akiyama, and his students would be taking over soon, so the team spent most of their time packing and getting ready to leave. At Commander Matsuyama's request, Sam and Steve had taken the dogs over to the other side of the airfield to put on a demonstration of their capabilities for him and his staff. That had been more like play than work, and the two dogs enjoyed all the attention they got.

The demonstration had given them just enough exercise that they were ready for bed when Sam turned out the light in the hut.

A little later Gunny heard someone calling his name. It was the Good Man, and Gunny was glad to see him again. He was about to go up to him when he sensed something to his left, and when he looked, there was Luke. Luke had never been with him and the Good Man before, but they seemed to know each other.

There was another strange thing, and it took Gunny a minute to realize that they were all standing in a field of soft green grass with a scattering of trees. Before, when he had seen the Good Man, they had just been in an empty, gray space.

"Gunny, Luke, I've got someone here I want you to meet. Guys, this is Rusty."

As the Good Man spoke, a dog walked out from behind him. He was a little smaller than Gunny, and he was all brown and white spots, and he had one funny-looking ear. He walked confidently up to Gunny and Luke and stood calmly for them to sniff him. Gunny was not surprised to find that the dog smelled like Old Bone. It was a different Old Bone smell, but it was definitely Old Bone.

This didn't bother Gunny anymore. If a man could smell like Old Bone and be a Good Man, then there was no reason why a dog couldn't be the same. Of course, there was the Bad Man who smelled like Old Bone, but that wasn't something Gunny wanted to think about.

After Rusty had sniffed him and Luke, he stepped back a few paces and with a smile on his face dropped into a play bow. In an instant Gunny and the other two were running, rolling and play fighting all around the grassy field.

Gunny felt like a young dog, strong and fast. All three of them could run and jump like dogs in the prime of life.

The Good Man watched them with a broad grin and tears running down his face.

"Good dogs! Good dogs! Oh, what a bunch of good dogs!"

When they finally exhausted themselves, they walked over and lay in the grass around the Good Man who stroked and petted each one in turn.

"Gunny, Luke, you've done a great thing. Me and Hanks are on our way home, and the others will be following soon. We owe it all to you, and I can't thank you enough. We'll see each other like this one more time and then someday, a few years from now, we'll be together for real, and you'll understand."

Gunny didn't understand the Good Man's words, but they made him feel like he did when The Man gave him his rope toy when he made a find. Feeling tired, comfortable, and safe, he drifted back to sleep.

EPILOGUE: ONE YEAR LATER

And when he gets to Heaven
To Saint Peter he will tell;
"Another Marine reporting Sir -
I've served my time in Hell."

Epitaph on the grave of PFC William
Cameron, H/2/1, Guadalcanal, 1942, but in
various forms dating to 1917

Ogden Valley, Utah
Wednesday, 6 June

AFTER THE TEAM CAME HOME IN JULY, Tom Sanders kept everyone informed of the progress in the recovery of the remains in the gully. When Tom deployed to Vietnam shortly after the New Year on another search with Team Liberty, that task fell to Sam. Thus, it was Sam who passed the word that the recovery had been successfully completed and that a full military funeral was planned for all five of their Marines at Arlington National Cemetery in June.

Sam had been thinking since he had returned home from Iwo Jima about a gift for Steve to thank him for what Luke did to save Gunny's life. After several weeks of research and study, he had commissioned an artist to do a portrait of Luke. He wanted something more than just a copy of a photograph, he wanted a realistic picture that expressed Luke's character and personality. For a couple of months, he provided the artist photos and descriptions of what Luke had done in Afghanistan and Iwo Jima. When the artist understood what his subject had accomplished, he offered to significantly reduce his fee, an offer Sam gladly accepted since this was turning into an expensive project.

Rebecca had been somewhat skeptical of this idea, but when she saw the completed work, she agreed that it was perfect. The artist had portrayed Luke in three-quarter profile in the middle of a search in the sparse brush of Iwo Jima. Luke was looking back over his left shoulder for his next command from Steve, and the scar along his side was clearly visible. It was a beautiful picture of a dog, but what captivated the viewer were the eyes. At once full of both joy and intelligence, Luke's great dark eyes were indeed the mirror of his soul. It was a portrayal of a good dog doing what he had been born to do.

Sam also wanted to get something for Alicia. Despite their rough beginning together, they had become friends, and he had grown to respect her and what she did, but he was stumped on what would be an appropriate gift. Then he got an e-mail from her that solved his problem.

Alicia had asked him if he could help her find a dog that she could train to work crime scenes with her the way Gunny had done. Sam had said that he would have to think about it.

As soon as Sam finished his reply to Alicia's e-mail, he looked up a number and made a call with his fingers crossed and hit the jackpot.

The funeral was scheduled for Wednesday, June 13th. At the request of Robby's family, the team was meeting at the Durance farm near Roanoke, Virginia on Monday the 11th. On the 6th of June, Sam and Rebecca loaded Gunny and the very carefully wrapped painting into the car and headed east.

It was a nine-hour drive to their first stop near Albin, Wyoming. Dubya was now thirteen but healthy and active and still capable of treating Gunny like a young puppy. Gunny loved it.

After a pleasant evening spent bringing Marsha up to date on all of Gunny's adventures, they were ready to go early the next morning.

As soon as they got Alicia's present loaded.

◆ ◆ ◆

Durance Farm
Near Cave Spring, Virginia
Monday, 11 June

Sam and Gunny stood in a small, well-tended cemetery under the shade of two old oaks and looked down the hill across Interstate 81 toward the Shenandoah Valley. There were thirty or more graves scattered around them in no particular order dating from the first Robert Durance to Durances and Durance kin from the current day.

It had taken some searching, but Sam finally found what Robby's brother had told him was there. It had been Gunny who had found the grave. Sam had seen him with his nose to the ground, and his tail slowly wagging and gone over to investigate. When Gunny saw him coming, he had gone to a sit, and his mouth had relaxed into a grin. Sam walked up to him and began to scratch him behind the ears.

The scent was very, very faint but Gunny recognized it immediately. It was the Old Bone smell from the dog who was with the Good Man, the dog he called Rusty.

Tucked in a corner a little bit away by itself the grave was a small mound topped by a faded wooden plaque whose hand-carved epitaph was barely readable:

RUSTY

1932 - 1944

Good Dog

"You act like you know this guy, Gunny. This was Robby's dog, the Marine you found in the cave. He must have been a hell of a good dog. Just like you, right buddy?"

The team was staying at the Durance farm before traveling to Arlington the next day for the funeral services. Although it was still called a farm it was, in fact, a boutique vineyard and the original farmhouse with its many additions was an upscale country inn. The population of southwestern Virginia had exploded in recent years, and most of the original Durance farm had been sold off to developers. The area around the cemetery, however, had been donated to a land trust and was safe from development in perpetuity.

The team members were enjoying their luxurious accommodations and looking forward to a big dinner and wine tasting that evening.

Sam looked down at Rusty's grave and thought for the thousandth time about how he would feel when it was time to let Gunny go. Gunny was ten now, and he only had a few years left. It would be nice if he could find a peaceful little spot like this for him. He'd have to think about that.

Later the team gathered at a table under a shade tree on the lawn for a drink before dinner. Sam shook hands with Tom, Steve, Ed Akiyama, and Professor Okada, and he got a surprisingly warm hug from Alicia. Sam then introduced Rebecca.

"How long have you two been married?" Alicia asked.

"Forty-seven years."

"That's wonderful! How did you do it?"

"Trust me," Rebecca said with a rueful smile, "it wasn't easy. Having him gone a lot helped."

Steve, in particular, enjoyed his laugh at Sam's expense.

"All right, dear, now that you've had your fun, would you be so kind as to go and retrieve the presents?"

"Why, yes, dear, of course. Whatever you ask." Rebecca replied with a wink at Alicia.

As Rebecca walked away, Steve said, "I didn't know we were exchanging presents."

Sam looked at Steve, "I had to do something to thank you and Luke for saving Gunny's life. If Luke hadn't done what he did not only would Gunny be dead, but we wouldn't have found Robby."

Rebecca walked up with the painting covered by a cloth and said to Steve, "When Sam told me what he was doing I wasn't sure it was a good idea, but I have to admit he got it right. I hope you like it as much as I do."

Steve accepted the painting from Rebecca and lifted the cloth. He stared down at it for a long minute, and when he turned it around for the others to see, tear tracks were running down both sides of his face.

"Sam, I can't thank you enough for this. It's wonderful. It's the best gift you could have given me. Thank you."

"No thanks necessary, Steve. Semper Fi."

As Rebecca walked back toward the house, Sam announced, "OK, Alicia, the next one's for you."

"For me? Why? I didn't save anybody's life."

"Just wait, you'll see."

A minute later, Rebecca came back with a chubby bundle of golden fur in her arms.

"Is that a puppy??? For me?" cried Alicia.

"Yep, meet your new crime scene dog."

As Rebecca handed the nine-week-old Golden Retriever puppy to Alicia, he stood up in her arms and began to lick her face.

"OK," Alicia asked, "How did you manage this?"

"Pure luck. As soon as I got your e-mail in February, I called Gunny's breeder, and they had a litter due in late March, and she was able to reserve a pup for us. He'll be a working dog. His mom is one of Gunny's mom's daughters, and the dad is an avalanche dog from Colorado. He'll probably drive you nuts."

"He's precious!" Alicia said.

"Precious?" Tom said, "Did Dr. Alicia Phillips just say 'precious'?"

After everyone had played with the puppy for a minute, Sam looked around and said, "Speaking of dogs, where the hell are Luke and Gunny?"

After ten minutes of searching, they found the two dogs lying side by side with their heads between their paws next to Rusty's grave.

"I thought we left all the weird shit back on Iwo."

"Steve, I think once you know what to look for, you'll find weird shit all around you," Sam said.

♦ ♦ ♦

Arlington National Cemetery

Arlington, Virginia
Wednesday, 13 June

The five Civil War-era caissons each with their six black caparisoned horses stood at the center of the parade ground in front of the Memorial Chapel. Flanking them were two platoons of the ceremonial guard from Marine Barracks Washington, D.C. arrayed in their Dress Blue uniforms. To their rear were the one hundred sixty members of the Marine Band in their red and white uniforms headed by the Drum Major with his tall bearskin hat. In front of these formations was the Color Guard of the Marine Corps with the National Ensign and the Marine Corps Battle Colors.

One by one the Body Bearer Detail, six Marines selected for their size, strength and military bearing, carried the flag-draped coffins from the Memorial Chapel to the caissons while the Band played the Marines' Hymn at a slow-march tempo. Behind the casket marched another Marine carrying a box displaying the medals awarded to each man.

Based on the reports from Team Liberty Iwo Jima, it had been determined that all five of the Marines had been killed while advancing to try to help their comrades pinned down in the Amphitheater. The Commandant of the Marine Corps had directed that Corporal Jeff Hanks, and Privates Ed Hobbs, Larry Lawrence and Simon Laskey each receive the Silver Star Medal, the Nation's third-highest award for bravery in combat. There had been strong sentiment to award Private First Class Robert Lee Durance III the Medal of Honor, but without any American eyewitness to his actions that was not possible. Instead, the Secretary of the Navy awarded him the Navy Cross, the Nation's second-highest award. All five men also received the Purple Heart Medal to recognize their fatal wounds.

Each time the detail emerged from the Chapel, the Marines of the ceremonial guard, moving as one man, brought their M-1 rifles topped with gleaming bayonets to the position of "Present Arms." As the coffin passed the Color Guard, the flags were slowly lowered to half-mast.

When the caissons had all been loaded, the move to the gravesite began with the Band in front marching to the slow beat of drums muffled with black cloth. They were followed by the first platoon of the guard, then the caissons with their mounted escorts from the Army's 3rd U.S. Infantry, and then the second platoon.

Leading the procession of dignitaries, family members, and invited guests were the Commandant and Sergeant Major of the Marine Corps and the Commanding General and Sergeant Major of the Fourth Marine Division.

Immediately behind them in a place of special honor marched Team Liberty Iwo Jima with their special guests Dr. Edward Akiyama and Professor Ichiro Okada. Rebecca was also there at Tom's request. At the insistence of the other team members, Sam and Steve walked in front with Gunny and Luke.

Behind Team Liberty was a long line of several hundred mourners led by Robby Durance's brother pushed in his wheelchair by his grandson, a Marine Sergeant whose Dress Blue blouse bore medals signifying his service in Afghanistan. Behind them came the limousines carrying those who could not walk the mile to the final resting place of the Marines of 1st Squad, 1st Platoon, Baker Company, 1st Battalion, 25th Marines.

It took over thirty minutes for the slow-moving procession to complete the route. During that entire time, the only sounds were the slow beat of the drums and the measured steps of the honor guard.

It was an unusual June morning in the Washington area with blue skies, low humidity, and comfortable temperatures. It was calm and peaceful in the shade of the trees along the road, and the prevailing mood among the marchers was one of pride and dignity rather than sorrow.

Five graves had been prepared side by side in the World War II section of the vast cemetery. When each casket had been moved to its position over the open graves, the services began.

There were three services because Jeff Hanks was a Catholic, Robby Durance, Ed Hobbs and Larry Lawrence were Protestants, and Simon Laskey was a Jew. The three chaplains, two men, and one woman, each commended the souls of young men dead for seventy-three years to their God.

Next, in a series of intricately choreographed movements, the Body Bearer Detail raised the flag from each casket and folded it to form a starred, blue triangle. Since these were all enlisted men, the honor of presenting these flags to the surviving next of kin fell to the two Sergeants Major.

In the final act of tribute, seven Marines raised their rifles three times and fired the last salute.

By unspoken agreement, the members of Team Liberty Iwo Jima stayed behind while the rest of the mourners and dignitaries departed. They just wanted a few last moments with their Marines.

They stood quietly for several minutes wrapped in their own thoughts and memories. As they began to walk away, Gunny and Luke both stopped in their tracks and turned toward a tree a few yards away. A second later, they both sprang forward catching Sam and Steve by surprise and tearing the leashes out of their hands.

The Good Man and his dog were there under the tree, and there were four other men with them. Gunny recognized all of the Old Bone scents at once. These were the men he had found when The Man had told him it was Time to Go to Work. Luke knew them, too.

They were all talking and saying, "Good boys, good dogs," and "Thank You."

After a minute, Robby and Rusty stepped forward and sat on the ground next to him and Luke.

"We can't thank you two enough for bringing us home."

Then, standing up, he spoke to the rest of the team. "And thank all of you. One day you will understand what all this means. We'll see you again then. In the meantime...Semper Fi."

Bending down, he patted both dogs on the head, and then he and Rusty walked back to their friends, and, slowly, the six images faded away.

"OK," Sam said, "Did anyone else see and hear what I just did?"

The rest of the team was too stunned to do more than nod their heads.

"Gunny, come!"

"Luke, come!"

The two dogs trotted obediently back; their eyes, their whole bodies were glowing.

"What in the hell was that?" Alicia asked. "Have we just seen what happens after ... after..."

"After we die?" Tom said, "I don't know, but I don't think I'm in a hurry to find out. He, Robby, said, 'one day,' we'll understand. It didn't sound like he meant one day soon."

"What do we do now?" Steve asked.

"I don't know about the rest of you," Sam replied, "but I'm going to find a bar that allows dogs and have a drink. Probably several."

"Sounds like a plan, Marine. Lead the way."

What I'd really like to do right now is have a long talk with Brother Francis, God rest his soul. I wonder if he knows how many other ghosts are stuck on that desolate little island waiting for someone to bring them home.

AUTHOR'S Q AND A

Q. Are you and your character Sam Webber one and the same?

A. No, Sam is taller and better looking than I am, and it's purely coincidental that my dog's name is Gunny.

Q. What about your other characters, Tom, Jim, Steve, Alicia, Luke, and Gunny. Where did they come from?

A. Except for Gunny, they are entirely fictional, but, as I said in my Author's Note, they are composites of people I've known all my life. Gunny is Gunny, and he has done all of the things described in the book either in training or on actual searches. I was going to give him a different name, but I just couldn't think of a better one. Two of the supporting characters, Marsha and Kurt, are real people, and I can thank them for getting me started in search and rescue.

Q. Do you have other books available or in the works?

A. I've written two other books in the Sam and Gunny K9 adventure series, *Ghosts of the Buffalo Wheel* and *The Very First Dog*. I'm pleased to say that my first two books were selected as finalists for best novel in the Dog Writers Association of America writing contest; *Ghosts of Iwo Jima* in 2017 and *Ghosts of the Buffalo Wheel* in 2018. *The Very First Dog* will be released early in 2019.

For more information, to ask more questions or to make a comment please see my website at www.ghostsofiwojima.com

ABOUT THE AUTHOR

Joe Jennings is a K9 handler with a search and rescue team in northern Utah. He and his dog, Gunny (the real Gunny), are certified for live find in both wilderness and avalanches, and human remains recovery on both land and water. They have been on over eighty searches across the Intermountain West. Joe is also a retired U.S. Marine and a veteran of the Vietnam War.

Joe is the author of two books in the Sam and Gunny K9 adventure series, *Ghosts of Iwo Jima* and *Ghosts of the Buffalo Wheel*. Both of these books were selected as finalists for best novel in the Dog Writers Association of America writing contest; *Ghosts of Iwo Jima* in 2017 and *Ghosts of the Buffalo Wheel* in 2018. A third book in the series, *The Very First Dog,* will be released early in 2019.

Made in the USA
Monee, IL
21 August 2020